Do you promise…

Not to Tell

Chapter One

If Detective Inspector Jo Rodriguez had been looking for an effective fitness regime, he could hardly have done better than the number of times he shot to his feet at the entrance of his senior officer into his old office at Stockport which he was once again occupying, on a temporary basis.

Jo didn't need the extra exercise. With six children at home, most of them sporty, his life was far from sedentary.

He was currently standing in for Detective Chief Inspector Ted Darling. Ted had, unusually for him, and with much persuasion, agreed to take some leave, with a major murder case not yet wound up. The delay was due to outstanding DNA results from their prime suspect, a man so far known only as Tonton. Those results were now well beyond reasonably overdue, even allowing for pressure of work at the lab.

Even Ted had had to concede that, apart from phoning the lab daily, sometimes several times, to try to chase them up, there was nothing much he could do that Jo couldn't do equally as well. So, still unwillingly, he had boarded a plane with his mother and his partner and flown off to spend a few days on holiday in Germany. They were going as guests of Met Police DI Oscar Smith, who had worked with Ted on a couple of cases and they'd forged an unlikely alliance.

The holiday was to be followed by one of Ted's training sessions with his special skills instructor, Mr Green, in the Welsh mountains, to which Smith had also been invited. An invite which had had more of a royal command feel to it.

'Gentlemen, please, there really is no need,' Superintendent Debra Caldwell told Jo and Detective Sergeant Mike Hallam, who shared the same office, as she did every time she visited them. The two men had both lost count of how many times that was, on average, per day. The pressure on all of them, her in particular, with no result to date on a high profile triple murder case, was taking its toll.

Twin newborn baby girls, and their mother, savagely killed and no charges yet brought against anyone was not a good look for a police service under pressure for rapid results from all quarters.

There was simply something about the tall, immaculately turned-out 'Ice Queen' which unfailingly provoked the positively Pavlovian reflex in both men. Which was probably why these visits almost always saw all three of them remaining standing throughout their conversation.

'Is there any further news yet on those DNA results, inspector?' she asked Jo, as she did on every such occasion.

'Still nothing, ma'am, and I have chased them twice already today. They just keep saying there's a backlog at the lab and they're doing all they can.'

'As you can appreciate, I am coming under considerable pressure from executive level for a conclusion. Is there no other solid evidence anywhere to link your prime suspect to the crime? What about eyewitness testimony? Still nothing on that score? Surely the killing of two defenceless newborn babies, and their mother, is sufficiently appalling for some of them to start to talk? If only to remove themselves from any suspicion of complicity.'

'Up to now there's nothing concrete from that either, although we are still trying,' Jo told her, dropping the ma'am as far as he risked going away from formality. 'Certainly nothing to convince CPS we have anything like a case with legs. Nobody seems willing to talk frankly for the moment, despite all our best efforts.'

'Have you conducted any of the witness interviews yourself?' the superintendent asked Jo. 'Is it just possible that the intervention of a more senior officer might emphasise the seriousness of the case and loosen tongues more readily?'

It took a lot of self-control for Jo not to do an eye roll at that. Especially as he saw by the expression on Mike's face that the DS was thinking exactly the same thing as he was. Ted Darling had seemingly superhuman powers, judging by the amount of paperwork he got through in a day, in addition to his usual role as Senior Investigating Officer, with all the associated admin that entailed. Jo was only just keeping up, going flat out, without even thinking of taking on interviewing witnesses to add to his workload.

'I'll certainly give that a try, if you think it might help. And I'll chase up the lab once more. I will keep you posted, as soon as I hear anything, of course.'

'Please do,' she responded. 'Oh, and have we attempted to establish whether this really is an unfortunate if unavoidable delay on the samples, or have the relevant ones perhaps been lost in the system, or even turned out not to be usable? And is someone there trying to delay the timing of when they have to own up to that?'

'I've been trying not to think of that possibility, with all the ramifications it would mean.'

'Please do think about it, inspector. The earlier we can anticipate such a problem, the sooner we can do something about it. I believe our suspect was difficult enough over the first sample. He's certainly going to be even less cooperative if we have to repeat the procedure, so please be prepared for such a challenge and devise a contingency plan to deal with it.

'I shall leave the matter in your capable hands,' she told him as she turned and left the office.

Both men sat back down at their desks to return to what they had been doing when she came in, Jo already with phone in hand to try chasing the lab yet again for the vital result.

'One thing I will never understand,' Jo said as he called up the saved number, 'is how Ted can stay on the wagon with the pressures he's under. I'll be glad to get back to the relative peace and quiet of my little corner of our realm, as soon as he's back. And I really hope that will be before we do discover that the initial sample has gone missing or something like that. The likely crap fallout from that scenario really doesn't bear thinking about.

'However it works out, I'll be more than relieved to hand over to the real boss on Monday morning when he gets back from his jollies. Whatever he's up to, I bet he's having more fun than we are.'

* * *

Except that Ted Darling currently had major problems of his own. For the moment, he was struggling to come up with a workable solution. And his predicament was anything but jolly.

He'd enjoyed his visit to Germany, as a guest of Oscar Smith, far more than he'd anticipated. He and Trev had taken Ted's mother Annie with them, on her first trip abroad and her first ever flight, She'd loved every minute of it, especially the flight. Unlike her son, who only ever flew when there was no practical alternative.

The three of them had stayed in Smith's grandmother's spacious house and found her delightful company. Under her influence, Oscar was on his best behaviour and had proved to be a thoughtful and considerate host. Ted and Oscar had flown back on Friday, earlier than Trev and Annie, for their rendezvous with Ted's old special skills instructor, Mr Green. He'd issued one of his invitations which was more of a three-line whip and to which 'no' was never an acceptable response.

They were supposed to have been joined by Sergeant Jock McLintock, an old acquaintance of Ted's, but he'd had to cry off at the last minute for a reason even Green had had to accept as valid.

Ted had spent much of the flight back, and then the drive, in his car, from the airport to the North Wales meeting point, trying to impress upon Smith how dangerous and unpredictable a man Green was. Someone not to be trusted. He stressed that Smith should certainly never lower his guard in front of him.

As soon as they'd made the rendezvous, in a small, little-used parking area, seemingly miles from anywhere, and Green had done his usual trick of appearing as if from nowhere, Ted realised he could have saved his breath, for all the good he had done.

He had to turn his head away to hide the wince he couldn't help making, when Smith had stepped forward, hand outstretched to shake, and begun, 'It's a pleasure to meet you, Sarn't Major. Ted's told me a lot...'

Which was as far as he got before one of Green's DMS-booted feet flew towards him, took every ounce of breath out of him without doing serious damage, then planted firmly on the back of his neck as he hit the ground, pinning him, gasping and retching, like a floundering fish.

'I thought Gayboy would have briefed you better. First rule of combat is always know your true enemy. And believe me, Monkey-boy, for the duration of this training exercise, I am not only your enemy, but your worst possible nightmare.'

The nickname was inevitable. Each of Green's 'victims' was given one on his courses, to dehumanise them. 'Monkey' was a reference to Smith's former regiment, the Royal Military Police. And Ted had briefed Smith on the likely initiation ritual. As far as he was concerned, from now on, Oscar was on his own. He'd have to manage as best he could.

Such things were simply Green's outdated, now often outlawed, but brutally effective, training methods. They worked by either making or breaking participants. Ted was fervently hoping Oscar would be up to the challenge as he didn't fancy having to carry someone his size down from the mountains if he wasn't. Even if Green deigned to lend a hand, which was unlikely.

Once a visibly shaken Smith had managed to get unsteadily back on his feet, looking a little subdued and still rather green round the gills, things followed their usual pattern for such sessions. Ted's and Oscar's phones were both seized and locked securely into a box under the seat of

Green's battered old ex-Army Land Rover, from which vehicle he hauled three loaded Bergens. He threw one each to Ted and to Oscar, slung his own on his back as if it weighed no more than a handbag, and set off at his usual blistering forced march pace, which Ted knew to his cost the man could keep up for hours at a time.

They bivouacked for the night close to their target, the Crib Goch ascent of Yr Wyddfa – Mount Snowdon.

Ted was a lot fitter than Oscar but he had to admire the guts and the tenacity of the man who, after his bad start, was determined to give a better account of himself when they set off on the Grade 1 ascent the following morning at first light. Even when Green pushed the pace hard enough to shave many minutes off the average time.

There was no opportunity to admire the views from the summit as, no sooner had they reached it, than Green was plunging off in a direction totally new to Ted, which showed little sign of recent use. His chosen route twisted and jinked so much that by the time they had reached what Green declared to be their stopping place for the night, even Ted's usually excellent sense of direction had deserted him and he had no real idea of which direction their final destination lay in.

Still, Ted told himself in consolation, one more night under the basha, then back to his car the next day in time to drop Oscar off at the airport for his return flight to London, and to pick up Trev and Annie after their flight back from Germany. Then return to work on Monday morning to relieve a Jo Rodriguez who would no doubt, by now, be thankful to hand over the reins.

* * *

'So now what the fuck do we do? Start CPR?'

Oscar Smith sounded annoyed as much as anything. As if Green was lying at their feet, showing little sign of anything but ragged, shallow breathing, by his own choice, the following morning, shortly after breaking camp.

They were still miles from anywhere, with no sign of the car park where they'd left their vehicles, when the man had suddenly dropped like a stone and remained unresponsive to Ted's shouts and shoulder-shakes.

'Not unless you're determined to kill him,' Ted told him, checking again for vital signs. 'He has a pulse, although it's slow and faint. We need urgent medical assistance.'

'Yeah, and he's the only one with a phone, which is presumably locked, so what are you planning on doing? Lighting a fire and sending up smoke signals?'

Oscar was no doubt busy thinking of that return flight, which he was clearly looking forward to after such a testing time. Ted ignored his rant, carefully manoeuvring Green into the recovery position, maintaining his airway and reaching in his own pocket for the space blanket he always carried there when in the mountains.

'Even if we knew which way to go for help and one of us made it there, he could quite probably croak before help arrived. Maybe we should try carrying him down?' Smith suggested.

Even he sounded dubious of his proposal so he continued, 'Ideally, we need to get into his phone. Call out a helicopter and get him a casevac to the nearest hospital.

'Get his phone out. We've got three tries, at least.'

'We've got two,' Ted corrected him. 'If we get it wrong three times, even if he comes to, we can't bank on even him knowing his unlock code off by heart, the state he's in. So it might be better to carry him down.'

Ignoring him completely, Smith was rummaging through Green's clothing and triumphantly produced a mobile phone from one of the zipped thigh pockets in the man's trousers.

He looked at it dubiously as he said, 'Not even sure this old thing is sophisticated enough to have a screen lock.'

He was jabbing at it as he spoke, then went on, 'But it does. Fuck. Any bright ideas as to a number that might mean something special to him? I'm assuming he's not daft enough to use his birthday?'

'I don't know that anyway,' Ted told him. 'Ours is hardly that sort of a relationship.'

Oscar Smith was suddenly animated, talking half to himself. Like a man finding himself unexpectedly on familiar ground. Using his brain to solve a problem which appeared on the surface to be insoluble. One where time, and the odds, appeared to be against him.

'SAS, you said? This is probably going to be too obvious, but it could be a double bluff so it's worth a try.'

His fingers were working quickly as he spoke, but he then shook his head. 'Incorrect PIN. So not 1941, the year The Regiment was formed. Did he serve in anything else?'

'You've only got one more shot,' Ted reminded him. 'His code could be anything, even his Army number, or a part of it. What makes you think it's connected to his military service?'

'Because I was a soldier and I know how they think. And I know what my code is. So, any other regiments?'

'Paras before that,' Ted told him.

Smith fingers were flying now, then he gave a triumphant air punch and a 'Yes!' as the phone obediently unlocked and he found himself staring at a home screen photo of a laughing small child, sitting on a fat Shetland pony, being led by an unrecognisably smiling Mr Green.

Smith only had time to tap in the first number of the emergency services as he opened the phone app before Green shot to his feet to snatch it from him.

'Well, it took the useless pair of you long enough to come up with something which would have worked if I really had been at death's door. It was like being at the mercy of a Brownie pack. I'd have died of old age or boredom, never mind anything critical, listening to the pair of you fannying about with no clear plan.

'And you, Monkey-boy, before you start thinking how clever you are, know that if you breathe a word about getting into my phone, to anyone, I will find you, and I will hurt you.

'By rights I should keep you up here another day at least until one of you finds a brain cell from somewhere and starts thinking proper survival strategy, but I'd end up killing one of you and that would be too much paperwork.'

And with that, he turned away and plunged onto a barely discernible track jinking its way down from the steep peak, at a pace to challenge a mountain goat.

Chapter Two

Jo Rodriguez was deliberately not using Ted's office in his absence. He was keen to make the point that he was there in a caretaker role only and he was definitely not Ted. He also preferred being back at his old desk so he could easily consult Mike Hallam, who already knew all the ins and outs of the case.

After the Ice Queen's latest visit, as well as chasing up the lab yet again, Jo had gone through the various interviews with witnesses to the triple killing, to see if he could spot one where he thought he might perhaps get something more from someone than previous interviewers had managed to. He remained sceptical but needed to show the Ice Queen he'd taken heed of her words, ready for her next appearance.

'There's a possible one here for me, Mike. Isabella, she's called. A Spanish-speaker. So at least we'd be saving on the cost of an interpreter. She's said very little to date. She's from the Dominican Republic. If we could get her in for interview today, I could at least have a go, although I'm not holding my breath.'

'I don't even know where the Dominican Republic is, but I'd say we need to try anything at this stage,' Mike told him.

'It's in the Caribbean. Shares an island with Haiti. The official language is Spanish, which is why I think it might possibly be worth my while to try interviewing this young lady myself, in her native language, if necessary.'

Mike frowned at that as he said, 'This is probably going to come out all sorts of politically incorrect, but it's only genuine ignorance on my part, and I know you won't take it the wrong way. But Haiti. Doesn't that have a link to voodoo, so might that not fit very well with this case? All this mumbo-jumbo stuff about killing twins to protect the planet? Or have I been watching too many of the wrong sort of films?'

That made Jo chuckle as he said, 'I own up. That was pretty much the first thought which crossed my mind, too. In fact it seems to be a complex issue, as religion often is, and I've only had time to skim read.

'In a probably leaky nutshell, Haitian Vodou is a different thing altogether, with nothing much in common with witchcraft, pins or wax effigies, as far as I can tell. I'd definitely need input from an expert, but I think I could do worse than try talking to this young woman. At least it's something I can wave at the Ice Queen to show I'm doing my best, and taking her suggestions on board. With luck, it might be enough for her to reduce her royal visits to one or two a day.

'I'd best go down to see Kevin, to ask for someone from Uniform to go and bring her in. I'll go in person. If I do it by phone, he won't see me literally on my knees begging for his help when I know how short of officers he is.'

Once he stood up, Jo realised he probably needed a trip via the bogs before he went downstairs to grovel to Inspector Kevin Turner for the loan of an officer to go and bring the potential witness in for further questioning. He'd been rather mainlining on the black coffee to try to keep alert enough to find the elusive breakthrough they so desperately needed, preferably before Ted's return on Monday morning, and it had taken its toll.

Jo had developed the habit of moving quietly. He always said, not entirely in jest, that having six children, three of each, the odds of finding at least one of them at any time getting up to something they weren't supposed to, were high. Having a father who could appear silently from nowhere was quite a good deterrent, in the home at least.

He made little noise himself when he went into the toilets so he could clearly hear the distinctive sound of sobbing being hastily stifled at the noise made by the door closing behind him.

Officer welfare was another part of Ted's role which Jo had had to take over in his absence. He had no idea who it was in that cubicle. Not even whether it was one of the Serious Crime Team, because several had been away from their desks when he'd walked through the main office.

Whoever it was, it was his duty to find out and to see what, if anything, he could do to help.

He went to the nearest handbasin, ran the water noisily and washed his hands. For extra effect, hoping it wasn't overkill, he sang a couple of lines from 'Guantanamera' as he washed then dried them under the hot air blower.

He opened the outer door, still singing to himself, then he simply let it close without going through it, stopped singing and calmly waited in the silence.

Big, solid DC Dennis 'Virgil' Tibbs was the last person Jo would have guessed to be the one crying his eyes out. He'd have put money on it being Maurice Brown, known by all as Daddy Hen because of his fondness for children or anyone in need of protecting. Maurice was currently desk-bound and assigned to collating. He'd been cleared of a trumped-up rape charge against him, but he'd made serious procedural errors for which he was undergoing further training before returning to full duties.

Virgil visibly jumped to find Jo waiting there, as he was busy rubbing away the tracks of tears with the back of his hand.

'Are you all right, Virgil?' Jo asked him. 'This is a tough one for all of us. Especially those of us with kids. No shame in that.'

'Sorry, Jo. I didn't think there was anyone in here or I'd have stayed where I was. I thought I heard whoever it was go out.'

'I'm a sneaky sort of parent. Ask any of my kids. And I can move as quietly as the boss in stealth mode when I need to. But seriously, there's no shame in having feelings. I can't take you off the case. We're low enough on numbers as it is, but I can take you for a pint after work, if that would help?'

Virgil was quietly crying again at his words.

'That's kind, Jo, but I need to get back to the wife …'

The outer door opened at that point and a young constable from Uniform started to come in. Jo immediately stepped to block him from seeing Virgil, or from coming any further.

'Closed for maintenance,' he told him. 'Go and find another one.'

From the look on the young officer's face, Jo dreaded to think what he imagined was going on.

With a hastily muttered, 'Yes sir, sorry sir,' he beat a swift retreat.

Jo stepped closer to Virgil and opened his arms.

'All my kids say I give good dad hugs, if that would help? And there's honestly no shame in having feelings. It shows you're human, and caring.'

His words made Virgil cry more, now with his face against Jo's shoulder and comforting arms around him.

'I'm as bad as the wife. I thought the hormones thing only affected women when they're pregnant. But I'm as bad as she is. We're having another baby. I'm going to be a daddy again. I think that's why this case is getting to me so much.

'Thanks, Jo, I promise I'll get my shit together soon. Just please don't tell any of the others you found me like this. And definitely don't tell the boss.'

* * *

'I don't suppose there's any chance you have blues for this Dinky toy of yours? Only I'm likely to miss my flight if you don't keep your foot down flat all the way to the airport,' Oscar Smith told Ted once they were finally down from the mountains and had had a typical Mr Green debrief.

That had consisted of him hurling their phones and the car keys at them and haranguing them about the precious minutes they'd wasted debating what to do when he'd collapsed, before doing anything useful.

'Comes to something when it takes a Monkey to solve a problem. We'll meet again, soon, and I'll expect much better from both of you.'

'And that, coming from Mr Green, is high praise indeed for you, Oscar,' Ted had told him as he unlocked the car to let Smith get in, which was when he posed his question.

'But no, even if I had blues, we couldn't justify using them. We've got a two-hour drive ahead of us, so if you check in online at some point, you should just about make your flight. I'm going to be at least an hour late to pick up Trev and Annie, unless theirs is running late, so I'll need to text him at some point when we stop.'

'We can't stop!' Smith's voice went up at the mere suggestion. 'I've got his number, I'll text him to explain, but I can't miss my flight so get your foot down.'

'I did tell you to book a later one, just in case,' Ted told him mildly. 'But fair play to you, Oscar, we'd have been a lot later if not for you. I'd never have got the unlock code because I don't know army regiments like you do, so we would have ended up carrying him. Until he deigned to tell us it was a bluff, which would probably not have been until we reached the bottom.'

'How did he do it, though? I really did think he was a goner for a moment there.'

'A lot a serious martial artists can do stuff like that. Slowing their own heart rate. Especially the ones who do a lot of meditation. I did wonder if it was genuine, but clearly we had to behave as if it was in case he died on us. The inquest would have been fun, for sure, if that had happened.'

'And did he mean it? About meeting again?'

'Another thing you should know about Mr Green,' Ted told him as he changed down for a twisty section of road, 'is that he never says anything he doesn't mean.'

* * *

Jo Rodriguez was doubly lucky with his planned interview of the Spanish-speaker, Isabella. He'd found Kevin Turner in a better mood than he'd feared and able to send someone out fairly swiftly to bring her in for further questioning. Jo had also found the crime team's newest member, DC Alison O'Malley, in the office and available to be a chaperone for the interview.

'Do you speak any Spanish?' Jo asked her, as they made their way down the stairs to wait for their interviewee to arrive.

'Enough to order *dos cervezas, por favor,* when my boyfriend and I go there on holiday, but that's my limit.'

'I'll be interviewing in Spanish so you'll just have to trust me not to be bullying her into saying anything to get some sort of testimony out of her.'

Ali laughed at that.

'I somehow don't see you as the bullying type, although I know they're usually clever at hiding their true nature. You might even find she does actually speak English and is just stalling for time, like some of the other witnesses seem to have been doing.'

She was right. As soon as Jo introduced himself and Alison, then launched into what was clearly a fluent stream of Spanish, the young woman told him, 'I do speak some English but I was afraid of making mistakes and perhaps being ...' she added a few words in Spanish, looking at Jo for a translation.

'Arrested and charged,' he supplied helpfully. 'And I can assure you, I only want to know the truth. If you've done nothing wrong, you have nothing to fear. You are being interviewed as a witness, not a suspect at this stage. I would strongly suggest you tell us anything and everything that you know. You can do that in Spanish if it's easier for you.'

'Do I need *un abogado*?'

'A lawyer. That is your choice. If you want one, I can arrange one for you. All I'm interested in is what happened at the Welcoming you attended where those two baby girls were killed. Newborns. Slaughtered before they'd barely taken their first breaths. And their mother, too.'

Their witness was crying now, soundlessly. Tears rolling down her cheeks and splashing onto the table in front of her.

Ali was starting to get worried. She'd never seen Jo like this. He was working himself up into such a state she was getting concerned that none of the resulting statement from the witness would be deemed admissible because of undue pressure if he carried on like this unchecked.

She laid a hand on his forearm, feeling the tension in his muscles. The whole case was bad enough for her. She couldn't begin to imagine what it was like for a doting father of six children.

First she fished a clean tissue out of her pocket and slid it across to the witness. Then she waited until she started to recover and the tension slowly left Jo's body.

Once she felt the situation was suitably defused, she looked at the woman opposite her and smiled in what she hoped was an encouraging and non-threatening way.

'Please, if there's anything at all you can say to help us, it would make such a difference with this case.'

She glanced sideways at Jo, not sure if she was about to overstep the mark, but desperate to get the breakthrough they needed – someone who might, finally, agree to go on record and tell them exactly what they had seen at the Welcoming where the two baby girls had been so brutally murdered. And, crucially, who else had been there and could potentially identify the person who had actually carried out the killings.

'This isn't the first such case, either,' Ali went on. 'Another police force nearby is also investigating the sudden unexplained death of a baby girl, a twin, shortly after she

Ted grinned at him as he said, 'Now, anyone with a suspicious mind – like me – might think that such a warm welcome, nice though it is, smacked of a degree of relief at handing over the reins. Am I right?'

'Spot on,' Jo told him with a laugh. 'We were doing well until I finally heard from the lab. The DNA sample from Tonton was unusable. A fault on the seal, they said, but as they delayed so long before owning up to it, I'm wondering if there's more to it than that. But the long and the short of it is, we need to get another one from him, which they have promised faithfully to rush through for us.'

Jo knew Ted well enough by now to know he wasn't likely to go off on one, shout, swear and blame all and sundry. At his worst, he might just karate kick the door or jump on his wastepaper basket. But he didn't seem inclined to do even that. He simply shook his head and sighed as he said, 'These things happen, unfortunately. I'll get the wheels in motion for a second sample to be taken, probably in the face of a lot of opposition. But we'll get it done. All is not yet lost.

'Any positive news, to counterbalance the bad?'

'There is, as it happens. Her Majesty has been harassing me for results all week, as you can imagine. She went as far as suggesting I should interview some of the witnesses myself. I wasn't sure if I could do any better than anyone else. But then I got lucky and found a Spanish-speaking one.'

He told Ted about his interview with the young woman, of her finally agreeing to provide a statement and if necessary to testify in court, as long as she could be assured of her personal safety in case of reprisals from anyone connected to the group.

'I'll need to arrange a translation of the interview, of course, but subject to assurances, I think she's a credible witness, and one who will go on to testify.'

'Excellent. Thanks, Jo. I'm taking it as a given that there was no question of coercion or intimidation of the witness to get her to talk?'

'I did lay out for her how appalling a crime it was, in case she'd been deluding herself. But no, everything by the book. I had Ali O'Malley in there with me, for a female presence, although she admits she only knows holiday Spanish. And everything done as it should be, with recordings. It should stand up to any defence cross examination.'

'Excellent. Just checking, although I know I can rely on you. Anything else I need to know before you go off back to Ashton?

'There is, although he wanted me to promise not to tell you. I couldn't promise that, of course. You need to be in the picture.

'I found Virgil crying his eyes out in the bogs. The case has been getting to him. He was trying not to let anyone know, going in there when there was no one about. Or so he thought, but I did my sneaky dad routine. He'd have heard the door when I went in there but I let him think I'd left so he came out and I saw him. And he was mortified.'

'Virgil?' Ted queried. 'He'd be the last person I'd have expected to hear that about. It's very out of character. Is he all right?'

'Broody, boss. He's just found out his wife is expecting their second child and that seemed to set him off. I only mentioned it so you could keep half an eye on him, although like I said, he didn't want me to tell you. I've not put it in my written report, but I thought you should know.'

'Thanks, Jo, I'll keep an eye. Clearly I can't take him off the case, short-handed as we are, but I'll keep a watching brief.

'Right, then, I have the conn, Mr Sulu, you can safely beam yourself back to your own nick, and thanks for your steadying hand on the tiller.'

Jo laughed at that, used to the boss's sometimes obscure film and TV series quotes.

'Do spacecraft even have a tiller? Oh, and when it comes to translating the interview, be sure to inform whoever books the translator that although my wife is on the list of those qualified to do such things, she clearly can't translate an interview I've undertaken. It would be an easy thing to get wrong as she's listed under her maiden name, although she would stop, of course, as soon as she saw mine.'

'Noted, and thanks again, Jo.'

Once he'd caught up with the team for morning briefing, Ted intended to spend the rest of the day going through notes left for him and taking an overview of any case progress in his absence. He knew he could rely on Jo to be on top of everything, but overall responsibility was his so he needed to be sure nothing at all had been missed or left to chance.

He also wanted to make time to have a quiet word with each team member, to see how they were bearing up. He was still surprised that it had been Virgil who'd seemingly been the first to crack, so he'd definitely need to keep a close eye on him, without letting him know that Jo had betrayed a confidence.

His first port of call needed to be to Superintendent Caldwell, as a matter of courtesy, if nothing else. He'd also assured Jo that he would be the one to tell her the bad news from the lab.

She was never one for chit-chat, although she did ask about Ted's holiday, and also about his training with Mr Green. She'd had experience of him in her own Firearms days, though not of his more extreme methods.

Ted gave her brief highlights but then launched into their current problem with the DNA sample. There seemed little point in delaying the bad news.

'I see. And what is your gut feeling telling you?' she asked him.

'I know spoiled samples can happen, for all sorts of reasons. What I'm failing to understand at the moment is the delay in telling us what had gone wrong. They knew we were desperate for those results. Jo and I have both been chasing them constantly. Up until Jo's interview with the young woman, those results were what we were banking on for starting to build a solid case.

'I appreciate someone somewhere is trying to cover their back, but it's gone beyond the ridiculous now. I've not yet informed CPS. They're clearly not going to be happy. We need a positive result on Tonton's DNA for us to have any chance of a 'beyond reasonable doubt' on him.'

As Ted's deputy in his absence, it had been Jo who was liaising with the Crown Prosecution Service, updating them on any developments in building a case against their suspects. Something else he would be pleased to hand over to Ted now he was back.

'Would you like me to have a word – an official one – with the lab?' the superintendent suggested. 'It's bad enough that the error occurred in the first place but to keep us in the dark all this time is unforgivable. The delay could well give a sharp defence lawyer grounds to pursue bail for this Tonton person since we really have very few reasonable grounds to keep their client in custody on what we have to date.

'Let's face it, we don't even have the man's identity, so that DNA could be vital in establishing exactly who he is.'

'That would be helpful, ma'am, thank you. I'll take any help that's going at this stage.'

'And what about officer welfare? How are your team bearing up with this case? It's a highly distressing one, especially for those who are parents, I imagine. Clearly you don't have the option to stand any of them down, but we must be seen to be pro-active in taking care of their mental health.'

She was right, Ted knew. Times were changing. In his early days there had been little thought to any such thing. Officers were simply supposed to accept that distressing cases went with the role. Nowadays there were so many safeguarding rules in place it sometimes appeared hard to know how they could be expected to do their jobs whilst following them. Especially in a unit like Serious Crime.

'Jo has been keeping a watching brief in my absence, and I'll continue to monitor all of the team.'

The Ice Queen was studying him closely. She was getting to know him well. Understanding that he would go to almost any lengths to protect his team members, and that could include not wanting to reveal a weakness unless it became impossible to conceal.

He'd never yet let her down. She would simply have to carry on trusting him to do the right and responsible thing, if it became necessary.

* * *

Ted had spent most of the day updating himself on everything which had been happening in his absence. As he'd expected, Jo had left him detailed reports and had done a good job of running the team.

As back-up, Ted took Mike Hallam out to lunch at their local pub, The Grapes, to ask him, in the informal setting of its back room, where they were the only customers, about welfare within the team.

It was clear that Jo had kept his word and told no one except the boss about Virgil. Ted formed the firm impression that Mike knew nothing about it and was not simply keeping quiet in turn.

'It's a tough one for everyone, this, boss. Probably the worst I've worked on. But you know our team. They're solid, and they look out for one another, as best they can. We really could do with a numbers boost, though, if you can pull some strings and score us some more bodies. I'm just worried that, stretched as we are, if we did have to stand someone down for any reason, there just isn't anyone to cover for them. Not to mention if something else happens which gets dumped onto us.'

'I know, Mike, and heaven help us if we do suddenly get another crime within our remit. Just cross your fingers that there's nothing else heading down the track in our direction. And whatever you do, don't tempt fate by even thinking of anything else turning up. We'll just have to hope the local scallies give us a bit of a break for now.'

* * *

As soon as Kevin Turner walked into Ted's office mid-afternoon, with only a brief courtesy knock, Ted had a sinking feeling that his earlier words had come back to bite him.

He looked at Kev, took in his harassed expression and stood up to put the kettle on.

'Cuppa?' he asked. 'You have the look of someone needing one.'

'As long as it's not that weak green weasel's piss you drink,' Kevin told him, pulling out the spare chair and sitting down. 'I wouldn't mind proper builder's tea, or a coffee if you have it.'

'And I hope you're not going to ask me for officers, for a change, because you know how we're fixed. I haven't got enough for my own needs currently, never mind yours as well,' Ted added as he put the kettle back on.

'Sorry, but I am. We've just got a case which has Serious Crime written all over it. It certainly needs one of your team to attend, if only to consult and tell me who other than you I can offload it onto as it's not one for us, that's for sure.'

The kettle hadn't long boiled so Ted made the drinks, put them on his desk and sat down opposite Kevin. He'd known him a long time. Long enough to know that if he said it was one for Serious Crime not Uniform, he was almost certainly right.

Kevin launched into his spiel once he'd taken a gulp of his coffee, wincing at the heat.

'We had a call today to go to a house where neighbours had been complaining of a very bad smell. And not your average blocked drains smell, either.

'My officers gained entry and found a very dead body in the kitchen. Like five or six days dead at least, they reckon. Male. Still waiting on final ID. No signs of intruders, no weapon about, but very clear signs the deceased had been ripped to shreds – half eaten, one of my officers put it – by something like one or more very large dogs.'

Ted was frowning now as he asked, 'And you think this is serious crime because ... ?'

'Because all the neighbours interviewed so far are adamant the man didn't have a dog. Didn't like them. Scared of them, even. Never been seen with one, and there were no traces in the house to suggest he'd ever kept any. No food for them, no dog bowls, no leads, no beds.

'And, this is the clincher for me, there were no dogs found on the premises, although all the doors were closed and locked. So who put them in there in the first place and why? And who removed them and where did they go?'

'Dogs as a murder weapon? I suppose it's possible. Tell me at least there's some CCTV of the area to give us a steer.'

'I would if I could but I can't. All of the cameras anywhere about have been taken out with what looks to my officers' admittedly untrained eyes, compared to you, like a high-powered air rifle.

'So is that enough for you to at least send someone to check it out? CSI are already there and Professor Nelson was on her way to consult, the last I heard. This has the makings of such an unusual one, the coroner wanted her input right from the start. Whatever's happened at that house, she might be able to tell us if it's a horrible accident, or a suspicious death, even before she gets the body for post-mortem.'

'There are definitely no dogs anywhere near still?'

As soon as Kevin heard that, he knew that Ted would be attending himself in the first instance. Ted's nervousness of dogs was an open secret.

'None at all located anywhere, but if it makes you happier, I'll make sure there's at least one taser-trained officer with you at all times,' Kev assured him.

'Thanks, Ted. I knew I could rely on you. Murder by offensive dog is a totally new one on me.'

Chapter Four

Before he went to the scene himself, Ted phoned the police dog section. He wanted someone who knew dogs and all about them to meet him there and talk him through their initial thoughts. This sounded like something which was going to need expert input from the start.

As a trained firearms officer, he should be able to tell for himself easily enough what had been used to take out CCTV cameras in the area, but he knew little about dogs. The first thing he needed to know was what sort of a brute would have killed someone in their own home, and in what had been described as a frenzied attack.

Like many people, he'd seen news reports of pet dogs being killed by other dogs. Increasingly by the breed known as XL Bully dogs, while not under proper control. Experts were saying it was only a matter of time before there were human fatalities, and there were growing calls to have the breed banned.

Ted was hoping that an expert police dog handler would be able to answer a lot of his questions, starting with exactly what type of dog they were looking for. With a bit of luck, the officer he'd been promised to act as a consultant would arrive at the house where the body had been found not long after he did.

He told Mike Hallam where he was going and why. Mike looked shocked at the news.

'Sooner you than me, then, boss,' he told Ted. 'You know I don't have a strong stomach at the best of times and that doesn't sound like a pleasant scene for anyone.'

Ted took his official car, guessing there would already be people flocking to the scene to try to get a look at what was going on. No doubt the local newshound, Penny Hunter, would be there already and would make a beeline for him as soon as he showed his face. At least with use of the blues he should be able to clear a space for himself to get through any throngs.

He was right about Penny. Hers was the first recording device to be thrust under his nose before he'd barely had chance to open his car door.

'Is it true that the dead man kept illegal fighting dogs which turned on him and killed him, chief inspector?'

'Penny, I've literally just got here. As soon as I have any details, I will let you know, but I can make absolutely no comment at all at the present time because I simply don't know anything and I'm not going to guess.'

An officer from Uniform was trying his best to stop anyone unauthorised breaching the cordon. He lifted the tape for Ted and noted his name, saying, 'Word's got out quickly on this one, sir. There's a lot of determined rubberneckers, for sure.'

'Is it just you to keep them back?' Ted asked him, reaching in his pocket for one of his Fisherman's Friend lozenges. From what he'd heard so far, he was likely to need something to help with the smell when he got inside.

'At the moment, sir, yes. There's another unit on its way to help but they've been diverted to another potentially serious incident. There's also two officers on door-to-door, talking to the neighbours. I'll manage for now though.'

Ted kitted himself out in coveralls, gloves, mask and shoe covers before making his way inside, immediately assailed by a smell he knew all too well from previous cases. He hoped his lozenge would be enough to help him through.

The stench was bad enough as he stepped through the front door. It grew worse as he walked down towards the kitchen at the back, where he could see that all the action was taking place.

He was pleased to see that the Crime Scene Manager was one he'd worked with before and knew to be someone quietly efficient. He'd need to discuss with her as soon as he could to develop a strategy for how the scene would be processed.

Other investigators were beginning their work on the scene under her direction, collecting and bagging samples, carefully labelling and sealing everything as they went.

It made Ted even more suspicious about the excuse of a faulty bag rendering the DNA from Tonton unusable. There was certainly no sign of risk of such a thing here, from what he could see. It could well be a different thing altogether at the lab, possibly, but it still sounded suspicious.

The body of a man was lying in the kitchen at the end of the hall, in a second open doorway which appeared to lead to a living room. The smell was cloying, overpowering, the body clearly not at all fresh. No wonder neighbours had phoned to report it.

Home Office pathologist, Professor Bizzie Nelson, was working around the body, seemingly unaware of the odour. Her assistant was taking photos from every available angle.

Ted had tried to prepare himself mentally for what he was likely to see, but the reality was worse. Far worse. Whatever animals had done this had clearly possessed very strong jaws. The man's throat was ripped open, his face partially devoured, and at first glance it looked as if his limbs had also had sections eaten.

There was blood everywhere, as well as excrement, both human and dog by the look of it.

Bizzie Nelson glanced up and greeted him. Formally, as always, in front of others.

'Ah, chief inspector. This is an unusual case for all of us, which is why I was asked to attend the scene as soon as possible. You know I don't make snap judgements, but on first examination of this room, it would seem that the deceased met his end at the jaws of a very large dog or more probably, dogs. Luckily for us, there are no longer any animals on the scene.

'Your victim died at least five to six days ago. I'll be able to pin that down more precisely once I get him on my table. It seems to have been the odour of decomposition which prompted reports from neighbours to the police. There's a small upper window open above the sink there, which would have let the smell out.

'Not yet knowing what type of dog did the damage, I don't know if they would have been likely to give tongue like hunting dogs whilst attacking. I would certainly have expected the victim to make some considerable noise, at least in the early stages, but even that doesn't seem to have produced any reaction from the neighbours. There may, of course, have been no one at home at the time of the attack.'

'I have a police dog handler coming shortly who might possibly have some input for us about what the breed of dog might have been, plus any other relevant details,' Ted told her.

He didn't voice all of his thoughts aloud, with some investigators present whom he didn't know. He wanted no leaks of any sort on this incident before he had a better idea of what was going on.

He wasn't about to jump to any conclusions – it wasn't at all his style – but if the intel on the deceased not having dogs of his own was solid, and he had no reason to doubt it, the dogs may well have been introduced into the house, left to do their job, then removed again and whisked away long before the body had been discovered.

He turned his attention next to the back door. The most likely point of entry for the dogs and whoever brought them. Too risky at the front, with passing traffic and possibly nosy neighbours. But the rear entrances to the houses were accessed from an old service road, Ted could see by looking out of the back door, beyond which was derelict land that looked as if it might once have been a market garden. It now boasted nothing more interesting than old mattresses and discarded furniture, and led in turn to a steep embankment above a railway line. There were no other houses close enough at the back for occupants to have seen anything much going on.

There was no sign of forced entry to the back door, which suggested that whoever put the dogs inside must have had their own key, found the door unlocked, or the householder either knew them, or saw no reason not to open the door to them.

If they didn't have a key, they could simply have taken one from the house when they'd gone back to retrieve the dogs, after leaving them to do their job, then locked up on leaving.

'Do we have an ID on the deceased yet?' Ted asked of those present.

'Not yet confirmed, but the neighbours who reported the smell said the occupant was a Frank Turnbull, who lived here alone and was on long-term sickness benefit, as far as they knew,' the manager told him. 'No accurate age but suggestions are forties or fifties. No mobile phone found anywhere yet, not on the body, nor in this part of the house.'

'Thank you. We'll need to do door-to-door, as soon as I have enough officers to arrange it. We're a bit stretched at the moment on the existing case.'

'Are you any further forward with the mother and baby killings?' Bizzie Nelson asked him.

Ted gave her a look above his mask which he hoped she would interpret as him not wanting to say too much in front of the CSIs as he said, 'We've hit a bit of a roadblock at the moment.'

It wasn't that he had any reason to be suspicious of any of the Crime Scene Investigators. He was simply paranoid about anything to do with such a complex unsolved case leaking out to the media from anywhere.

Bizzie was as sharp as a tack, always. She read the message behind his words and said simply, 'Do please let me know if you need any more input from me.'

Before Ted could go any further, there was a brief tap on the open door to the hall which led from the front entrance. A man in civvies stood there, looking round. With everyone in overalls and masks, it was impossible for him to tell who was who working on the crime scene.

'I'm looking for DCI Darling, please. I'm Sergeant Woods, from the dog section. I believe you need a consult.'

'Don't come anywhere near my suspicious death scene without full kit on!' Bizzie bellowed, before Ted could get a word in. 'And chief inspector, can you please deal appropriately with whoever let him get this far without.'

It wouldn't fully become Ted's crime scene until the professor turned it over to him. For now, she called the shots, and made sure everyone knew that.

Ted didn't leave the kitchen to go out of the front door, or he would have needed a fresh suit, shoe covers, gloves and mask, but he showed the sergeant where to get his own, to make sure he was suitably kitted out before he let him back inside.

'Sorry about that, sir. Believe it or not this is my first potential murder scene, although I've seen plenty of bodies through other causes. Stupid rookie mistake, though.'

'Don't worry about it. You weren't to know the professor hadn't finished. I should warn you, though, that the scene isn't very pleasant. The body wasn't found for around five or six days, for one thing, we believe, and the wounds are horrific. That's what I'm relying on you for. To tell me if they were inflicted by a dog or dogs, and if so, what sort of an animal it might be.'

'Luckily I'm not squeamish, so I'll certainly do my best to help you, sir.'

The sergeant kept well out of the professor's way until she indicated that he could move closer.

'There is, as you can see, sergeant, significant crushing injury to the trachea. That, and the fact that the jugular veins and carotid arteries were punctured, would have made death quite swift, mercifully. If it was indeed canine jaws which caused the injuries, it would have had to be a very powerful animal. The dog hypothesis looks probable but I can't confirm anything before I've carried out further tests to be sure.'

'Ma'am,' the sergeant began, before Bizzie stopped him in his tracks.

'Please not ma'am, sergeant. I am not royalty. Anything but. Professor will more than suffice.'

'Well, professor, stating the obvious here, if you'll excuse me, it would take a very big and powerful dog to inflict that degree of crushing injury. And the bites certainly do look canine at first glance.

'Without knowing your findings to date, I would also suggest there were two dogs at work here. If you look there,' he pointed from a safe distance, 'it seems likely that there were two strong sets of jaws pulling in opposite directions.

'Please excuse me if I'm going beyond my remit, but it also looks to me as if the animals may have consumed some of the flesh, as there appear to be some chunks missing, unless you've located them.

'That's very unusual with normal, domesticated dogs, unless they are literally starving. So in this case, I would certainly consider the possibility that they'd been deprived of food for some time to make them much more likely to attack.

'Did the dogs belong to the deceased?'

'We're still investigating that,' Ted told him. 'One of the neighbours who phoned about the smell said he didn't have any dogs, but that they'd heard some barking, as well as other noises coming from the house a few days ago.'

'From the look of the damage to the deceased, it would have taken very swift, expert intervention to have been any use to him, even if someone had dialled 999 then.'

Bizzie was listening attentively to what he was saying. She could tell he knew what he was talking about. She was a dog lover and owner herself and hers had always been bull terriers. The current one, Spilsbury, was so soft and friendly that even Ted was not particularly afraid of him.

'So are you able to make any deduction of what type of dog might have inflicted such injuries, sergeant?' she asked him. 'Very clearly something large and powerful, of course, but something which would be capable of attacking someone to this extent.

'I grew up with mastiffs and now have bull terriers. I remember well the gentle nature of the mastiffs, although they were of a size to inflict damage similar to this. I'll need to wait until I get the body back to my lair to calculate dimensions, force of the bite and other such details, but I would be interested in your first thoughts.

'We should, at least, be able to extract DNA from the dog dirt and other samples, so if we ever find a likely animal, we should be able to confirm its involvement that way.'

'It takes a particular dog to do this to a human being, except in dire necessity. I agree about the English mastiffs. They tend to be protective, especially of children in their care, but not aggressive. Certainly not to this degree.

'My first thought, going by the likely power of the jaws would be an XL Bully. Because of their size and power – we could be looking at a nine-stone or more dog here – some unscrupulous types keep them specifically for intimidating anyone they need to.

'They can certainly be trained to attack, especially if they're ravenous. Looking at the amount of dog sh...' he corrected himself just in time, in front of the professor and a senior officer he didn't know, 'dog dirt they left in here, it looks as if they may well have been left here for some time. Days rather than hours. Perhaps to make sure they did the job they were put here for efficiently.'

'Forgive my ignorance of all things canine, sergeant, but would the dogs make any noise while doing what they did?' Ted asked him. 'Barking? Growling loudly enough for neighbours to hear? I think there was mention from someone about hearing barking but we're still at the stage of getting initial info.'

'Hard to say, sir, it would all depend on how they were trained and for what purpose. Some owners of attack dogs get their vocal chords cut so their victims don't hear them coming, and there's no noise to alert anyone around. It's sometimes done with fighting dogs, too, or for other clandestine activities, where the owners don't want to draw any attention to what they're doing.'

He was interrupted in his flow at that point by the hesitant voice of the officer on the door, calling quietly, 'Chief inspector? Sir? There's an officer out here who says he needs to talk to you urgently, if you're able to come to the door, please.'

Ted excused himself and walked back towards the front door, stopping well short, again not wanting to go out then having to don fresh coveralls to return.

There was a man in civvies with the Uniform officer. Not someone Ted immediately recognised, but who had his warrant card out and held up for him to see.

'DCI Darling? I'm Sergeant Sean Duffy. Organised Crime. I think this might be our crime scene, not yours.'

Chapter Five

'I think this is probably something we need to discuss in private, sergeant,' Ted told him.

'Nothing much to discuss, but I'm happy to tell you why that is. I agree that we need to do it somewhere in private though, no disrespect to anyone present,' Duffy told him.

'My car's nearby. I would suggest we go and sit in that and I'll listen to what you have to say.'

Ted was already heading for the front door, peeling off protective layers as he went, then dumping them in the used items receptacle.

Once they were safely inside Ted's service vehicle, out of the way of the gawkers, now being kept back from the crime scene by more officers who had arrived while Ted was inside the house, he turned to Duffy.

'You're welcome to make your case, sergeant. I'm not prejudging, but the crime is on our patch and it certainly falls within my team's serious crime remit. So on what basis are you staking a claim for the Organised Crime Group?'

'We've had Turnbull in our sights for some time now, keeping a discreet eye on him. We have reliable intel that he's a drugs dealer for one of the main gangs we've been monitoring.'

'Not constant observation, then, if someone's managed to get in and do this to him,' Ted told him drily.

'You know what it's like with officer numbers. I'm sure your team's missed stuff because you don't have enough feet on the ground when and wherever you need them most. That's what's happened with this. I'd pulled bodies from here for something bigger going down, so they've got at him when no one was watching.'

'An insider tip-off, perhaps, then? The gang struck when they knew the coast would be clear? Or just a lucky coincidence for them? I should add here that I don't like coincidences. Don't trust them. They make me nervous, because in my experience, there's usually much more to it than that.'

'What's concerning me most now is that I've had an officer visiting Turnbull regularly to score from him. We're pretty certain Turnbull doesn't know he's been supplying a copper, but this is all sounding worryingly as if someone within the gang knew, or was suspicious.

'From the little I've heard so far, this has all the hallmarks of a punishment killing. By the sounds of it, one to send out a very strong signal to any of their foot soldiers to be bloody careful they know exactly who they're dealing with at all times.

'The other possibility is that Turnbull might have been upping the prices and taking a cut off the top, or keeping money back and stupidly thinking he could get away with it.

'I'd be lying if I said the thought of a leak from within my unit had never crossed my mind. It's the logical conclusion to start from. I just can't see any of my team doing that. But I suppose that's what everyone says when it happens amongst officers they work with every day, and have possibly done so for years.'

Ted knew only too well how true that was. Every officer in his own station had been shocked rigid when a long-serving and well-respected sergeant had been found to have been selling information to the press on a regular basis, to fund a gambling habit which was spiralling out of all control.

'So if you've had the deceased under obs for some time, you can perhaps tell me if the dogs which killed him were his own.'

'Not that I know of. Bear in mind I was sending one of my officers into that house on a regular basis to score and I wouldn't have been comfortable doing that if I'd known there were potentially dangerous animals in there. And my officer never mentioned any signs of any dogs, which I'm sure he would have.

'Turnbull might have had the idea he needed protecting if any of his drugs deals went bad, but everyone for miles around knows which gang he sells for and believe me, those twisted bastards are capable of far worse than any dog. That knowledge alone was probably enough of itself to give him all the protection he would need. Needed. Which is what makes me think the gang had him taken out themselves for some reason.'

'So you've been letting Turnbull carry on dealing in the hopes of getting closer to the gang through your undercover officer?'

'Pretty much, yes. That's why I'd prefer to take this case with my team. We're all over that gang already and we are really close to nailing them now. This could be the breakthrough we've been looking for.'

'Except it's on my patch, and as I said, a murder like this one is very definitely one for Serious Crime. And I hope you're not suggesting you wouldn't share intel with us in some idea of taking all the glory.'

Duffy made a snorting sound.

'I don't play games. Certainly not "who-can-piss-highest-up-the-wall" ones. I'm just interested in getting this pile of shit off the streets. We've been trying to for long enough, so far with no success. We so nearly had them once before but they walked free from court because the witnesses we had suddenly all got struck down with extreme memory loss. Related, no doubt, to one of them mysteriously receiving such serious injuries it's uncertain if he will ever walk again. And, funnily enough, he has no recollection about how he sustained them, but claims he must simply have been drunk and done it to himself.

'The case against them collapsed at committal stage, so we're going to have to build a much stronger one next time, or we stand no chance of getting it even that far.'

'Given that we're both complaining of shortage of officers, the logical thing would seem to be to run this as a joint op,' Ted told him.

He saw the sceptical look on the sergeant's face and went on, 'It makes sense. We'd both need clearance from higher up, but I don't imagine there would be any resistance, given the circumstances we're both in.'

Duffy laughed as he said, 'Oh, yes, you got the Ice Queen down here, didn't you? I've heard she's one who always likes going by the book and of course, in my unit, we often have to go off-piste. Way off. But I agree with you. It seems, on the face of it, to be the best thing for both of us, if we get the nod.

'How do you want to play it now? Ideally, I'd really like to view the scene while I'm here, if the body's still on site.

If nothing else I can give you a positive ID on the deceased, as I know Turnbull by sight from the many covert photos and film footage of him we have.'

'Aah.'

Ted's signature stalling sound, when he was working out how to frame something he was about to say.

'If you have his prints on record, that would help. As far as facial recognition goes, it might be a bit tricky to give a positive ID, given the injuries he sustained. But yes, the body's still here. Professor Nelson hasn't yet released the site. You may already know her, or know of her. She's a stickler. The best there is. She won't miss a trick, but she's very bluntly spoken, if you've not encountered her before. And don't, whatever you do, address her as ma'am. She hates it. Always professor.

'After you've seen the body, it's probably best if we each go back to get the authority we need for a joint op. Then, if that's okay with you, can you come over in the morning first thing, with any of your officers you want to include, so we can do a joint briefing and go from there?'

The sergeant still looked hesitant. Ted guessed he and his team were a solid unit, not used to working with what they might perceive as outsiders, with different skill sets. Working together seemed to Ted to be the logical thing to do, but he'd been prepared for a degree of resistance.

Finally, Duffy sighed and told him, 'Subject to approval from the top, it probably is the best way to play it.

'I'll just go and take a look at the dog's dinner, then I'll see you tomorrow. I'll bring a couple of my team along for the ride, if nothing else comes our way in the meantime which ties them up.'

* * *

Ted went to put his head round Kevin Turner's door when he got back to the nick, to update him, before he went to see the Ice Queen.

'Was it as bad as the first responders are saying?' Kev asked him.

'Every bit, if not worse,' Ted told him frankly. No point in dressing it up as something it wasn't. 'We're going to need to keep an eye on whoever attends the scene. It's not something they're likely to forget in a hurry.'

Kev snorted.

'I know it's not PC to say it but in our day we were supposed to suck it up and get on with it, no matter how bad it was. Now we seem to be doing more hand-holding than coppering these days.'

'Careful, Kev, your inner dinosaur is showing. Times have changed. And in fairness, this one is up there with the worst I've seen. The poor sod had been partly eaten by dogs, and I only hope he died quickly before they started on that. Not to mention the smell and that wasn't just from the body.'

'Spare me the details, Ted. I only said we were supposed to. I'll admit to you, if you promise not to tell anyone else, that I'd have been the first one out the door to puke, by the sounds of things. And I have a phobia about dog shit, if that's what you're referring to. Always have had. I can even smell it on your clothes, and I'm assuming you wore coveralls.

'Cats are even worse. No idea how you cope with all of yours.'

'There's another twist to the case as well,' Ted told him, then recounted his meeting with Sean Duffy and his claims on the case for Organised Crime.

'You're not tempted to turn the whole thing over to him and his team? It would certainly solve your manpower problems. And yes, talking political correctness, I know I should say "officer power" but like you said, I'm an old dinosaur at heart.

'Good luck with it all, Ted, however you run it. And before you ask me for any more bodies, the answer's no. A resounding no. I simply don't have any more to offer you.'

Ted had a slightly more promising response from Superintendent Caldwell when he went next to update her.

'In anticipation of a second big enquiry coming your way, I have already started to put feelers out for more officers,' she told him.

'In fact, there is a chance of a joint op with Organised Crime,' Ted replied, then gave her the full details of his encounter with Sean Duffy.

'On the face of it, that might help alleviate the shortage of officers, might it not?'

'It might, but there again it would mean working with a team who may well have different ideas, methods and values to ours.'

'Clearly, as the senior ranking officer, you would take overall responsibility.'

For a moment, Ted was sorely tempted to respond with something flippant about having plenty of spare time to run both the latest case and oversee the progress on their outstanding triple murder simultaneously. He decided against it. He suspected the Ice Queen might not see it for what it was.

'Sergeant Duffy and a couple of his officers are coming here for morning briefing tomorrow for a pooling of intel and an idea of how we go forward, working together.

'So I better go and brief the team on what else we now have on our plates.'

Ted had phoned ahead on his drive back from the crime scene at Turnbull's house and asked Mike Hallam to make sure as many of the team as possible were in for an end of play briefing on the latest case.

At worst, Ted could put Maurice on the dog case. He was good at talking to people, so he would be helpful working on taking statements from neighbours. Because of the restrictions he was currently under, he would need another officer, preferably female, with him at all times, but he would be a lot better than nothing.

Maurice was good with people in general. Too good, sometimes. It was his softness which had got him into hot water and had so nearly cost him his job, and his liberty. But the consequences of his actions had scared him so much that he was highly unlikely to do anything as daft ever again. He'd play it strictly by the book in future. Certainly for some time to come.

DC Jezza Vine, too, with her acting skills, had the ability to interact with anyone, so would be a possible.

He'd need to liaise with Mike to see who he could most easily do without on the Tonton murder case.

Once all of the team were back in and at their desks, Ted told them all about the crime scene he had come from. Bearing in mind what Kevin Turner had said to him, Ted had sloshed on a bit of the emergency aftershave he always kept in his office desk, in an attempt to disguise any hint of decaying body, any of its functions or anything related to the dogs.

'So because of their connections to the deceased, Organised Crime are staking their claim on this case. Subject to approval from higher level for them, that's how we'll work it. Superintendent Caldwell has already given her approval.'

'Who would be in overall charge, boss? Who would any of us working on it be answerable to?' DS Rob O'Connell wanted to know.

'I'd stay as SIO overall, so the buck would stop with me for anything and everything.

'So as long as the other team gets the go ahead, we'll be joined for tomorrow morning's briefing by Sergeant Sean Duffy and two of his unit to discuss this latest case. We'll do that first thing, then do updates on our own case, once they've left.'

* * *

Ted was, as often, the last of the team to leave the office at the end of the day, but with Jezza Vine not all that far in front of him so they inevitably left the building at around the same time.

As they reached the car park together they saw a forlorn-looking Maurice Brown sitting in the driving seat of his personal vehicle, the driver's door still wide open.

The engine was making uncooperative noises, clearly refusing all attempts to start, and sounding weaker each time Maurice tried the key.

'Are you all right, Maurice?' Ted asked him. 'I know nothing about cars, and I can't give you a lift home because I've got the bike and no spare helmet, if you can't get her to go.'

Maurice was still trying, to no avail.

'Woah, bonny lad,' Jezza told him, hurrying across to him.

'She's clearly refusing to start for a good reason and all you're doing by keep trying is running the battery right down. I can take you back if the worst comes to the worst. But d'you want me to have a look? Pop the bonnet and I'll see what's what. I might just spot something obvious.'

'I don't know anything much about cars,' Maurice told her, starting to get out.

'No, stay where you are. I might need you to give her a try when I've fiddled a bit. But don't touch anything until I tell you to. Not with my hands in amongst the working parts, for sure.'

'Do you know anything about mechanics, then?' Maurice asked her.

Jezza lifted her head to give him a grin as she told him, 'No, Maurice, nothing at all, that's why I offered to help, you great daft lump. I'm going to sabotage it so it never goes again.

'I had a good mate, in sixth form, and he taught me the basics, at least. Enough to know yours hasn't seen the inside of a garage for far too long. And my father had a classic car. A real old beauty, but he neglected his, too, so he let me do some of the maintenance on her. Like a lot of people with plenty of money, he was a real penny-pincher.'

If either of them had been looking at Ted instead of at Maurice's car, they'd have seen a slight change in his expression. A small frown as his mind went off in search of some vague memory of something Jezza's words had triggered.

It was only a few minutes before Jezza was telling Maurice to try turning the engine over once more. This time, after a few brief coughs and splutters, it caught and ran. There was still a slight miss there, to a trained ear, but it was at least going again, much to Maurice's relief.

'Now promise me you'll get the poor thing booked in for a service as soon as possible. It's in a shocking state. Let me know when and where and I can pick you up to bring you into work.'

'Thanks, bonny lass, I owe you a big one. Night. Night, boss.'

Jezza echoed his, 'Night, boss,' and added a, 'See you in the morning.'

Ted replied with the same then paused, watching a jaunty Jezza, clearly pleased with herself, walk over to her own car and drive out of the car park.

A Jezza who, Ted had now found out, knew her way round the inside of a car's workings.

Chapter Six

'Hello, it's me,' Ted called out as he let himself in through the front door, immediately assailed by various cats, led as always by the youngest, Adam.

'And here was me thinking it was my secret lover, paying a risky visit, hoping you weren't home yet. One of these days, you two are going to pass on the driveway.'

Trev's voice, coming from the kitchen, sounded happy. Knowing his partner, Ted suspected there was already a bottle of wine open and being consumed.

Ted smiled as he appeared and told him, 'He and I have an agreement. We stay in contact so our paths never cross.'

Then he added, 'I'm going to go straight up and jump in the shower then get changed. I've been at a very grim crime scene and I feel the need to get clean.'

'Oh, gross, is that the dog thing? I heard a brief mention on the news. That sounded bad enough, but I bet there's more to it, so I don't blame you. D'you want me to get your suit cleaned for you? Was it as bad as that?'

Ted was busy taking off his shoes, then his jacket, sniffing at it as he did so.

'Kev claimed he could smell the crime scene on me but he might have been winding me up. He's getting increasingly grumpy with the shortage of officers. I'll sponge it down and hang it up in the bathroom while I shower. That should fix it, thanks.

'I'd like to watch the local news once I've cleaned up, if you don't mind. I want to see what they're saying about it, in case there's been any leaks of the details.'

'Not a problem. I suspected you would. Don't be too long in the shower, though. I'm making a German dish, the one Annie raved about. She's safely back home and still enthusing about her holiday. She really was taken with Oscar. She keeps calling him a proper gentleman.'

Ted laughed at that as he said, 'He can be, but it's not the first description of him which would spring to my mind. He's clever, though. I have to admit that. If not for him, I could well still be stuck lugging Mr Green down from the summits of Snowdonia.

'Right, shower, change, then I'll be ready to eat whenever it suits you.'

* * *

Ted had asked Mike for an early meeting the next morning, before the joint briefing. He wanted to pick his brains about the best possible use of officers, now their team would be involved in two major cases.

'I'd have said Maurice, any time, for interviewing potential witnesses around the dog crime scene, boss. We both know he can get almost anyone to open up and talk to him. But it's such a grunt for an officer of his experience and ability to have to be chaperoned, the dozy pillock. Pardon my language.'

'When's the last of his retraining courses, before we can put him back on full duties again?'

'Not for another couple of weeks, I think. No vacancies anywhere before then, which rather says something about the state of some officers, if so many of them need training updates. Especially for something as basic as a male officer not going in alone to talk to a vulnerable woman.'

'That reminds me, you talking about so much retraining needed. I'm supposed to be meeting with Chief Superintendent Marston at some point to discuss recruitment issues. The theory being that if we're more selective at that stage, we might not have as much of it to do down the line. Let me know if you have any input for that, please.'

'Boss, for all his many faults, I wouldn't like this team to be without our Maurice, nor anyone like him. He might not have got through a tighter selection process but I think he's a worthwhile addition to the team, most of the time. It's just a shame that when he does get it wrong, he does it in a big way. He's doing a good job on collating, though. He's trying so hard to redeem himself he's not letting anything at all iffy slip through. I think he's even surprising himself with how thorough he's being.'

'Who else were you thinking of putting on the dog case?'

'Jezza's the logical one. We know how sharp she is, and she doesn't seem to get worried by the gory ones. There are going to be a lot of very nervous people to interview on this one, if they know, or suspect that there's an organised crime gang connection.

'What's Steve on, for now?'

Mike looked surprised.

'Are you thinking of him working with Organised Crime? They might eat him for breakfast, as timid as he is. He's currently doing a further deep CCTV trawl for the Tonton case, and he started on the dog one as soon as he had enough details. He's found functioning cameras further away from the scene and he's already spotted a few things which need a follow-up.

'Surely Virgil would be a better bet for Organised Crime, boss? On his own admission, we know he can play the hard man gangster role to perfection and he's not easily intimidated. Plus he does seem to be struggling a bit on the Tonton case, unusually for him. I know it's a distressing one but it seems to be more than that.'

Ted hadn't yet shared with Mike what Jo had told him. He was clearly going to have to, but now was not the time.

'I think it might be one for Rob, perhaps, if Sergeant Duffy would be happy having another sergeant on the case. The Super's also pulling in whatever officers anyone can spare from elsewhere to join us here, so we should, at least, be less stretched than we have been. We ought to be able to find the right officers for the various roles, with a bit of luck.

'Right, that sounds like people turning up so let's go and brief, and see what our friends from Organised Crime want from us, which we can realistically provide for them.'

Sergeant Sean Duffy had brought two of his team members with him, whom he introduced only as Tosh and Wolfie. He didn't specify their roles within the team but it was the one called Wolfie who supplied the most detail about Turnbull, the dog victim, so Ted deduced he may have been the undercover officer buying from him.

Tosh resembled the average nightclub bouncer or bodyguard, and Ted could easily see Wolfie at a rave or festival, scoring drugs without setting off any alarm bells.

Ted invited Duffy to begin by giving a brief biography of the gang and their methods. The sergeant summed up succinctly in few words.

'Nasty. Very nasty. Think of the worst things you've come across as coppers and I guarantee this lot can top it. It's why we've never tried to put anyone into their inner circle. The risks are just too high. Off the scale.

'It's important your team understands that, any of you who will be working with us. Do not underestimate the risks involved. I can't stress that enough. I won't go into too many details, but not everyone who joins us stays the course, for one reason or another.

'And they're into a lot more shit than drug dealing, although that's a large part of their empire. Human trafficking and under-age prostitution is another big chunk of what they do.

'We call them the Co-op Gang, although they have their own name for themselves. Slightly tongue in cheek, that. Those of you who know your social history will know the Cooperative Society movement began in our area with a group called the Pioneers. And this lot certainly rely on cooperation to keep them where they are. Enforced, mostly, of course. Anyone who's shown any sign of talking has either disappeared altogether or been left with such severe injuries they'll remember the warning for the rest of their lives.

'You're all police officers. I'm not trying to scare you. I just want everyone to be under no illusions about what this lot are capable of. I've lost officers before because the risks got too big for them. Usually because the risk expanded to their families, and that was a line drawn, so they've asked for a transfer or quit the force altogether and moved away. Abroad, sometimes.'

Ted was looking round at his team whilst the sergeant was speaking. Gauging reactions, trying to spot any signs of distress which would help him decide who to propose to work with Duffy's team.

'And just in case any of you are in any doubt, or think for a moment that I'm exaggerating to put you off, I'll tell you this. A very good officer on my team found pictures of his daughter on the internet. Extreme pornographic photos of her. His daughter was thirteen at the time.

'Photoshopped, of course, and cleverly done, but still. Her face, unmistakably, and he had no idea where they got that from. But not her body. A very distinct warning as to what the Co-op Gang can do when crossed. Not only is that officer no longer on my team, he's one of those who is no longer serving at all. He quit in the face of that, and he was a huge loss, believe me.'

'What about this latest case, sergeant, and the use of dogs to do the gang's dirty work for them? Is that new?' Ted asked him.

'They're certainly known to be part of the dog-fighting scene, and they've certainly used dogs before to intimidate and to hurt, but never to such extremes, as far as we know.

'Another dealer tried muscling in onto their patch. A man known to be soft about his little yapper lapdogs. Two of them. Don't ask me what sort. Hairy. Can't tell one end from the other. After they got eaten – and I'm using that word in the literal sense – by some great slavering brute owned by one of the Co-op Gang, the bloke packed his bags and did a moonlight, never to be seen on their turf again.

'Now that news of this latest punishment killing has got out, even people who have previously fed us the odd little titbit are likely to be hiding wherever they might think it's safe to do so. The gang have killed and maimed before, of course, it goes with the territory, but this takes it to a whole different level.'

There was silence for a moment as Ted's team considered the enormity of what Duffy had been saying. All of them had had experience of violent deaths in various forms at some point in their careers. The details of this one were off the scale of anything any of them had encountered before.

'Do we know if these dogs have been specifically trained to kill on command?' Rob O'Connell asked. 'Or were they starved into doing what they did? I'm just thinking that might be relevant for anyone who might suddenly find themselves face to face with one of the big brutes. Does it need a command from someone to launch a lethal attack, or would the dogs do it of their own volition?'

'If it helps, I talked to a Sergeant Woods, from the dog section, about that very point,' Ted told them all. 'From his summary of the scene, he said the dogs had clearly been sent in hungry – starving is probably a better word – so not only would they attack the first person they saw, they would also eat whatever they could find.

'His estimation was that they had been left in there more than twenty-four hours and probably for as long as two days. In other words, unless Turnbull had had a firearm to hand and been not only prepared to use it but to discharge it accurately, twice, in quick succession, he had no chance of surviving.

'And believe me, unless you're very experienced with handguns and using them under extreme stress, that's much harder than many people might imagine. Especially the way it's often portrayed on TV or in books, for instance.'

He turned next to Duffy as he said, 'So apart from my assurances of our full cooperation with your team if we work this murder case together, what further help do you need from us? A pooling of resources between us makes most sense to me, given how short-handed we both are.'

Ted was making it clear he was not prepared to relinquish the case, even if it stretched his team to the maximum.

'I was thinking, initially, of putting DS O'Connell and DC Vine onto interviewing neighbours who may be potential witnesses to anything to do with the Turnbull killing.'

Ted nodded to both officers in turn, for the benefit of Duffy as regards identification.

'They will, of course, keep you informed of any and all leads they might turn up related to your Co-op Gang.'

'A word in private, before we go any further,' Duffy said tersely.

Ted stood up and led the way to his office, instructing Mike Hallam to carry on in his absence.

As soon as Ted closed the door behind them both, Duffy launched into his objections.

'Look, this is not at all me being a misogynist, but we tend not to use female officers in the front line on cases related to this particular lot for very good reasons, although we have plenty of them, and cracking good ones, too. The Co-op gang have some fairly strong cultural and religious views about the status of women. Barely seen and never heard, for one thing.

'Putting in an IC1 female and expecting any likely witnesses to talk to them is optimistic. And any female officers should logically come from OCG as they know the gang members and their main associates.

'Yes, I know it's off our gang's home turf down here, but they're well known. Their reputation precedes them. Even people who don't know them are going to be wary, once news is out there about exactly what happened and who was behind it. And we both know most of the details have leaked already.

'Your DS, yes, he looks a useful sort, as long as he knows our structure and doesn't try to step on any toes, but a female officer, unknown to us, when we have trained ones of our own? It would worry my whole team, that. One more thing for them to look out for, to make sure nothing happened to her.'

'But on the law of averages, some of the witnesses around where Turnbull lived are going to be female and IC1. I hear what you say about ethnicity issues, but that's very much a mixed ethnicity area. I think you'll find that might not be as much of an issue as you fear.

'As I said, the murder is our case, but I'm happy for us to cooperate. That includes, of course, respecting my choice of my own officers.

'DC Vine – Jezza – is an experienced and talented officer. She could have gone much higher in rank already, but her personal circumstances mean she's not interested. She has drama training, so she can interact with almost anyone by being whoever she needs to be. Her hobby is kick-boxing, so she has a degree of self-protection, though clearly not sufficient of itself for extremes of violence, or up against firearms.'

Duffy still didn't look convinced but he said, 'Fair enough. As long as you note my objection to your choice so it's on the record, should the worse come to the worst.'

Once Duffy and his officers had left, Ted put his head round his door and asked Steve to step into his office. As ever, Steve did so looking like someone entering the dock in court fearing a guilty verdict and a harsh sentence.

'Nothing serious, Steve,' Ted assured him. 'I need to take a look at a closed file from some time back and I know you would be far faster at finding it than I would.

'It's also something totally off the record, so I can't ask anyone I don't know well, and trust completely, to retrieve it for me. And I need to know I can rely on the total discretion of whoever does dig it out. I know I can usually rely on you, Steve. I hope that would always be the case, regardless of the circumstances.'

Steve flushed as the boss looked at him, looking as serious as the DC could remember having seen him before.

'Yes, sir, of course.'

'Good, thank you.'

Ted mentioned a name and saw Steve's eyes widen, his Adam's apple bob up and down around something rather like a gulp.

'Total discretion, Steve,' Ted reminded him. 'I'm counting on you.'

Chapter Seven

Duffy and his officers had left, after a short briefing with Rob and Jezza on what was needed from them initially. After their departure, Ted wanted another few words with his team before any of them went out to do anything.

'The Co-op Gang are dangerous. You now know that, beyond any doubt, with the further intel from Sergeant Duffy. But there's another danger I don't want any of you to forget about or play down, and that's those dogs. That risk could potentially impact on any of you, whichever case you're working, because we simply don't know where they came from, or where they are now. We don't even know if they're still on our patch or not.

'With no CCTV functioning near to the Turnbull house, we're in the dark about how they got into that property and how they were taken away.

'According to the dog section officer, now they have attacked once that we know of, and killed their victim, they should be considered as extremely dangerous and capable of doing the same thing again, either with or without a command from their handler. So whether you're working on our case or something else, and wherever you're asking questions, it might well be worth dropping in some about large, possibly out-of-control dogs in the neighbourhood you're in. It's the sort of thing people are often happy to talk about, if only to report noise nuisance from barking dogs.

'Sergeant Woods, from the dog section, was fairly certain from the injuries to Turnbull that they were XL Bullies, or a breed of the same size and type. If you don't know what they look like, do your research and familiarise yourself. And whatever you do, don't try being a hero. I'd rather learn you hid in your car while some large but harmless woofer went past than hearing about you taking a risk and getting yourself seriously injured, or worse.

'I'm sure you all know – it's no secret – that I'm nervous around most dogs, except my mother's little Corgi and Superintendent Sampson's docile Iggy, so I'm not going to judge anyone else who is. The last thing I want from any of you is heroics. If you spot anything like these dogs, call it in and at least get back-up from a taser-trained officer before you go anywhere near. If you're not sure whether they could possibly be the right dogs, take photos and send them in. And get yourself to a place of safety while you're waiting. We don't know what the ones in the Turnbull case look like, but Sergeant Woods might at least be able to tell us, from photos, if they could be the same type.

'Rob, Jezza, all of this goes double for you because Sergeant Duffy wants you working on finding witnesses anywhere near the Turnbull house. And for all we know so far, the dogs might live close to there.

'We need them found, identified, DNA tested, then we'll go straight for a destruction order, given the seriousness of this case and the strong probability that they could do the same thing again.

'Steve, I'm hoping at some point you're going to report a miracle and tell us you've picked up the dogs' trail on CCTV somewhere further afield. As with anything else which presents a serious risk to officers and members of the public, we need those dogs found and appropriately dealt with, as soon as possible.'

'No sightings at all so far of any dogs of that size and type, sir,' Steve told him. 'Of course if they were transported in a closed van, they wouldn't be seen on camera. That might have been part of the reason for the shot-out cameras in the surrounding area, to make it harder for us to know where they came from and how they were recovered.'

It was an unusually assertive speech from Steve. He'd certainly not have said as much, sounding so confident, had the OCG officers still been present.

'Thank you, Steve. Right, everyone, you all know what you're working on for now, so let's get to it, and report back here at end of play, hopefully with some updates on either case,' Ted told them all.

* * *

'Promise me you won't tell anyone but I'm as windy as the boss about a possible encounter with those dogs,' Rob O'Connell told Jezza as she drove them out towards the Turnbull house.

'I didn't realise you don't like dogs,' she told him.

'It's not that so much. It's the thought of another trip to hospital so soon. It doesn't seem all that long ago I got stabbed. I still have the occasional nightmare about that. And that's not for public knowledge either, please.'

'I have to confess I'm a bit worried about an encounter, too. Normally I'd be optimistic my kick-boxing abilities would help, but I'm honestly a bit wary of putting my feet anywhere near jaws like those. If I got my timings wrong, being up close where I'd need to be, I wouldn't give much for my chances of getting away. Especially if I only had one leg left!'

Jezza was making light of it, as she so often did, but Rob could still hear the slight note of anxiety in her voice.

'And what the dog section officer told the boss about some of those dogs having their vocal chords doctored worries me a lot, because that could mean we might not know there were dogs in any house we were about to go into,' she added.

Jezza changed down and brought the car to a halt at traffic lights which were just turning to red then asked, 'So how do you want to play it, then? Should we stay together, so we might be able to watch out for one another like the boss said, or split up and go in alone?'

Rob gave a dry chuckle at that.

'I think I'd sooner face a very hungry XL Bully than go back and tell the boss you got eaten by one because I let you play the lone crusader. We stay together, at all times.

'From the printout Maurice gave me of houses where there was no one answering when the first responders were going door-to-door, there aren't sufficient numbers of them to risk the wrath of the boss by splitting up.

'Let's start with the closest houses where no one's yet been interviewed, and see how we get on from there.'

They started with the adjoining semi to the crime scene, which was still taped off, with an officer on site to make sure no over-eager members of the press or public tried to get close enough to film or photograph the interior. It was an officer both Rob and Jezza recognised so they exchanged a nod of greeting from the next driveway as they went to knock on a shiny bottle-green front door.

There was no reply to Rob's first knock, so he tried again, more loudly, and was rewarded with a voice from inside, calling out, 'I'm coming! Wait a bit. It takes me a bit of time.'

They heard shuffling footsteps then the door opened and part of the face of an elderly woman peered at them through the narrow gap left by a safety chain.

Rob and Jezza held up their identity cards as Rob said, 'DS O'Connell, DC Vine, Greater Manchester Police. Do you have a few minutes to answer some questions, please, Mrs ... ?'

'Leather,' she told them. 'And it's Miss Leather. Florrie. Is this about what happened to poor Frank next door? I saw something about it on the TV, and I couldn't believe it.'

'Would it be all right if we came inside to ask you a couple of questions, Miss Leather?' Jezza asked her. 'Rather than standing on the doorstep?'

'Oh, I am sorry, how silly of me. Yes, please do come in. Go straight down the hall to the kitchen at the end. I keep it warm in there and I could put the kettle on for you if you like.

'You two go on ahead. I'm very slow on my feet today. Yesterday was my day for getting my bunions done and they're very sore today. I suffer badly with them. They're herrideterry, you know. They run right through my family.'

Jezza had to make a conscious effort not to smile at the mispronunciation, which tickled her sense of humour.

She and Rob sat down and said a polite no to a brew, thinking of time. Then Jezza started on the questioning, by silent agreement between them.

'Did you know Mr Turnbull well?'

'Oh yes, I would say so. He moved in next door quite a few years ago. A very nice man. Very kind. He would often do little jobs to help me out, although he said I shouldn't tell anyone that. He was on sickness benefits of late, you see, after a bad accident, and he said he could lose them if anyone thought he was capable of doing work of any sort.

'I don't really know what happened to him to leave him like that. He just said he'd had a very bad fall and injured his back. But he was always so careful when he did little jobs for me. But then I suppose he would be, not wanting to have another bad fall, p'raps.

'And he had so many friends, so they must all have thought highly of him, like I did. There were people coming and going to his house all the time. So many visitors!'

Jezza and Rob shared a loaded glance. They could well imagine the true nature of his visitors.

'Do you happen to know any more details of the injury which meant he was on the sick?' Rob asked her. 'Any idea of where or when he had this fall, perhaps, or what might have caused it? And did it involve a hospital stay at all?'

Rob was thinking they might be able to find out more details if the man had been hospitalised.

'He just told me he'd had a very bad fall. In town. A good while back now. All those old slippery stone staircases around Underbank. They can be lethal, especially if they get a bit damp. He said he'd gone full length, from the top to the bottom, and broken a lot of bones. He was in hospital for quite a few weeks, but when he got out, that's when all those friends of his really started rallying round, and making so many visits.'

'And did you ever see any of his friends bringing dogs with them when they came to visit him?' Jezza asked her.

'I can't say that I did, love, but I'm really not the sort of lonely old woman who sits staring out of the window all day long.'

'And you didn't hear the noise of any dogs, coming from next door, before Mr Turnbull was found?'

'I didn't, love, no, but then I have to admit my hearing isn't as sharp as it was. I have to have the telly on quite loud to catch everything, because I don't like trying to follow on the subtitles. They go too quick for me to keep up. That's why I was so glad to have such a nice kind man for a neighbour because I'm sure he must have been able to hear my telly through the partition wall.'

'Was it unusual for you not to see him for a couple of days at a time?' Rob asked her.

'No, not really. Like I said, I wasn't always looking out for him.'

'And you didn't notice anything at all which made you wonder if anything was wrong next door?' Rob persisted.

He knew she was not one of the neighbours who had phoned in to report the bad smell. It must surely have been very strong next door. Rob even thought he could get a lingering whiff of something unpleasant, but he realised it could just have been his imagination, knowing what had happened on the other side of the wall.

'A smell, you mean? One of the other neighbours told me about that, when I got back from the chirriopoderist and saw all the cars and commotion everywhere.'

Jezza hid another smile at the woman's further unusual pronunciation.

'I'm afraid not, love, no. I'm on some tablets which means I've got very little sense of smell or taste. It makes meals very boring these days, but at least they keep me going, I suppose.

'Poor Frank. It somehow seems worse that he wasn't found straight away. I'm surprised none of his friends didn't sound the alarm when they didn't see him. There must have been some bobbing round in that time. It seemed like there always was.

'And they said on the telly that there was dogs in the house when he died. I don't understand that. Frank didn't have dogs. He didn't even like them. He told me he was really afraid of them because he'd been chased one time by two really big ones and he'd thought they were going to attack him.'

'And you definitely never remember any of his friends bringing dogs with them when they came to visit him? Could they possibly have done that while you were out?'

'No, I never saw any. Not even left in the garden while they was inside. But they wouldn't, you see. If they was his friends they'd know he didn't like them so I don't think they'd have brought them.

'Poor Frank,' she said again, sounding genuinely sorry. 'Whatever did happen to him, I hope he didn't suffer too much. He really was a very kind neighbour. I shall miss him.'

'So, the dodgy drugs dealer with a heart of gold, who was kind to little old ladies,' Jezza said ironically as she and Rob left the house.

'Wouldn't be the first time we've heard two entirely different versions of a person who's been on our radar,' she went on. 'And it's got me wondering if it might possibly have been that encounter with dogs before which caused him to have that bad fall down the steps that left him on the sick.'

'A first and final warning from the gang that he wasn't doing things exactly as they expected him to? That could very well be,' Rob agreed.

'D'you think it might be worth our while to have a short walk round the back of the houses and then up in front? I know most of the cameras have been shot out but we might just spot something that's been overlooked to date. You never know. We're starting with pretty much nothing so we can't do worse than that.'

Rob nodded at her suggestion.

'There's an outside chance we might find an undamaged camera somewhere that's been overlooked, so we'll at least know where we could start pulling in footage from. Maybe a private one. And with a really big dollop of luck, we might just possibly find the point at which the dogs were loaded into a vehicle, which would help Steve in his CCTV trawling.'

They both knew there had been searches made already but it wouldn't be the first time something had been overlooked on the first one.

They walked round to the service road at the back of the houses, both pulling on gloves in case they needed to pick anything up, Jezza arming herself with an old branch she found lying nearby, so she could poke about more effectively.

They had gone a fair distance down the old road when Jezza stopped, prodding cautiously with the end of her stick at something at the edge of the formerly cultivated land, half-hidden in some long grass.

'Rob, look away now if you don't have a strong stomach. But my finely-honed detective skills tell me I've just found a pile of dog puke. And unless I'm very much mistaken, it's a pile of puke which contains what looks to me very like a human tooth.'

Chapter Eight

Ted was on the phone to the Crown Prosecutor in charge of the case against Tonton for the killing of the twin newborn girls and their mother. He needed to update her on the situation with the first DNA sample.

She listened in silence, then said, 'Well, it's a bit of a bugger, for sure, but it's not the end of the world. His legal team, if we get close to committal proceedings, will doubtless scream blue murder, pardon the pun, and try to make an application for bail on the grounds of unacceptable delays on the part of the prosecution.

'Mind you, from what you've said about him, he may be arrogant enough to opt to defend himself, of course.

'We can easily counter the claim of unacceptable delay by saying their client delayed things in the first place by not cooperating with giving the sample when he is legally obliged to consent to a DNA test. He was treated patiently and politely when it could have been heavy-handed. Not to mention refusing to cooperate by giving his identity. So we've got some Brownie points to spare there, and that might just enable us to keep him in custody until we finally do get some results.

'But please promise me, Ted, you're going to be all over this in person, like a rash, from now on, because if it goes wrong again, your Tonton is going to walk, and there will be nothing at all we can do about it.'

'I have camping gear, Rachel. I'll go and pitch my tent in the doorway of the lab, if that's what it takes,' Ted promised her.

She laughed at that then went on, 'And presumably you're still no nearer a proper ID on the man? It's presenting all sorts of problems not having his real name and some idea of his background, at least. Not even of his country of origin and his status here. He might well be an illegal, for all we know.'

'He's a real international man of mystery so far. No hits anywhere from his fingerprints. None from facial recognition. And as you say, we don't even know if he's in the country legally or illegally. None of this should be possible in the technological age, but he seems to defy all the systems so far.'

'Well, let's get this second DNA sample done and processed in world record time and see if you can't solve the mystery once and for all.

'The circumstances around our strong opposition to the mere suggestion of bail for him haven't changed. In fact, they become stronger the longer he remains unidentified and uncooperative.

'You know as well as I do that it's impossible to second-guess magistrates and that some of them have made the most bizarre decisions with sometimes catastrophic results. I'm banking on even Their Worships thinking twice before liberating our mystery suspect who appears to have no name, no antecedents and no known fixed abode.'

* * *

DC Alison O'Malley was one of the team still working on

the Tonton case, which was a long way from finished.

Even before the delay caused by the missing DNA, the prosecution file was still looking far from convincing. With too few exceptions, witnesses were unwilling to talk much about the suspect Tonton. Even most of those who had been present at the brutal slaying of newborn babies had little of any use to say, for reasons Ali didn't profess to understand.

Ali was the newest member of the Serious Crime team and had hit the ground running with such a complex and gruelling case.

She was currently working with DC Maurice Brown. He was collating all witness statements and highlighting for her any which needed follow-up for clarification or extra detail.

Ali liked Maurice. Instinctively trusted him, and felt his nickname of Daddy Hen was well deserved. She was sad for his current restricted status, purely through his kindness and instinct to help anyone in trouble. She felt conflicted, too, as it was an ex-boyfriend of hers who had caused all of Maurice's current problems, and she'd never even guessed at the dark side to him.

Maurice had passed her a statement taken from one potential witness to the killing of the twin babies and their mother. A woman who at least spoke enough English to have given her statement in that language. She'd been interviewed initially by Jezza, and Maurice had felt from reading the transcript that there was at least a possibility that she might be persuaded to say more, if she spoke to the right person.

Ali knew she wasn't bad at vulnerable witness interviews, but she knew someone who was far better. Someone who could get almost anyone to open up to them.

She went across to the office in which DS Mike Hallam was working on something at his desk. He was in charge of who went where, and for what, and was being even more vigilant than usual after the boss's warning about the dogs on their patch.

Mike listened to what she had to say then asked simply, 'And you're asking me to sanction this rather than the boss because ...?'

'He's not in his office at the moment, sarge.'

She said it with such a straight face that Mike had difficulty keeping his own the same. It was the kind of thing Jezza would come out with. He knew the truth was likely to be that she considered him a much softer target than the DCI.

'All right, take Maurice with you. But he's your responsibility. Don't let the great soft lump do anything else daft or he risks being out on his ear. Make sure he keeps a safe distance from your witness, physically, and emotionally. And that he doesn't get overfamiliar in how he speaks to her. No calling her bonny lass or pet or anything else open to misinterpretation. Especially someone whose first language might not be English, let alone Geordie.

'But how confident are you that this witness will say any more than she has already? I don't want to send two of you out on a time-waster mission.'

'I've watched some of her interview. She was nervous, on edge, but I had a feeling that might have been the setting, as much as anything else. A police station can be intimidating, if you're not used to being in one, even if you've done nothing wrong. We both know that.

'Rightly or wrongly, I just had the feeling that if we could go to her house and have more of a chat situation, over a cuppa, then between me and Daddy Hen, we might just be able to get her to where she'd feel comfortable making a statement. If not to us today, then perhaps she might agree to come in at some time and make a formal statement on the record.

'What do you think, sarge? It must be worth a punt and an hour of our time? If nothing else, we could ask around about the dogs whilst we're out there. We might get lucky.'

'I think you're right, Ali. As long as you promise me faithfully you'll chaperone Maurice properly, every minute, I think the two of you stand a good chance of getting something out of this potential witness.

'Ask for permission to record the whole thing, from the minute this woman opens the door to you. Always assuming she does, of course. And check in with me as soon as you can so I know there are no problems.

'I hope it goes without saying that if you happen on any big, ferocious dogs while you're out and about, you do not approach, under any circumstances until you've called back-up and got yourselves to a place of safety.

'Good luck.'

Ali couldn't help smiling as she walked over to Maurice's desk. He was working away quietly on his allotted task but there was an air of gloom and despondency about him which he couldn't hide.

'Maurice, get your coat, you've pulled,' she told him. 'You and I are going out into the big wide world together. I've got permission from the DS for you to come with me to do a follow-up interview on someone I think might just possibly tell us more than they did in their initial interview, if we talk to her away from the station.

'It's only a hunch, a so-called woman's intuition thing, and I may be completely wrong. But are you up for it?'

He was looking at her with such anticipation on his face that Ali felt an unexpected lump in her throat. She thought of the saying of throwing a drowning man a lifebelt and now understood exactly what that might look like.

'I'm well up for that, if you think I can help, bonny lass. Lead the way, and I promise to be on my very best behaviour.'

* * *

The address Ali had for the potential witness turned out to be a tiny but neat ground-floor flat in an older, large house, clearly divided up for the money-making potential of multiple occupancy.

She'd had no idea whether they would find the woman at home, but it was only moments after her knock that the door opened to a young woman, perhaps early to mid-twenties, who was hastily adjusting a headscarf before she spoke to them.

Ali and Maurice both held their warrant cards up for inspection as Ali said, 'Hello, I'm DC Alison O'Malley, this is DC Maurice Brown. I know you've kindly been into the station to give a witness account of what happened when you attended a Welcoming where two babies and their mother died. I wonder if you had time to go through one or two further points with us, please?'

'I have to go to the police station again?'

There was no mistaking the anxiety in her voice and on her face as she asked the question.

'No, that's not necessary for the moment,' Ali assured her. 'It's just to go over a few things, for clarification. But I would like to record our conversation on my phone, if you're happy with that?'

The woman was looking from one to the other of them, still hesitating. Maurice was doing his best to look non-threatening, but saying nothing for the moment. Ali had, as instructed, given him a reminder on the drive over to try to avoid his usual terms, like 'pet' and 'bonny lass', because they might present cultural problems, and the last thing he needed right now was anyone else complaining about inappropriate behaviour from him.

'Unless we're disturbing you, and you have somewhere else you need to be?' Ali added.

'No, please, come in. I was just surprised to see you here. I've already told all I know. And yes, it is ok to record.'

She stood aside and indicated for them to go into the smallest kitchen Ali had ever seen. There were only two chairs by the tiny table, and even with Maurice being polite and remaining standing, the room felt crowded. Ali noticed he was careful to position himself, as best he could, somewhere the woman would hopefully not have to squeeze past him for anything.

The woman – Sara, her name was, Ali knew from the notes and the interview – looked restless and fidgety. Not necessarily a sign of anything unusual in that. Having two police officers, one of them large and bulky, in such a small space, could have that effect on anyone.

Sara offered to make tea but Ali refused politely, not wanting her to have the perfect excuse to have her back to them whilst they were talking.

'As I said, I've seen your interview but I would really like it if you could tell me some more details about the group you joined. In your own words. What drew you to them?'

Sara frowned at the question, so Ali rephrased the idiom.

'Why did you want to be part of the group?'

'I worry for world population. There are simply too many people on the planet. We need not so many for everyone to survive. The earth too. I don't believe in killing anyone. But for people to make choice not to have children, or only one child, and encourage others to be like that also. That, I think, is good. The right thing to do. That is what I thought this group was about. I did not know they supported killing.'

She paused and half-rose from her seat saying, 'I need water ...'

Ali motioned her to stay where she was and said simply, 'Maurice will get you a drink. Maurice?'

Once again, Maurice was careful not to get too close to Sara as he got the drink and put the glass within her reach.

'How did you become involved with the group, Sara?' Ali asked her.

'I found them online. I was looking for discussion groups. About overpopulation. I went to some of the Circles. I thought they seemed nice people, with good ideas which were in likeness to mine.'

'And what about the Welcoming you attended? What made you want to go to that? Can you explain to me why a group about overpopulation would be welcoming more children into the world?' Ali asked her. 'Was that not contradictory to their stated beliefs?'

Sara frowned at the wording. Maurice spoke then, with a glance as Ali to see if she had any objection to him doing so.

'We're wondering why a group wanting to do something about too many people on the planet would want to celebrate more babies coming into the world.'

'I thought the group was like some countries have done. They celebrate one baby for one family, but no more. I did not know there were two babies this time. I was very shock when the baby came and when Tonton ...' she paused, her voice breaking, then took another gulp of water to steady her nerves before continuing, 'when Tonton did what he did.

'I was making a scream. Crying. I could not look. I did not see anything else. Others too were crying and screams. We were trying to get out. To get away. It was terror. I could not see anything else. I keep my eyes closed. Turn my face away, and put my hands over ears. Like this.'

She demonstrated her actions, genuine terror still registering on her face. Both Ali and Maurice formed the clear impression that she was giving them a true account of the horrors she had seen and heard.

'You didn't say all of this in your interview at the station, Sara,' Ali told her. 'Why was that?'

'I was afraid. Very afraid. I didn't want trouble. I have come here to train, as physiotherapist, and I don't want to be made to go back to my country. I didn't know what to do and they said I was being filmed.'

Maurice put on his most non-threatening expression, used his softest tone. A voice which made almost anyone want to talk to him. To confide in him. The method which had earned him the nickname of Daddy Hen in the first place.

Ali sat back and listened. If anyone could get this frightened young woman to talk to them, and possibly even to agree to testify against Tonton, Maurice would be the one to do it. She was banking on that.

'Sara, if you did nothing more than go there to find out about the group, no one is going to accuse you of anything. But this Tonton is clearly someone very dangerous. We believe that the three people he killed at the Welcoming you attended are not his only victims. Not the only people he has killed.

'But we need proof. Eyewitnesses. People who were there who will go to court and say what they saw. We can arrange protection for anyone who will do that. And as soon as we have statement from witnesses, we can make sure Tonton stays in prison, for a very long time.

'Will you do that, Sara? Please?'

* * *

As Ali and Maurice were driving away from the flat, Ali turned to her passenger with a beaming smile.

'Maurice, that was a masterclass in dealing with a reluctant witness. I can now see where your nickname comes from. She'll almost certainly want you to do the second witness interview with her on tape, so I hope there's a way round your restricted duties to allow for that. I'm sure there will be, especially when we go back and report to the boss that we've now found someone else ready to testify against Tonton on the record. Sara's testimony, together with Isabella's, should finally be starting to build a case with some chance of success.

'So now we're on a roll, shall we just do a drive around and see if we can spot any big brutes of dogs anywhere?'

Chapter Nine

Ted listened without interrupting as Ali and Maurice reported back on their visit to the latest potential witness and the hope, as long as she didn't get cold feet, of someone else willing to testify against Tonton, subject to safeguards.

'Good work. Very good work, both of you. Maurice, when you confine yourself to doing the things you excel at, without crossing boundaries, life gets a lot better for all of us.

'Get everything written up and on the file as soon as possible, please, and I'll update CPS. It may well make up in some small measure for the cock-up with the DNA. Keep in touch with this witness so she doesn't feel used and abandoned. Make sure she knows we have her welfare at heart.

'I also want CPS advice on when we interview Tonton again, and drop into his lap the hot potato that we now have two eyewitnesses to the killings who are ready to testify against him. At least to the killing of the first baby, even if one of them stopped looking after that. That should shake things up nicely, and probably give us further grounds to oppose any attempt to have him released on bail, because of the DNA delay. We can now legitimately claim we'd be worried about him interfering with any eyewitnesses.'

Maurice was still grinning ear to ear at the praise when he went back to his desk. Mike Hallam was now in the main office, checking something with Steve, and noticed his expression, and the smile on Ali's face at the same time. There'd been no sign of Mike when they'd got back, which was why they had gone to see the boss in his absence.

'Can I take it you two had a successful visit and we might finally have some good news, at last?' he asked them.

'About as good as it gets, sarge,' Ali told him. 'I couldn't find you when we got back, so we went straight to the boss. Another eyewitness, prepared to testify. She'd clammed up a bit in her interview when she came into the station because she was worried about her status, and had no idea how safe it was for her to talk in here, on the record.'

'And is she a credible witness? If she was nervous about what she said to officers in the station, how well do you see her standing up to robust cross-examination from the defence team? And how's her English? Good enough to stop the defence claiming she didn't know what she was saying when you spoke to her?'

'I would say she's very credible, sarge. But to allay fears, Maurice and I thought we'd arrange an interpreter when she comes back in to give another statement on the record, so we can clarify anything that might need it as she's interviewed. That way there's even less margin for error.'

Mike smiled to himself. Ali was sounding like Jezza again with such an off-pat answer. But she and Maurice, working as a team, had done good work. It was the first time he'd seen Maurice look pleased with himself since he'd had all the worry and stress of the false allegation against him.

'Every single detail noted and on the file as soon as possible, please,' he told them. 'Good work from both of you. Maurice, as you're collating, you'll have to chase yourself up if you don't get everything done sharpish.

'And when you've done that, which needs doing as quickly as possible, you need to flag up any other witnesses who might potentially talk more to us, once they know that some of the others have started to. Goes without saying that no word of who it is who's talking should go further than this room, so I'll give a general reminder about that once everyone's back in.

'But the two of you – Ali, Maurice – you've played a belter there. We're a good bit further forward than we were a few hours ago.'

* * *

Trev had already left to teach his English class by the time Ted had wrapped up everything he needed to do for the day and got home.

There was something simmering on a low light in the oven and giving off inviting smells, which made him realise he couldn't even remember if he'd eaten anything at lunchtime, never mind what it might have been.

There was a fresh loaf in the bread bin, so he cut off the crust, spread it generously with butter, smeared it with jam, folded it in half and sank his teeth into it.

Brechdan jam. He could almost hear his mother's voice, telling him the Welsh for jam sandwich. He could also hear in his head her telling him to cut the bread, not fold it over, which wasn't polite. Memories from when he was very small, before she'd left him with his father and lost touch with her only son for so many years.

It had been good to spend time with her last week. The rift which had long existed between them had slowly healed, and most of that was down to Trev's influence.

Ted felt a sudden urge to speak to her, so once he'd finished his mouthful, he pulled up her number on his phone and rang it.

'Teddy bach? It that you?'

It gave him a guilty pang that she always sounded so anxious when he phoned her out of the blue. As if he was about to tell her some bad news – something she didn't want to know.

'Hello, mam, I was just eating a *brechdan jam*, so I thought of you. Especially because I folded it instead of cutting it.'

She laughed at that but there was still a note of worry in her voice when she went on, 'Are you not at home yet? Not eating a proper meal with Trevor?'

'It's his English class tonight, but he's left us something in the oven for later. Promise not to tell him I've been filling my face, but he might just spot the end of a loaf gone missing.

'I just wanted to check you were all right, mam, and settled back in after your holidays.'

'I had the most wonderful time, Teddy. Thank you so much for letting me come with you. And what a nice man your friend Oscar is. So very charming. But then his grandmother is a very gracious lady, with such good manners. She clearly brought him up the right way.'

Ted very nearly choked on his *brechdan* listening to her singing Smith's praises, but he wasn't going to disillusion her. Charming was another word which didn't spring readily to his mind when he thought about Oscar Smith, although he had been impressed at how polite and attentive he had been to the visitors. Almost certainly due to the influence of his

Oma, his grandmother, who seemed to keep him firmly under control.

'I'll have to go now, mam. As usual, Trev did the cooking but not the washing up or laying the table before he went out, so I'd better pitch in and get the place fit to eat in.

'*Hwyl, mam.*'

He always tried the odd word of Welsh with his mother. Ones he'd learned and remembered from his childhood. He knew how much that meant to her.

He could hear the pleasure in her voice as she replied in her native language, then he ended the call and made a start on reorganising the bomb site which the kitchen currently resembled, before Trev got back.

Ted was just putting the final touches to laying the table when he heard Trev's key in the door and his voice calling out, 'Tell your lover to put his clothes back on and sneak out the back way. Your husband's home.'

'Oh, you're safe to come in. He never comes in here. He's allergic to cats,' Ted replied as Trev appeared in the doorway, half obscured by a large bouquet of yellow roses.

'But I see yours has been generous,' he added at the sight of the flowers. 'Even if they do look as if they've been dragged through a hedge backwards.'

Trev chuckled, leaning in to kiss Ted.

'I wasn't expecting any such gift so I had to stuff them down the front of my leathers for the ride home, which is why they're a bit battered. I'm hoping they'll revive a bit if I stick them in water.'

'Why don't I do that for you?' Ted suggested, knowing that, of Trev's many skills, neatly arranging flowers was not one of them. 'You'd better take a look in the oven and see if your offering's ready.

'Who are these really from, if that's not an indelicate question?'

'Anna Wójcik. She came in just to say hello to everyone, now she's out of hospital, but she's not yet fit enough to restart English lessons. She says she does want to, though.

'Her late husband's sergeant's wife brought her in to say hello. Val Carver. Anna's apparently staying with them for the time being, until everything's been sorted out. She wants to stay in the country, and she wants to come back to the group for English lessons, once she's fully recovered.

'Understandably, she doesn't want to carry on living in the same house. Far too many bad memories there for her, although she does want to stay in the same area.

Trev had taken the food out of the oven and was dishing up. Ted put the flowers on the table as a centrepiece.

'Anna told me, with help from Val, that yellow roses are a symbol of friendship and especially of thanks to friends, where she comes from. Isn't that a nice gesture?'

Ted was thinking of all the trouble for his team caused by Anna Wójcik's late husband, Eric Leader. Of how, in particular, the man had conspired to wreck the career of Maurice Brown and to bring a kind and good, if misguided, man to his knees.

He could have said so much. Instead, he decided, as he so often did, to go for the diplomatic approach.

'A very nice gesture.'

* * *

'Right, thanks to some excellent interviewing by Ali and Maurice, we finally have someone else who's willing to testify against Tonton, for those of you who've not already heard of that breakthrough,' Ted told the full team the following morning.

'As soon as possible, I want a further interview of Tonton where that fact is put to him, to see what he has to say for himself. It's my bet he won't have been expecting any such thing, so to hear that might possibly rattle his tongue loose finally, although I wouldn't count on it.

'Our focus now needs to be on seeing how many other witnesses we can persuade to start saying more than they have up to now. No one likes to be the first to talk, but once someone does, and especially now we have two of them, it can often produce a snowball effect and we could get more. So let's try that, but without giving any hint about who is now talking to us. Not just for their own personal safety, but if we want to persuade more people it's safe to talk to us, they need to trust us. Completely.

'Maurice, you know the statements better than anyone else by now, so can you please flag up any witnesses we should start with. Any who seemed close to talking and who might now do so once they know they're not the first.

'Ali, I think you had one in that category. A young woman who may have been expecting twins. Can you follow up with her, please, see if she will definitely testify?

'There's also the link with Merseyside, via the killing near Billinge. Jezza, you were on that, so you need to hand that over to someone else to follow up, now you're working with OCG on the Turnbull case. Where are you up to with that? Rob?'

'We interviewed the next-door neighbour yesterday, boss. Apparently the victim had suffered serious injuries in a fall on our patch previously, which we thought might possibly also be connected to the dogs. Jezza found further traces which we presume were from the same dogs a bit further away from the Turnbull house. It's given us a new theory on the whole dog involvement thing. Jezza?'

'It is just a theory so far, boss. The fall was the reason why Turnbull was on the sick and couldn't work, so seems to be dealing pretty much full-time from home to make a bit of money. But prior to that, as far as the neighbour told us, there was nothing much wrong with him, and he was working, although she wasn't clear about his profession. Some sort of joinery work and doing handyman jobs, she thought.

'He often helped her out with little jobs and she said he was always very professional and careful with anything he did, especially working up ladders or anything like that.

'So unless he was drunk, it seems strange that he should manage to fall down an entire flight of stone steps in town, enough to do himself serious injury. I wondered if he might possibly have been running for his life from dogs on his heels. I thought I could do worse than dig into any reports of the accident and any possibility of eyewitnesses to it.'

'And you've run this past Sergeant Duffy, have you, before embarking on it? You and Rob are answerable to him too now, don't forget, so it's up to him what you work on.'

'First on my list after we've finished here, boss,' she told him glibly.

Ted hid a smile. He could well remember telling Mike Hallam, when Jezza had first joined their team, that she was clearly someone who preferred to run free of the pack. She got the results most of the time. She was still a free spirit, though, who liked to do things her own way, unless kept firmly under a watchful eye.

'It was clearly some time ago. Far back enough for him to have been put on long-term sickness benefit, from what you've told us, and we all know that doesn't happen overnight. So I'm not sure what useful evidence you could still turn up on it, especially if it was classified as an accident at the time. Almost certainly no CCTV left, for instance.

'The final decision rests with Sergeant Duffy, but whatever he says, don't spend too much time on it. With still such a long way to go to get any kind of a result on our own case, we need every available officer working on it.'

Ted headed back to his office, then noticed Steve was padding along at his heels. He held the door open for him, then shut it behind them.

'Yes, Steve? What can I do for you?'

'That file you wanted me to dig out for you, sir.'

Steve stopped speaking, hesitated, looking uncomfortable.

'Yes, Steve?' Ted asked again.

'I've located it, sir. Shall I send it through to you?'

'That's the general idea, please.'

Steve was still dithering.

'And please remember, Steve, you don't discuss this with anyone. Is that clear? Total confidentiality. I'm counting on you.'

Steve only managed a terse, 'Yes, sir,' before he turned and left the office.

Chapter Ten

Ted was at his desk early, before any of the team appeared. He wanted time to look through the file Steve had retrieved for him without any distractions, or any risk of anyone catching a glimpse of what he was looking at.

He was almost sure he was wrong with the niggling thoughts which had been playing around in the back of his mind. Almost certain. There was just that annoying little voice in his head which kept saying, 'but what if ...?'

He had no idea what he would do if that little voice proved to be right. Always supposing he could find any evidence for that possibility. He would cross that bridge when he came to it. If he had to.

The first thing which jumped out at him on his initial quick read through was a possible coincidence. And Ted neither liked nor trusted those.

The file was on a road traffic collision from several years ago. A double fatality. And one of the first attending officers had been a PS Lee, from Stretford. Not all that unusual a name, but it was the name of an officer, now an inspector, still at Stretford, who had dealt with the arrest of Maurice Brown after the rape allegation.

Ted's first contact with her had been a slightly bumpy affair. Quite rightly, she was determined to show that on her watch as duty inspector, there were no special favours for anyone. Especially not for fellow officers.

Something about the way PS Lee's detailed report had been presented reminded Ted of how Inspector Esme Lee phrased things. He might well be wrong. He might well be about to make a total pillock of himself by digging into a closed case for no valid reason at all.

But the niggle was there, and it wasn't going to go away until he had checked it out. For that, he would need to pose a few further questions and hope he didn't manage to ruffle Inspector Lee's feathers once again.

He phoned, more in hope than anticipation, but was told Inspector Lee was not currently in the station. The person who spoke to him promised faithfully to pass on his message asking for her to call him when she had the time. He wasn't holding his breath, though.

He closed the file, locked it safely away, then went out to the main office ready for morning briefing, as most of the team were now filing in. For once, Maurice wasn't the last to arrive. His success the day before had clearly done wonders for his self-esteem which had taken such a battering lately.

'Jezza, before we start, have you cleared your idea about Turnbull's fall with Sergeant Duffy, and is he okay with you working on that?'

Jezza gave him her sweetest smile as she said, 'I have, boss, and he's agreed, but with the caveat of not spending too much time on it.

'If nothing else, it might help us get those dogs taken out of the equation, if we can find a link to them, and that's got to be a good thing, surely.'

'I'd agree with that in principle, but your current specific brief, you and Rob, is Organised Crime and there's always the outside possibility that the dogs are unrelated to the Co-op Gang. As long as Sergeant Duffy really is okay with you checking out the incident, I'm happy with that. But, as I'm sure he's already said, don't get too bogged down on that, especially if it looks like it's leading nowhere fast.'

Rob O'Connell held the senior rank of the two of them, him and Jezza, but Ted knew how hard it was for anyone to stop or even deflect a determined Jezza on a mission. He'd have a quiet word with them both before they went anywhere, to set a few firm boundaries.

'The main focus for today is to try to persuade any more witnesses we can to testify against Tonton. With two definites already now, we're getting closer to being able to make a solid case against him, so let's keep going with that as our objective.

'Jo got us off to a good start with his witness, and now there's the one from Ali and Maurice, so we need to build on those. It goes without saying that you let slip no word or hint of who the persons are who've been talking to us.'

'Also, boss, if I can just say. Sara didn't witness the killing of the second twin or the woman. She told us she had her eyes shut and her hands over her ears when that happened. So her testimony is against Tonton only, not the husband,' Ali put in.

'Thank you, Ali, a good point,' Ted told her, then went on, 'So Mike, can you arrange a further interview with Tonton as a priority. Preferably get him brought in here, if getting secure transport soon enough doesn't throw up problems, because I want him left in no doubt at all that the net is finally closing around him.

'Maurice, we need that list of other possible witnesses who might be persuaded to testify from you asap, please ...'

'Already started it, boss,' Maurice told him. 'It shouldn't take me long to circulate, at least the first few.'

Jezza made a theatrical show of staring at him as if she didn't recognise him.

'Who are you and what have you done with our favourite skiving bonny lad?'

A ripple of amusement ran through the team at that. The affection between Jezza and Maurice often showed up in such teasing remarks. Ted said nothing other than a 'Focus, please,' then he went on, 'And Mike, who are we putting on interviewing Tonton this time? Preferably someone he's not been interviewed by before.'

'I thought Virgil, boss,' Mike told him. 'I'm hoping that might rekindle fond memories of him being arrested by him.'

'Never touched him, sarge,' Virgil told him, grinning. 'Well, only to cuff him, but nothing more. But yes, more than happy to give it a shot, although I can't promise to succeed where others haven't. I'll try my best brooding gansta looks and see if I can get any further with him.'

* * *

'I'm still not sure why you're so obsessed with the dogs, rather than any other aspect of the murder,' Rob told Jezza as she drove them out of the station car park towards the town centre, once morning briefing had finished and she'd done her research trying to pin down when and where Turnbull had had his serious fall.

'Several reasons,' she told him. 'Because of your little Faye and my kid brother Tommy, for starters. Plus anyone else who could potentially become a victim of those monsters unless they're found and destroyed. And preferably soon.'

She did a sneaky change down and foot down manoeuvre to get through traffic lights whilst it was still just legal to do it.

'Also if we can somehow show that the same dogs had previously been used to terrorise the victim into falling and suffering life-changing injuries, that should hopefully be a hole below the waterline of any defence case to try to suggest Turnbull had been willingly pet-sitting the dogs, who had never before been known to do any harm to anyone.'

'It's still all a bit sketchy, though. But since Duffy, Mike and the boss have all signed off on it, I'll accept I'm outnumbered. Just remember who's the ranking officer between us though. When I say enough, we give up on it and go back to taking witness statements near the scene.'

He said it in a joking tone. Rob was never one to try to pull rank and he knew how hard it was with Jezza anyway, once she was set on a course. But he was less convinced than she was that there was anything to this line of enquiry. He was prepared to give it a try, but with not as much optimism for success as she clearly had.

Jezza had found out the basic details of Turnbull's fall down the steps, including the report of a witness to the incident, the person who had called the emergency services when it happened.

That person had seen the fall, but had mentioned nothing as to what might have caused it and it had been treated as a straightforward unfortunate accident, although a serious one.

Jezza parked a short distance away from their destination, then she and Rob walked along to the small café, from where the 999 call had been made.

It was quiet at that time of day. The breakfast rush was over, and they found a woman inside, clearing and wiping down tables in the almost empty room.

'Mrs Barnard? Ruby Barnard?' Jezza asked her, holding up her ID. 'I'm DC Vine, Jezza. This is DS O'Connell. We're following up on an incident – a serious fall down the steps up the road – where I understand you were the person who called the emergency services. Have you got a few minutes to answer a couple of questions, please?'

The woman looked surprised, but no more than that.

'That poor man who fell down them, you mean? Eeeh, that was a good while ago now, love. How is he, the poor man?'

'His injuries meant he had to give up work,' Jezza told her, not wanting to go into too many details. Certainly not to tell her he was now dead, though not directly related to the fall, in case that information set off alarm bells and made the woman reluctant to say anything to them.

'You almost certainly helped him to survive the fall though, by calling for help so swiftly.'

'Well, I'm glad I helped in some way. I didn't hear what happened to him after he got carted off to hospital. Not that I expected him to come round with a bunch of flowers as a thank you or nothing like that.'

Her tone suggested she had probably hoped for some recognition at least for her Good Samaritan gesture.

'I was just about to have a cuppa, while it's quiet, before the mad rush starts. Would you like one?' she told them, as the remaining couple of customers finished their drinks and left.

It might have been a coincidence that they drained their cups at the sight of what was clearly a police visit but Jezza noticed and didn't think it was. Some people, even if innocent of any crime, still preferred to distance themselves from police business when they could.

Jezza and Rob both politely refused drinks, not wanting to spend more time than they could really justify on something which might not advance them in any way.

The woman poured herself a cup of tea which looked strong enough to trot a mouse across, then indicated they should all sit down at a table whilst it was quiet.

'Can you tell me how you came to notice him fall? This place is not all that close to the steps,' Jezza asked her.

'Just a coincidence, really. I'd gone out to bring the menu board in for the day because I was getting ready to close up. A man came hurrying past, like all the devils in hell was chasing him. Of course I glanced back the way he'd come but I couldn't see anyone coming after him, so then I looked at where he was going. I was thinking "if he's not careful he's going to knock someone right off their feet, running like that. Running like a mad thing."

'Then he got to the top of the steps and like half jumped to get onto them, but then I saw that he lost his footing and he went flying, all arms and legs thrashing about. I had my phone in the pocket of my pinny so I hurried a bit nearer, because there didn't seem to be anyone else about who'd seen what I saw.

'I could see straight away he'd fallen most of the way down and he was just lying there, crumpled up, so I called an ambulance, quick as I could. I didn't go down because I don't know no first aid or anything, and I'd left the caff open so I didn't want anyone to go in and rob the till while I was out. I thought I'd leave it to the professionals.

'I heard later on the news that it was a bad fall, poor man, but I wasn't surprised, from what I saw.'

'Did the police take a witness statement from you at some point?' Jezza asked her.

'Yes, love. A nice young bobby came round the next day. Only a bit of a lass. Looked like she should still be in school. I told her everything I'd seen, she thanked me for calling the ambulance, then went on her way. That's the last I heard about it all.'

'And you didn't see anyone else about anywhere? Nobody else who might perhaps have seen what happened? Who might possibly have seen a reason why the man was running so fast?'

'No, not really. Well, when I was walking back to the caff, there was a man standing next to his van on the other side of the road, looking in that direction. I saw him looking so I called out something like "some poor sod's had a nasty fall down them steps. I've called the ambulance." Something like that.

'He called back summat about that sounding serious. Then he finished giving his dogs a drink and put them back in his van.'

Jezza tried hard not to throw a grin of triumph towards Rob as she said, 'He had dogs with him? Do you know what sort they were?'

'Eeeh, I know nowt about dogs, sorry. Great big slobbery things though, both of them. The kind you wouldn't want to meet on a dark night, that's for sure. The gobs on them would scare you something shocking, for one thing.'

'Do you remember any specific details about them, perhaps? Colour, size, or anything like that?'

'Not really, love, sorry. Bloody big brutes though, both of them. They'd be up to here on me, for sure,' she indicated with one hand at hip-height. 'One was just like a dark brown colour, the other had white splodges on it. The van was a Transit, though. A white one.'

She said it with an air of triumph, as if it was going to be a valuable clue.

Jezza thanked her, but as she and Rob were walking back to their vehicle, she said, 'Well, that narrows the vehicle down to a few hundred thousand, at least.'

'Good call on the dogs angle though,' Rob conceded. 'But if you start with the "I told you so" I'll have to do something drastic, like tell the boss to keep you chained to your desk for the rest of the case.'

* * *

Ted hadn't really expected to hear back from Inspector Lee, without him chasing her. His message had been a bit vague so he thought she might, at best, have filed it under tasks to do at some indeterminate future date, once she'd caught up with all her own paperwork.

She surprised him by phoning him just as he was sitting down to a brew and a bacon barm, after Steve had volunteered to go out on the sandwich run.

'Inspector Lee, sir, returning your call, as requested. What can I do for you?'

Her tone was polite, neutral, which was a good start. He would have to feel his way carefully from here on.

'Thank you for calling back. This is a long shot and is probably going to sound rather odd, but it's something I felt I needed to check out for myself.

'You were a first responder to a double fatality road traffic collision, some years ago now ...'

'Sadly, that's happened more than once in my career to date, so you'd need to narrow it down for me, please. And bear in mind, I might not have all the details logged in my memory banks.'

'Fortunately, the car in this case might ring a few bells because I imagine they wouldn't be all that common. A classic car like that, and not a common one. British racing green,' Ted told her, and added the location of the incident and more precise details of the car.

'Ah, now that I do remember because as you say, not something you come across every day. What can I tell you that wasn't in the reports, including the inquest report, which I assume you've read?'

'I have, yes. Misadventure verdict, because of the high levels of alcohol in the driver's blood and evidence of excessive speeds. I just wondered if there were any other contributory factors which were considered but didn't go anywhere.'

'Not that I recall. It seemed to be a clear case of driver error. He wasn't wearing a seat belt so was thrown clear on impact, which is why we were able to get blood-alcohol samples, and he was a good three times over the limit. He'd also been caught on camera earlier, twice, doing well over the speed limit.

'The wife was less fortunate. She was wearing her seatbelt and it seems she couldn't get out of it when the car exploded in flames.'

'Were there any other signs of what caused him to lose control?'

'Apart from being pissed as a fart, if you'll excuse the expression? There was extensive fire damage to the vehicle so it wasn't easy to determine anything much from that, although one of the forensic examiners said one of the steering rods had sheared but that could have happened on impact. It was all pretty mangled from the collision, and then the fire which started. It had gone down an embankment where it went off the road and that would have increased the momentum prior to impact. It hit a tree near the bottom of the embankment.

'I remember there was a suggestion at the inquest that the owner had short arms and deep pockets when it came to paying to maintain his vehicle properly, so that might possibly have been a factor, but with the rest of what was found, the coroner was happy to record Misadventure.

'Unless you know something I don't, sir? And if you do, I hope you would share it at your earliest convenience, although I've no idea if the case could even be reopened after all this time, after that verdict.'

'No, I don't really know anything. It was just a coincidental series of circumstances which set off my suspicious mind. But you've now allayed any concerns so I can safely forget about it.

'Thank you, inspector, you've been very helpful.'

Chapter Eleven

Ted wanted a quiet word with Virgil before his interview with Tonton, which was scheduled for the following afternoon, when suitable transport with a prison guard could be made available.

As senior officer, Ted was responsible for the welfare of all the officers on the team. Times had changed in the service. Where once no officer would have dared showed emotions within the workplace, even in toilets where they might have thought to find a bit of privacy, it was becoming acceptable to show feelings. There were now safeguards in place to deal with the traumas of the job.

Virgil was one officer Ted had never thought to see brought low enough for tears in the station. He'd always been a joker. The first with a smile and a humorous comment. Ted hoped it was simply the emotion of another baby on the way which had brought him down. As things stood he couldn't afford to lose any officer, certainly not one who had always been as solid and dependable as Virgil.

Ted called him into his office and invited him to sit down.

'I just wanted to check that you're all right to be working on the Tonton case, Virgil. I imagine it's particularly hard for those with children of their own.'

Virgil shifted in his seat, looking embarrassed.

'Jo told you then, boss?' he asked. 'I asked him not to and I was really hoping he wouldn't.'

113

'You know he was obliged to. I'm responsible for your welfare, so he took on that role whilst deputising for me. He had to include it in his handover. He had no choice.

'So I'll ask you again. Are you going to be all right interviewing Tonton? Mike clearly doesn't know about the episode in the gents, which is why he chose you, and I haven't said anything to him. I'm doing it on a strictly need-to-know basis.'

'I'm fine now, boss. I'd only just found out the wife is expecting again and I think I was feeling soppy and broody. I'd really like to have a go at Tonton. He strikes me as so arrogant. I'm not claiming to have better interview technique than anyone else, but I really would like to have a try with him, if you think I can do it.'

'I'm hoping the "have a go at Tonton" is just a figure of speech,' Ted told him. 'We need him to talk, but we don't want any suggestion of incorrect procedure to come back and bite us at the eleventh hour. We've got precious little testimony against him to date so we can't afford for any we do have to be challenged.

'Strictly by the book, please. With this one more so than ever. I imagine he'll want legal representation for interview and we don't want to give the defence any ammunition at all to fire at us when they next try for bail. Which they will. At every available opportunity.'

'Sorry, boss, a very inappropriate turn of phrase. But I really would like to try with him, even though he's probably not going to say any more than he has done already, which is pretty much the square root of nothing. And you know, I hope, that you can trust me not to punch his lights out, no matter how tempting it might be.'

'Thanks, Virgil. And when we make a bit more progress, I hope you'll let me get the drinks in for a team get-together to celebrate your good news.

* * *

Rob and Jezza were on a video call from their car with Sergeant Duffy of the OCG. They were giving him an update on what they had learned about Turnbull's fall, with the added nugget of an eyewitness claiming to have seen two large dogs close to the scene.

'Might not be the same dogs,' he cautioned them. 'There's probably more of those big Bully bastards than you might imagine. But it's another lead and a good one, so run with that for now. See if you can get any more sightings around Turnbull's house and – the holy grail – anyone who may be willing to talk to you, if they've seen them.

'And we got the DNA results back in record time on that tooth you found, Jezza. Lab are falling over themselves after that big cock-up with one of your samples. The tooth was a positive match for Turnbull, so well done on that.

'You could do worse than walk past the murder site again, going a bit further out than anyone's checked before. See if you can pick up where any cameras haven't been shot out, then try for a look at what they might have picked up.'

'Sarge, out of interest, is there a charge involving using dogs as a lethal weapon?' Jezza asked him. 'It's not something I've come across before and I'd hate to think we get as far as finding the dog owner then they get off with a pat on the head and a rap on the knuckles for a lesser charge like having dogs dangerously out of control.'

'Definitely one for CPS to sort out, that, Jezza. Above the pay grade of us humble foot soldiers. And certainly not one I've come up against before, either, but you can bet this won't be the last such case we hear of. The dogs can at least be seized if we find them, though, as a danger to the public. We have enough to demonstrate that. But good work, both of you, and take care on the dog trail. Watch each other's backs.'

As the call ended, Jezza turned to Rob to say, 'I know you should never judge but I must say I was pleasantly surprised by that. I'd have sworn Duffy was going to be old school, "no pats on the head from teacher for doing the job the bloody taxpayer is paying you for", and all that sort of stuff.

'So, back to the crime scene once more, see if our luck holds and we can turn up some CCTV or another witness. Or preferably both.'

'Sounds good to me. As long as we can grab a takeaway coffee on the way there. A strong one, if our day is going to consist of more rummaging around in dog puke.'

* * *

'Ted? Bill.'

Terse as ever, from the retired sergeant who now acted as first point of contact with any member of the public going into the station for any reason.

Since he'd been given the role, efficiency had improved beyond measure. With his length of service, there wasn't much he hadn't seen or heard before. Genuine issues were channelled where they needed to go with efficient speed. Time-wasters were politely filtered out and sent on their way with a pile of leaflets to study. And Bill's instincts never failed him.

'Yes, Bill,' Ted told him, knowing it would be nothing trivial if Bill was phoning him about whatever it was.

'I have two women down here, with a big bunch of flowers, which they want to give to Maurice in person. But I know he's in quarantine, as far as contact with the public goes, so I thought I'd best check with you first.

'For what it's worth, one of the women says she's the wife of a Sergeant Carver, and I know that name from that case Maurice got caught up in.

'Look, we both know Maurice is a bit of a prat. But he did a bloody silly thing for a good reason, and a lot of us can relate to that. So can I let him come down in person to get his flowers?'

Bill had certainly done risky heroics himself. He'd once jumped onto a moving car in which a child was being abducted, refusing to let go, making it impossible for the kidnappers to drive off. The subsequent collision had ended his active service days but gained him a medal for bravery.

Maurice had tried to help a vulnerable woman in danger and gained nothing more than a written warning and restricted duties.

'I'm quite happy to chaperone him while the women give him the flowers. I'll even body cam it all, if you want me to, but I'd like to see him get his flowers, if he can.'

'Are they yellow roses?' Ted asked him.

Bill's voice turned instantly suspicious, as if he thought he was being sent up in some way.

'What are you, psychic?'

Ted laughed at that, then said, 'No, Trev got the same thing last night. The woman in that case goes to his English classes.

'As long as the whole encounter is recorded so there's no doubts or misunderstandings, I'm happy for Maurice to get his flowers. I'll send him down.'

Maurice looked stunned when the boss told him. His morale had been down as low as it possibly could be after all he'd been through with the false allegation. He was only now, slowly, starting to pick himself back up and rebuild his confidence.

He found Anna Wójcik standing by the front desk when he went down, an enormous bunch of yellow roses in her arms, a shy smile on her face, which still showed yellowing signs of the damage inflicted on it by her late husband.

'Hello, Maurice,' she told him, holding the flowers out to him. 'This is for say thank you for helping me. Yellow flowers for thank you and for friends, where I come from, and you were like a friend to try help me.'

Maurice couldn't stop himself. His eyes filled with tears, which started to slide down his face, now beaming his pleasure at the gesture.

'You're welcome. You're so welcome. I was just doing my job.'

Bill was rolling his eyes at all the fuss. He reached under the desk and stuffed a few paper tissues at Maurice.

'We won't keep you, Maurice,' Val Carver told him. 'I'm sure you're busy, but Anna wanted to thank you in person.'

As they left, Maurice wiped his eyes and blew his nose then turned to Bill. There was something he'd been meaning to ask him for some time now but he'd never found the right moment.

'Sarge, when I came in to answer bail that time and you were asking to see photos of the bairns, that was you giving me an alibi, wasn't it? You weren't really interested in my family, were you?'

Bill gave an exaggerated eye roll as he said, 'Hallelujah! No wonder they made you a detective.

'Maurice, I'm about as interested in your sprogs as you would be in my cockatoo. I think you're a bloody idiot to have got yourself into so much shit. But I also think you're a decent idiot who wouldn't hurt anyone, certainly not a woman, so I believed you were being set up by someone a lot cleverer than you. Which is probably almost anyone.

'Now piss off back upstairs and get on with the job the public pay you to do.'

Maurice was beaming from ear to ear as he went back upstairs, clutching his flowers. Coming from Bill, that had almost been a kind comment.

* * *

Ali O'Malley waited for a response to her knock on the boss's door before going in. She needed his sign-off on something once more.

Ted had actually been hoping to get away at a halfway decent time. He was eager to get to the junior self-defence class he ran with Trev. Except lately it was mostly Trev doing everything, as Ted's work so often restricted his leisure time.

'Boss, our eyewitness is coming in tomorrow to make a full statement about Tonton. I've been liaising with Virgil over timings so there's no risk of the two of them seeing one another. Our witness would be bound to be put right off if that happened, despite any and all assurances that he couldn't get at her.

'What I wanted to ask you about is can I have Maurice in on the interview with me, please? He honestly did make all the difference when we spoke to her before. And he was so careful to go by the book. He didn't even call her bonny lass. Not once.'

Ted smiled at that.

'That must be your influence, then. All right, he can be involved, but make sure you remind him very firmly about his boundaries. In fact, send him to me before the interview and I'll do the same.

'You both did good work in getting your witness this far, so the last thing we need is it all to go pear-shaped through Maurice saying something which gets lost in translation and puts her off saying anything more.'

* * *

'Now that looks promising,' Jezza said, looking into one of the gardens further along from the scene of the fatal dog attack.

So far every security camera they had seen still in place had been vandalised and she and Rob reckoned there may have been more which had been taken down for repair or replacement.

For a moment Rob couldn't see what she was referring to, so he asked her what he should be looking at.

'There, in that tree. Well camouflaged by the leaves and by its own colouring. One of those nature trail cameras. Very hard to spot, which is probably why there's no immediate sign of damage to it.'

'What were they hoping to photograph from up there?' Rob queried, 'And would it even cover enough to catch our dogs, if they did go past here?'

Jezza gave an exaggerated eye roll as she replied, 'Birds, maybe? Or squirrels? That's the sort of thing people usually have those for. Maybe urban foxes, too. And those trail cams often have quite a wide angle and range, I think, depending on the settings.

'It's not all that far from where the puke with the tooth in it was, so there's at least an outside chance of it having caught something relating to the dogs, unless the shots from the night in question have been wiped.'

'We can at least see if there's anyone at home, but we might be better off doing that via the front door rather than tramping in from the back garden.'

It took some insistent knocking before the door was opened to them by a short, bald man peering tetchily out at them through thick-lensed round glasses. Jezza thought he looked disconcertingly like Richard Attenborough in the role of the killer John Christie in the classic film of 10 Rillington Place. She knew she was more of a film buff than Rob so was hoping he hadn't had the same thought or the two of them risked inappropriate expressions while trying to talk to the man. Assuming he would agree to that.

'What d'you want? I'm busy. I don't like Jehovah's Witnesses and I never buy from door-t-door salesmen.'

Jezza left it to Rob to identify them. She was having enough trouble not letting her amusement show at either of them being taken for Witnesses.

'We're neither of those, sir,' Rob told him politely enough as both of them held up their ID, which the man peered at with no signs of any lessening in his suspicious expression.

'We happened to notice your camera in the back garden and we wondered if you might perhaps have caught any shots which could be of help to us in our enquiries.'

There was a sneer not just on the man's face but also in his voice as he asked, 'The police are interested in ornithology, are they? My camera is set up specifically for birdwatching, although it does, inevitably, capture other shots.'

He showed no intention of inviting them inside.

Jezza tried her most charming look as she asked him, 'How often do you wipe the card, sir? We're interested in any shots at all from the weekend. Might you still have those?'

'I usually check it every day, but I'm a bit behind this week. I've had a bit of a bug so I've not even been in the garden. The current card has been in for probably a week.'

'Might it be possible for us to look through the contents, please?' Jezza asked, still biting her tongue to stay polite, knowing how much was riding on the possibility of something useful being on that card, tantalisingly close to them.

'Oh, you can't come in my house. I don't let people come in. Not unless you have a warrant.'

'In that case, if we give you a signed receipt, would you allow us to take it away with us, please, Mr ...?'

The man looked horrified at the mere suggestion, but continued, 'Hanrahan. And I don't like people in my house, I told you that, but I wouldn't be happy with you taking it away.

'You can come into the hall and stay there, with the door open. I'll get the laptop. Tell me the day that interests you, but I should warn you, there could be a thousand or so photos to go through.'

* * *

'Don't you just love cooperative members of the public?' Sergeant Duffy said ironically when Rob and Jezza were back at their car, with the SD card finally safely in their possession, updating him on developments. 'And I bet you your Mr Hanrahan would be one of the first to be protesting about the police doing nothing to tackle crime.

'Well done, both of you. Now make my day and tell me there was something worth seeing on the card.'

'Luckily he has his camera on a high shutter speed, mostly for bird shots, which is why he had so many,' Rob told him. 'But yes, a few halfway decent shots of two big woofers, and a man with them. Hard to make out much for now but we thought we'd go straight back to our nick and give it to our boy wonder with anything techie, young Steve. Hanrahan took a lot of persuasion to hand it over without a warrant, that's for sure.'

'Excellent. Bloody good work, both of you. And we've had a bit of a breakthrough at this end, too. I told you our gang are into everything. Porn films, for one thing. It's another thing they get people into – actually appearing in them – as one more way to have total control over them.

'We uncovered some pretty nasty stuff. As hard as it gets. And we've identified one of the gang's minnows appearing in it with an underage girl. With his own eleven-year-old daughter, to be precise. And not a mock-up this time. It's confirmed as genuine footage.

'We have him in custody now. Very much protective custody. But we're not prepared to offer him any amnesty for testifying. Not for shit like this.'

'Bloody right too,' Jezza blurted, white in the face and shaking with what appeared to be suppressed serious anger. 'Any man who would go anywhere near his own daughter should get the death penalty. Boiled in oil, then burnt at the stake. In public.'

Chapter Twelve

'Oh, you made it then? That's lovely. I wasn't expecting you, so this is a very nice surprise. The kids will be thrilled to see you.'

Trev was just about to close the door to the gymnasium, as most of the juniors were already inside waiting to start their self-defence class, when Ted hurried in, heeling off his shoes as he did so.

'Only just, and I didn't have time to go home first for my kit. I thought I'd come anyway, to watch if nothing else, because it's ages since I managed to get here.'

There was no physical contact between them. No hug or kiss, which was their norm. By tacit agreement, they kept it strictly professional in front of the children. Most of them knew instinctively that Trev and Ted were more than just friends, but both men were aware there may be parents who would object to their children being taught skills which inevitably involved physical contact by a gay couple. They were not about to deprive any of the youngsters of the chance to learn valuable life skills by making an issue of it.

Trev smiled at him as he said, 'Some detective you are! I put it in the boot of your car last night, on the off-chance you might manage to get here. So as long as you've not come in your service vehicle, for some reason, why not go and get changed while I start the warm-up?'

It always did Ted good to spend time with the youngsters. It made him feel that for once, he was doing something which showed immediate benefits and was potentially preventing crime. So many of the children who attended had already been the target of bullying and at least one of them of worse things. The more they attended, the more their self-esteem rose, the more likely they were to be able to say no to getting into anything undesirable through having the confidence not only to say it, but to mean it and reinforce it, if it became necessary.

As ever, Ted's biggest fan, Flip, now a proud police cadet, had eyes for nothing and no one except his hero. He looked ready to explode with delight when Ted later singled him out for a demonstration, and called him Cadet Atkinson in front of all the others.

It made Trev chuckle when he and Ted got into the car together after the session, Trev having walked down to the dojo as a warm-up. They'd waited to tell Bernard they wouldn't be staying on for their own judo session as Ted had a ton of work he ideally wanted to at least get into some sort of logical order before he went in the following morning.

'That was kind of you,' Trev told Ted. 'I thought Flip was going to burst with pride. He's such a nice boy. Will he make a good copper, d'you think, or is he too nice?'

Ted threw him a mock-offended look as he waited for a gap in the traffic to let him turn onto the main road.

'I'm a copper and I'm nice – aren't I?'

'You're very nice, which is why I put up with you being married to the job. I just wonder if Flip is too much so, though. He's very good at the technical side of what we teach, and he seems to be coming on very well with the judo. I just get the feeling somehow that he's always holding back.

Not giving everything he's got. Almost as if he'd back off if the going got really tough, and presumably that wouldn't be of much use in front-line policing.'

'He's young. He has a lot to learn,' Ted countered. 'And things are changing in the service all the time. I'd like to think there could be an opening for young people like Flip, by the time he's old enough to join up. Look at Steve. He wouldn't say boo to a goose but he's absolutely fantastic on the techie side. And surprisingly good in interviews as he looks so non-threatening, but his mind is razor sharp. Plus don't forget he arrested his own father for assault, and that takes some doing.'

They were interrupted by Ted's phone ringing in his pocket.

'Can you get that for me, please?' he asked Trev. 'If it's urgent, tell them I'll pull over and take it. If not, I'll call them when we get back home, or from work tomorrow.'

Trev fished the phone out and answered with, 'DCI Darling's phone.'

Then he heard Trev say, 'Oh, hello, Mr Marston, this is Trevor. Ted's driving at the moment ...'

Ted was making frantic signals to indicate he didn't want to take the call, so Trev went on smoothly, 'Traffic permitting we should be home in about twenty minutes, so he could call you then, if that's convenient?'

Ted smiled his thanks. They should be back in less than half of that, but the margin would at least give him chance to catch his breath and greet the feline reception committee before he had to talk to the senior officer who was, even at his best, pompous and somewhat demanding.

'I've been rather avoiding him,' Ted confessed when Trev had ended the call. 'I know we're supposed to meet to discuss recruitment and training issues in an attempt to improve the service, but with two such big cases still ongoing I feel I'm playing a precarious juggling game to stay on top of everything as it is. I've hardly begun to put together any proposals for him.

'I'll call him when we get back and try to give him a date, at least. I agree with what he's trying to do. I was one of the ones who brought it up, after all. I just don't know when we can get together for a discussion, the way things are.'

* * *

DC Steve Ellis certainly proved Ted right in his estimation of his technical skills the following morning. He was already at his desk when Ted, always early, went in, while there was still no sign of the rest of the team.

'Morning, Steve. How's it going with the contents of the SD card? Make my day and tell me we might get a positive ID from one of the shots.'

'I think we will, sir,' Steve told him, sounding unusually confident. 'I've pulled up quite a few shots which show a figure with two dogs. The camera was set at a very fast shutter speed, luckily for us. I'm just selecting which ones I can blow up without losing all definition. They're night shots, but we might still get some idea of hair colouring, clothing, that sort of thing.

'There's also a clear one of the dogs walking ahead of the man in amongst the shots, and we can very clearly see their markings and colour contrast in that one, which should help.'

'So they're off the lead, then?' Ted commented, looking at the images on Steve's screen. 'Is that even legal for big brutes like that? If not, that might at least give us a valid reason to go after them and seize them as a potential danger to the public. I certainly wouldn't fancy coming face to face with one, never mind two, but then I'm not a dog person at the best of times.

'Can you find that out for me, Steve? It could be a useful piece of information. Check with the dog section first. They should probably know off the top of their heads.'

'I did start to look, sir, but that breed's relatively new to this country so I'm not sure all the breed-specific legislation has caught up with them yet. I'll keep looking, though.'

'Good work. Try and get us some printouts in time for morning briefing. I'm just going to update the Super on our developments, if anyone's looking for me.'

Superintendent Caldwell listened to Ted's report then said, 'Well, that's a good development, potentially. I would assume that as long as the dogs' DNA matches our crime scene sample, we could get an instant destruction order, given the seriousness of what happened.'

'I would think so, but I need to consult with CPS on the available legislation for a case like this one. I suspect it's a new one for most of us. It's in place for dogs killing a family member, from what I've read so far, but if it exists for killing off anyone who crosses the owner, I've not yet found it. That's why I need to call them some time this morning to make sure we know how to proceed. That's if, of course, we can succeed in tracking down where the dogs are now.'

'Maximum precautions before anyone goes anywhere near those animals, if you do succeed in tracking them down, chief inspector. I want no heroics from anyone on this, and that includes you. Is that clear?'

'Oh, don't worry, ma'am, I'm a self-avowed coward where dogs are concerned. I'm not going near them unless I'm behind experienced dog handlers, taser officers and a few marksmen for good measure. And I'll remind the team of that, too. We need those dogs off the street, but not at the expense of injured officers, and certainly not of any civilian onlookers.'

'And how are DC Vine and DS O'Connell getting on working with OCG?'

'I've had good feedback from Sergeant Duffy. He's particularly impressed by Jezza. It was largely her work that put them onto the earlier dog incident, and got them the camera footage.'

'I hope he's not thinking of poaching a good team member. Although she could go a lot further than DC if she chose to.'

'Doesn't want to,' Ted told her. 'I bring it up at every single performance review and her answer is always the same. Likes it here, doesn't want to move. She probably doesn't really need to work much at all, if she doesn't want to. Well-off background, owns her own flat and, I believe, received a substantial life insurance payout on the death of her parents.'

'They died in an RTC, I believe.'

'They did, yes, leaving Jezza to look after her younger brother. And there was a sizeable trust fund to provide for his special needs, too.'

'Well, I hope she likes it here enough to stay with us. But we mustn't ever stand in her way, and we should do everything we can to support her if she does choose to make a career move.'

* * *

'Sir, I've now blown up all the relevant trail cam photos and enhanced them as much as I can but they're still a bit grainy,' Steve said at morning briefing, once all the team members were in.

'They've thrown up three people as a possible match. Two down here on our patch, one up on Rochdale's. All have previous for drugs, assault, including one serious GBH, and various other crimes.

'The GBH one, who's in our area, is the closest match of the three. It might be of significance that the defendant received a much lower sentence than anyone would have expected for such a serious assault. He pleaded guilty and made a big thing of it being an isolated moment of madness. and how remorseful he was. It was the first time he'd been charged for serious assault, although he was thought to have committed several, but witnesses kept mysteriously withdrawing their statements and refusing to testify.'

'That sounds familiar,' Mike Hallam commented. 'What do you think, boss? Start by paying that one a visit?'

'Not without a very thorough recce. I saw what those dogs were capable of so I don't want anyone to walk into that possibility. Certainly not without appropriate back-up. We might also need to liaise with OCG if there's a possibility he's also on their radar.

'Let's start with some basic fact-gathering to try to establish if he's even keeping any dogs at his place. And remember the possibility that they might have been doctored so they can't bark a warning.'

'But boss, some of the neighbours have mentioned hearing dogs barking in the Turnbull house, so doesn't that mean that the ones in this case hadn't been doctored so they should have the decency to warn anyone of their presence?' Jezza countered.

She and Rob had called in to give their updates, having already sent everything through to Sergeant Duffy. As he'd said, no point them driving all the way up to Rochdale to tell him anything they could do by phone.

'And what if those two are not the only ones there? There might be silent ones who could appear before any officers realised. We need these dogs taken out of the equation as soon as possible, of course, before they do any more damage. But we also need a very thorough risk assessment before anyone goes anywhere near.

'Mike, I'll leave that for you to organise, please. Keep me posted.'

* * *

The young woman who had spoken to Ali and Maurice previously had agreed to come into the station in the morning to remove any possibility of her seeing Tonton there, as he was to be interviewed further under caution in the afternoon.

To avoid any possibility of their vital eyewitness changing her mind, Ali had asked for an area car to go and pick her up and deliver her, then take her back home afterwards. Keeping it formal all the way was, she hoped, a way to reassure their potential witness that everything was being done by the book and with her well-being in mind.

Ted wanted to watch some of each interview live, to get a feel for how things were looking with the case. He could go through the recordings in detail afterwards, but sometimes watching in real time gave a better idea of how well any testimony would stand up in court, either as part of the prosecution case, or an indication on what was going to be the defence's line, in the case of Tonton.

Ali deliberately left as much of the interview as she dared to Maurice, poised to step in at any time if he looked in danger of saying the wrong thing. She'd given him a strong reminder and the boss had well and truly marked his card for him, so for now, his technique was impeccable enough to be used as a training video.

As before, the young woman seemed to have made a connection with Maurice. She addressed most of her testimony to him, seemingly completely at ease with him. She replied fully to anything Ali asked her for clarification, but it was always to Maurice that her attention returned.

By the time they had finished, Ali was as confident as she could be that it was damning testimony against Tonton, which they could use, and that the woman would make a good witness to present to the court. As long as nothing happened to change her mind in the meantime.

She sent Maurice back upstairs, then escorted the witness herself to where she could wait safely for her return lift, so that at no point was she left alone with Maurice, without it being in any way obvious.

She next got Virgil to come and watch the playback of the interview, so he could see and assess for himself the strength of the testimony against Tonton. She was cautiously optimistic, but the man had proved so difficult to get any information out of up to now that she didn't envy Virgil the task of trying yet again to do so.

'Well, if CPS think we've got enough to get to court, I would say that witness could well sway a jury. Even if she wants anonymity, which we both know can sometimes make jury members sceptical about testimony, I think if she gives her evidence exactly as she presented it to you and Maurice, we could be in with a sporting chance.

'So I suppose it's all down to me now. No pressure, then, eh? And first of all I have to get him to voluntarily supply a repeat DNA sample, so I don't have to start out by manhandling him.'

'Good luck, Virgil. Not adding to the expectations already riding on you, but I have a good feeling about this. I'll transcribe the witness statement for you so you can have it to hand to read from.

'It's a long shot, of course, but I'd bet money on Tonton not imagining for a moment that any of his flock would have the audacity to testify against him. And now, hopefully, the tide is turning against him.'

Chapter Thirteen

Virgil took time to read through all the available notes once again while he was waiting for the phone call to let him know that Tonton was on his way by prison van for his latest interview. He knew there was a lot hinging on whether or not he could be the one to get their prime suspect to say anything of use in the case against him, where others had so far failed to.

He was often successful in interviews. He put it down to luck as much as his appearance, which could be somewhat intimidating, although he was as soft as butter behind the facade and the banter.

After his reading, he was frowning as he went across to Ali's desk for another word with her.

'I'm trying to look at this testimony objectively, but as though I was on the defence team. So I can anticipate anything they might throw at the prosecution case if and when we can get it to court.

'Your witness wanted an interpreter, supposedly just to check on any unfamiliar words, although her English is good. It would need to be, because she works for the NHS, like my parents do,' he began.

'But you also got her to admit that the common language for these Circles and Welcomings and whatever else they have is English. So have all the people we've interviewed through interpreters just been taking the Mickey? Are there more of them who can speak English perfectly well and they've just been trying to stall for time by insisting on full interpretation before they answer anything? Has that been a ploy because there was some sort of arrangement between them to save Tonton at all costs? To give him the time to get away? And if we can show that, would that not give us a stronger case to go after more of them for a possible joint enterprise charge?'

'If I were to don my wig and gown to reply to my learned friend,' Ali told him ironically, 'I would say that there are quite a few native English speakers who would need some legal terms explained to them. In fact we've probably both been in court when someone in the box has had to ask for clarification on what something a barrister was saying to them meant in plain English.

'And I've struggled all along to understand why they are so protective of Tonton, even after they've seen what he's done. Surely by now they would realise he's not any kind of saint or holy man, and he needs stopping. Soon.'

'Well, I suppose it's all down to me now to make sure he is. If I can do it. And if by any miracle you and Maurice can turn up any more witnesses prepared to testify against him before I've finished interviewing him, I'd take you both out for a pint.'

Ali and Maurice were still trying to find any other members of the group who might be persuaded to talk more than they already had, once they were told that others of their number had now agreed to testify.

Maurice had been over the files so many times he could do them as a specialist subject on a quiz show. That knowledge, combined with how good he was with people, was returning dividends. Ali let him do the phoning round, whilst keeping one ear open on what he was saying, so she could genuinely tell the boss she'd supervised him at all times. The day was still young and he had already found two more witnesses who had at least agreed to the two of them going round to their houses to talk about the possibility of them giving further statements on the record. It was a good start.

Working so closely with him, Ali was getting to know him better and realising what an asset he was to the team, as long as someone kept reminding him of his boundaries.

In an illogical way, she somehow felt responsible for the terrible allegations her own ex-partner had levelled at Maurice. Although he had in reality done nothing more than bending procedural rules, he was paying a heavy price for letting his heart rule his head.

Ali couldn't help but ask herself if she should somehow have known how dangerous a man Eric Leader, her former partner, had been. She was supposed to be a detective and she'd lived with him for a time, without having any idea of what he was capable of.

She consoled herself with the thought that the one good thing to have come out of it all was the boss letting her work closely with Maurice, which had helped her to find out more about him. She'd been impressed by his diligence. He may be a plodder, and inclined to skive if the opportunity presented itself, but his dedication had got them a lot further forward than they had been.

A sentiment echoed by the boss when Ali went to update him and to check if he was happy with her taking Maurice with her again to talk to the next witnesses, both female. And also to ask him if they could do so as soon as possible, on the off-chance that they could then update Virgil, either before or during his interview with Tonton, of more people coming forward and being willing to testify against him.

'Definitely. You two are making a formidable team. It's just what Maurice needs right now. He's a good man. A good officer. He doesn't always engage his brain in gear before acting sometimes, though, unless we're careful. But this is a much better use of his time and talents, as long as you're there to keep an eye on him.

'Can you please ask Virgil to come in and have another word before he starts his interview. Thank you, Ali.'

Ali was smiling to herself as she left the boss's office to tell Maurice his special skills were needed once more. She'd certainly never met a senior officer quite as free with the praise and thanks as DCI Darling.

'Maurice, get your coat. We're on again. See if we can visit at least two more witnesses and get their agreement to testify before Virgil has finished with Tonton.'

'Me too?' Maurice asked her, to confirm, hardly believing his luck.

'You too, bonny lad. You're my new secret weapon,' she told him, all too aware that in taking on Jezza's role of looking after Daddy Hen, she was even starting to sound like her.

* * *

'Are you all set for this, Virgil?' Ted asked him while they waited to hear when Tonton had arrived. 'You've been over this latest statement in enough detail? Whatever you do, don't underestimate Tonton. We already know he's clever. Slippery and dangerous, too. He'll pick up on your slightest hesitation and exploit it, so you need all your confidence, plus absolutely all the facts and come-backs at your fingertips.

'He's arrogant as well, don't forget. He'll try to niggle at you to make you doubt yourself, so keep it simple, stick to the facts and don't let him get under your skin.

'I think you can do this, and do it very well. Just don't for a moment doubt yourself that you can. And with any luck, Ali and Maurice might have news for you before much longer about one or two more possible witnesses ready to testify. Leave him in no doubt that his flock are now starting to turn against him.'

Tonton showed not the slightest anxiety at being brought in for further questioning. If anything, his expression was one of bored indifference. He'd even dispensed with having legal representation, to which he was entitled, as had been explained to him.

He'd been handcuffed to the prison officer who'd escorted him as a potential flight risk for the journey, but he was not considered dangerous so the restraints were removed once he was sitting down in the interview room, facing Virgil, half smiling.

'Are you prepared to give me your real name now, or do you still insist on being addressed only as Tonton?' Virgil asked him, to start things rolling.

'As I have explained before, Tonton is the only name by which I now go.'

'And are you still unwilling or unable to give us an address? Somewhere you live, or at least stay?'

This time his smile towards Virgil was overtly patronising.

'Well, for the moment that would be At Her Majesty's Pleasure.'

'You've applied before for release on bail, and you now know there is no chance of that without a verified address. I'm giving you a further chance to supply one which we can check for suitability.'

'I have none.'

'And you were informed of your right to have a solicitor present for further interview?' Virgil checked, for the record. 'Is there one on their way, or have you declined that right?'

'I have no need of legal representation. I am an innocent man, wrongly detained for something I did not do.'

Virgil didn't want to reveal his trump card of witnesses now willing to testify just yet. He wanted to ratchet up the tension before dropping that particular bombshell, which, from Tonton's demeanour, Virgil felt sure was going to come as a big shock to him.

'Another reason for wanting your presence here today is that I require you to supply a further DNA sample. There's been some problems with the original one.'

Tonton frowned at that, his eyes flashing anger.

'That is hardly my problem. The sample was taken from me forcibly, without my consent. If something has happened to make it unusable, that's not remotely my concern.'

'I'm afraid you are obliged to provide another one, sir, which will be done, with or without your consent, before you leave here. As has been explained to you, your consent is not required by law. Please let me know, in light of that, if you want us to pause until your legal representative can come to advise you.'

Ted was watching the man's expression and body language through the glass from the next room. He could see straight away that Virgil had him on the back foot, but was still staying calm and polite in his questioning. So far a textbook piece of interviewing.

He wished he could stay and watch more live, rather than catching up later from the recording, but he still needed to speak to Chief Superintendent Marston. It had been the man's turn to be unavailable when Ted had phoned him back the previous evening, so they'd postponed their call to the following day. Ted checked his watch and saw it was due to happen in a little under forty minutes.

He'd stay as long as he could. He was keen to see Tonton's reaction at first hand when Virgil started to mention eyewitnesses now willing to testify. If anything was likely to shake the man out of his supercilious calm, that would be it.

'It's hardly worth troubling anyone for what is clearly another of your fishing exercises. If you had any solid evidence against me of any form, you would have produced it by now.'

'Well, you see, sir, the reason you have been brought here today is to inform you of new evidence which has only recently come to light, in the form of eyewitness testimony. The existence of new evidence would no doubt have been explained to you as part of the arrangements for you being brought here. You perhaps didn't appreciate the seriousness of the new evidence.

'There are now people prepared to testify under oath that they witnessed you picking up a twin newborn baby girl, in order to put her to death in the most brutal way. Shortly followed by the killing of the second twin girl, and then ensuring that the mother's husband, by this time in a severe state of shock, was directly involved in the killing his own wife by strangulation. Actions which you claimed to have done as a way to prevent further overpopulation of the planet.'

The second point was pushing it slightly, Virgil knew. The latest witness, Sara, had said she had her eyes closed and her hands over her ears after the first two deaths. But she had been present. She would have heard most of what was going on, and Virgil had been deliberately careful with his phrasing, using only the word "ensuring". Had Tonton had a lawyer present, they would, of course, have jumped all over what Virgil had said.

This time there was no mistaking the sneer of contempt on the man's face as he replied, making a show of lifting up his withered arm with his functioning one, 'Good luck with getting enough members of a jury to believe that someone as clearly disabled as I am would be able to do such a thing. Always assuming that you can convince them I had a valid motive to do it, rather than the fanciful nonsense you've come out with so far. Not to mention proving conclusively that I was even there at the relevant time.'

Virgil's sense of timing was excellent. He left just enough of a pause for the man to think he was winning on points, then he said calmly, 'You see, the problem there comes in the form of our expert witness.

'We are lucky enough to have one of the country's leading forensic pathologists to work with. A real thinker outside the box. She performed the post-mortems on all three of these victims.

'When we informed her of our main suspect – you, sir – and explained your disability, she became intrigued. So much so that she made a teaching exercise for her students of investigating if it could be possible for someone such as yourself to have carried out the killings in the way in which they happened, taking account of all the forensic evidence available to her from the scene.'

Again, Virgil was stretching things somewhat in that Professor Nelson had only looked into the feasibility of Tonton killing the babies, not their mother, either alone or with the husband.

'The results of the experiments were a resounding yes. It would be perfectly possible for what we believe to have happened, now confirmed by a credible eyewitness, to have done so ...'

Virgil got no further before the man known only as Tonton was halfway over the intervening table, his valid hand heading for Virgil's throat.

Virgil could move far faster than his size and build suggested. He jumped up from his chair and neatly sidestepped, at the same time pressing the alarm button to summon reinforcements, leaving Tonton clutching air and sprawling over the table.

Ted was the first through the door, ready, as ever, to defend one of his team if necessary, but Virgil had the situation under control, with Tonton now in a firm hold he could not escape from.

'Would you like some time to contact your lawyer before we continue this interview, sir?' Virgil asked the man.

Neither he nor Ted recognised the language Tonton replied in. But there was no mistaking the vitriol in what he was saying.

'I'll take that as a no then, sir, shall I?'

* * *

'Now, chief inspector, we need to compare diaries to find a

time when we can finally sit down together and discuss our ideas for better procedures so that we can ensure the very best possible recruitments into the service,' Chief Superintendent Marston began when he phoned Ted at precisely the appointed hour.

'As it happens I have a visit to the Lancashire HQ in Preston coming up shortly. I'll be travelling by train, so I thought I could break my journey in Stockport. I believe there is a perfectly acceptable hotel quite close to the station.'

Marston gave Ted the date to check. For one anxious moment, Ted wondered if the man was angling for an invitation to use his spare room. Ted was struggling to think of anything worse.

'So you and I could have our discussion at your office in the afternoon as I would need to leave for Preston early the following morning. Is that convenient to you?'

Ted put it in his diary, hoping that wouldn't lead to some crisis with either of the current major cases which would complicate matters.

'That's fine, sir, thank you. Noted. Would you like me to send a car to collect you?'

'That won't be necessary, thank you, the walk will no doubt do me good and it isn't far, if the map is accurate.

'One further thing. I did enjoy speaking to your partner, Trevor, on the telephone when I asked his advice on a gift for you that time. If it's not too presumptuous, I wonder if you and he would care to join me for dinner that evening, as my guests, and if you could perhaps suggest a suitable restaurant.'

It was such a surprise that Ted found himself accepting the invitation without even consulting Trev. He told Marston they would choose somewhere appropriate and make the table reservation.

'Excellent, that's settled. I shall look forward to it,' Marston said as he ended the call.

Ted thought he'd better quickly check with Trev if he was all right with what he'd been let in for without consultation, but his partner simply laughed when he heard.

'Oh Ted, sometimes, for a clever detective, you are so obtuse at reading people, and your gaydar skills are a disgrace. Your Mr Marston is actually rather sweet but so far in the closet he could never turn the key, never mind come out, which is why he is alone and lonely. Going out to dinner with two gay men will probably be the highlight of his year.'

'He's always seemed homophobic to me,' Ted told him.

Trev sighed. 'Ted, you're hopeless. Don't you think that might be because he's hiding his own true identity? Anyway it's so lucky we've no Kids' Club that evening because of the repair works to the gym. That means we won't have to cancel self-defence, and disappoint the kids. It's going to be great fun.'

145

Chapter Fourteen

'Well done, Maurice. Seriously, that was fantastic, the way you held it together in there. Textbook stuff. And you're definitely the one who got her to talk as much as she did. I was a spare part,' Ali told Maurice as she drove the two of them away from the home of the eyewitness they had just been interviewing.

'She was a nice lass. Naive, but nice. The thing I can't get my head round – not at all – is why no one reacted. After he killed the first bairn. Why did they all just stand there like sheep and let him go back to do it again? And then the mother too, and she was only a bit of a lass herself. Why?'

They'd stopped now at traffic lights. Temporary ones for roadworks. They'd been held up there on their journey out and knew they were on a long time lag so Ali killed the engine whilst they waited.

'It's easy to forget that you and I have had special training as police officers. We're trained to react in a certain way in particular circumstances. But the average member of the public hasn't had that, and they're often warned not to be a have-a-go-hero. Their instinct is often to freeze, or to go into self-protection mode, if they act at all.

'And unless any of them had been at a previous Welcoming involving multiple births – which none of the interviews to date have established – it could well have come as a complete surprise to everyone there, so they'd be in some degree of shock.

'Again, we both know all too well that you can't tell someone is a killer, or a psychopath or anything else, just by looking at them. No matter how well we think we know someone.'

There was no sign yet of the lights changing. Maurice took advantage of the moment to put one of his big hands gently on top of Ali's which was resting on the gear lever, ready to change out of neutral the moment the lights turned green.

'Don't beat yourself up, bonny lass,' he told her gently, understanding immediately what she was referring to. 'You couldn't know what Leader was really like. You had a lucky escape, in a way, but I'd bet any money that he was careful how he treated you because you were in the service, same as him, and he'd know what could happen to him if he tried anything like that with you. Nobody else thinks you should have known and done something. I certainly don't.

'Thinking about it, it was the same with the young lass we've just spoken to. She would have had no idea what was about to happen. And once it all kicked off, she would have been frozen, I suppose, like she said.'

The lights changed at that moment. Maurice removed his hand so Ali could put the car in gear and pull away smoothly.

'It would be nice to think she might be the first of a couple, at least, that we can let Virgil know about,' she said. 'I'm guessing eyewitnesses willing to testify against him never crossed Tonton's mind. Certainly not more than perhaps one member of his flock turning on him, and he might be conceited enough to think he could still talk himself out of that. The more people we can persuade to talk, the more rattled he's going to be.'

* * *

Their next potential witness was standing in the front garden of her tiny terraced house, looking out for their arrival. Ali had phoned ahead to let her know they were on their way.

She looked small, slight and somewhat anxious. Mid-twenties, from first impressions, and wearing clothing which kept her well covered, while her head was bare.

There didn't seem to be any prescribed dress code for the members of the Circles in their everyday lives, although all the females had been wearing long flowing dresses at the one which had been raided, and where Tonton had been arrested, after trying to escape.

Maurice stood aside to let Ali go first through the garden gate. He had no idea of the beliefs of the people they were interviewing and wanted to present the lowest level of threat he could if they were to get anything useful out of her. It was how he would always behave and he hoped it might show their next witness a bit of what sort of person he was.

He let Ali speak first and do the introductions.

'Aisha? I'm Detective Constable Alison O'Malley, this is DC Maurice Brown. Thank you for agreeing to talk to us.'

'Hello, my friend phoned me to tell me you were on your way so would be on time. Come in, please. Would you like some tea?'

Ali and Maurice exchanged a glance. They had asked the previous witness not to talk to anyone else, especially anyone they'd not yet interviewed again.

Aisha saw the look, as she showed them where to go, and smiled at them.

'Don't worry, we didn't discuss anything. She just phoned to tell me you'd left her house and to say that you were both very nice and kind so I should feel safe talking to you, if I wanted to.'

Her English was excellent, yet Maurice and Ali both knew from the interview notes that she was another one who had wanted an interpreter present when previously interviewed.

'Tea?' she asked them again, inviting them to sit down in a modest-sized but impeccably neat kitchen.

Both of them shook their heads as they took their places where indicated.

'Before we start, I know you requested an interpreter when you were interviewed at the station previously, yet your English appears to be excellent,' Ali told her. 'Are you happy to talk to us now without one? And would you mind telling us why you requested one previously?'

Aisha sat down in turn. There was a half-drunk mug of something on the table in front of her which she picked up and cradled. It looked like a gesture to give her something to do with her hands, rather than a real need to drink anything.

'The people attending the Circles are from many different countries and cultures. Some of them probably from places where there is very little trust in the police.

'When anyone new joins us, Tonton always reminds people that we don't talk about ourselves to anyone other than people we know from the Circles. I think, these days, that's true of a lot of groups like ours. They can often become the target of hate crimes if people get the wrong idea about

149

any religious involvement. Even though there's no type of religious aspect to our Circles.

'Also there's never been any question of anything at all illegal in what we have been discussing and doing, but most of us know, or at least feel, that not everyone amongst us might have a legal right to stay in the country. So we are careful what we say to anyone. And we've always been advised to ask for an interpreter if we're being interviewed by anyone official for any reason. A way to protect ourselves from possibly being made to say the wrong thing, or misunderstanding a question.

'Please excuse me, I'm sure you are not like that, but when you don't know the system, you can be suspicious.'

'You're clearly here legally since you're happy to talk to the police, so may I ask you what it is you do here? Are you in work?' Ali asked her.

'I'm a student, in Manchester, studying ethnomusicology.'

Maurice frowned his incomprehension.

'Well, your English is already better than mine. I have no idea what that means.'

She smiled at him.

'Not many people do, so you're not unusual there. Put simply, it's the study of music as a reflection of different cultures.'

'And are you now happy to tell us everything you can about what happened at the Welcoming ceremony you attended which eventually led to the arrest, at a later date, of the man known as Tonton? Would you agree to us recording what you tell us, on video, and would you, if necessary be happy to attend court and say the same thing there, in front of Tonton?'

'I will do, yes, and I'm sorry I didn't tell you everything the first time I was interviewed.

'I hope you will believe me when I say that I had no idea what was going to happen at the Welcoming. I'd never been to one before, and hadn't spoken to anyone else who had. I was so shocked by it all I didn't know what to do or say. But I now believe that all of us who were there must tell you exactly what we saw. Even if it means trouble for us. Some of us are already talking together about doing that. We must. Tonton must be stopped from ever doing anything like that again.'

* * *

Maurice drove on the way back, leaving Ali to call in to the station with an update on their progress to date, to be fed through to Virgil if he was still interviewing Tonton.

Not only had Aisha given them her full statement, she had also highlighted some names of others she believed might be willing to testify, once they heard they would not be the first to do so. They were first names only, some of them not uncommon, but it should be easy enough to pick them out from the list of those known to have been present.

'Excellent timing, Ali,' Virgil told her. 'Tonton got a little bit cross at some of the things I was putting to him so he lost it and tried to attack me. We've put him in a cell to calm down a bit so I'm having a coffee break for now and gathering my thoughts on where to go next with him. News of more witnesses is probably just what I need to press a few more buttons.'

Ali had the call on speaker so Maurice asked him, sounding concerned, 'Shit, mate, you all right?'

Virgil laughed as he replied, 'I thought I was pretty swift on my feet getting out of his way and sounding the alarm. The boss did Olympic-level speeds coming in from the next room to lend a hand if I needed it.'

'I thought he was an exception with all the pleases and thank yous he says to everyone, all the time,' Ali put in. 'It's nice to know there are some senior officers who would also wade in physically to the rescue of us mere mortals when necessary. I don't imagine they're all like that.

'We're just off to try one more witness who Aisha suggested as another possible, while we're out and about. I'll get a message through to you if you're still with Tonton, rather than wait until we come back in.

'This time it's a young man. I thought that would bring some balance. If we only present evidence from women who were there, it might possibly suggest some sort of extreme gender divide thing going on, which could potentially muddy the waters.'

'Are we sure it isn't that? Is our Tonton perhaps a woman-hater and trying to dress it up with some so-called philosophy about protecting the planet?' Virgil asked her.

'I have the feeling there are murky depths to our Tonton yet to be plumbed, so that's rather over to you. We'll keep you posted.'

The next address they visited had nothing impeccable about it in terms of tidiness, and certainly not of cleanliness. Theo Lee, the person they had come to interview, explained that he shared a small house with several other students and what they saw of the property made Ali and Maurice feel for the landlord of the property taking it back at the end of the lease, unless a few miracles had been performed by then.

Ali hadn't had much of a preconception about this possible witness. All she knew was that he was a young man, rather solitary, who had newly joined the Circles, but that he hadn't been present at the Welcoming which had ended with the killings. Some of the members had, though, got together afterwards to talk about what had happened. Inevitably, knowing human nature, although all would have been told that they should have no contact with any other potential witnesses or suspects.

It was likely to be hearsay, at best, but talking to him might go some way towards answering the question the whole team were inevitably asking themselves – did any of them know or suspect what the Welcomings were all about in the case of multiple births.

This time Ali and Maurice were not even offered a drink but looking at the state of the kitchen, especially the sink, they were relieved. The two of them exchanged a loaded glance, both clearly thinking the same thing at the same time. Apart from the glasses and the much darker hair, Theo Lee reminded both officers of their own DC Steve Ellis in appearance. A casting agency's stereotypical version of a computer nerd.

Theo didn't invite them to sit down, either. To their further relief, as the only chairs not piled high with dirty washing looked sticky and grubby.

As before Ali took the lead in questioning, asking Theo to tell them, in his own words, what he knew about the group, especially in relation to the Welcomings, seeking and receiving his consent to film the interview.

'Well, I never expected to hear all the things I did about what happened there,' he told them, his tone on the aggressive side of defensive.

'I'd found out about the group through a friend so I went along to a couple of the get-togethers –the meetings they call Circles. They seemed to be in tune with my own beliefs that overpopulation is the biggest danger the planet faces. I actually agreed with the principle behind the Chinese idea to make one-child families the norm.

'I heard them talk about these Welcomings but I really didn't want to go to one of those. It seemed to me to be intrusive, too personal. And I don't like babies very much, anyway. But then I heard what had happened at that one and I was horrified. I believe in restricting reproduction in whatever way possible, but not by putting babies to death. It's not at all what I thought these people were about.'

Ali looked towards Maurice once more. This wasn't sounding helpful to them by way of witness statement. Not only had Theo not been present at the Welcoming, but he wasn't saying anything which would implicate Tonton or any of the others in premeditated killing.

'So what was it about the group which interested you?' Maurice asked him. 'You said you'd been to a couple of Circles. So how many did you attend? And what made you go back after the first one?'

'I went to three, and what interested me was the talk of population limitation. Tonton was constantly preaching that as a solution, or at least a partial one, to the state of the planet. One-child families.'

'Did he actually say how he hoped to achieve that?' Ali asked him.

'He never mentioned actual killing, but he did say a lot of things about needing to restrict population by whatever means available.'

Once the two of them were back in the car together and heading for the station, Maurice asked, 'Is any of that enough to be of any use though, do you think? It's all a bit vague.'

'Not for us humble plods to work out, luckily,' Ali replied. 'We supply his statement, then it's up to a clever prosecutor to see what they can make of it by way of prosecution ammunition.'

* * *

Ted was on the car park when Jezza came out of the station at the end of the day. She and Rob had had a good day, with the possibility of a location where the dogs in the murder case may be being kept.

They'd fed the information through to Sergeant Duffy who was organising enough of the right sort of back-up for a raid on the address first thing the following day.

'Your turn for a breakdown, boss?' Jezza asked him, seeing him standing there peering under his car's bonnet, then walking over to see if she could help. 'Won't she start, even off the crank handle?'

Ted gave her one of his mock-serious looks as he said, 'My car is not that old, DC Vine. She starts, but I just thought the steering was feeling a bit wobbly coming in this morning.'

'Wobbly. I see. That's a good technical term.'

Jezza could never resist the opportunity to tease the boss she thought the world of.

'I just thought I'd have a look to see if I could see anything obviously about to drop off or if I could safely drive it round to the garage for them to check.'

Jezza was walking round the car, looking at the wheels. She told him, 'Well, at least your tyres look in decent order. Low pressure in one of them might give that feeling.

'The other possibility is something not right with the tie ends, but that's not really easy for me to check here, especially not in my work clothes.'

She was now leaning as far as she could into the engine compartment, trying not to touch anything, but seemingly knowing what she was looking for.

'If you're worried, boss, I would definitely take it to your garage and get them to have a quick shufti. Do you want me to follow you there in my car and run you home afterwards? It's no trouble.'

'Thanks, Jezza, but I'm sure it will be fine. It's not far and I can go slowly. The lads there know my little car well. I bought it from them. They'll be able to tell me in no time if there's a problem. And they'll give me a courtesy car if I need to leave mine there.

'Thanks for your help, though. It's good to know there's someone on the team with a bit of mechanical knowledge when I have none.'

As Jezza got into her own car to drive away, Ted said to himself, quietly, under his breath, 'Quite a bit of mechanical knowledge, it would seem.'

Chapter Fifteen

'Boss?'

Virgil noticed that the DCI didn't seem to be listening to everything he was telling him. That was totally out of character. He was usually sharp as a tack. Fully focused on the matter in hand. This time he looked as if his thoughts were elsewhere. A long way off.

'Sorry, Virgil, you were saying?'

In the end Ted had taken the decision the previous day, after Tonton's loss of control, that the man should be sent back to prison to cool down and returned the following day, when he would be kept handcuffed securely throughout the interview, with the prison guard staying with him in the interview room at all times. Ted was not only thinking of the safety of his officers but also that the move would prevent the defence team from claiming their client had been interviewed when under duress and not in a fit state to be questioned. Certainly without legal representation, which he continued to refuse.

At least Tonton was being held locally. Not much more than a half-hour journey away, unless traffic was particularly bad, which was better than it might have been.

'I imagine that what Theo Lee told Ali and Maurice means we might struggle to get a joint charge against all those present at the Welcoming,' Virgil went on. 'They both think Lee would make a credible witness, and I do too from what they've told me. He's very literal in everything he says. Everything factual, nothing emotional. The two of them remarked it was very like the way our Steve presents anything. Another computer science nerd, too, so just facts, no speculation.

'It certainly does explain why people would go to these Welcoming ceremonies, thinking they were exactly that. A way of celebrating new life. And it does seem as if earlier ones were nothing more sinister. A happy occasion, celebrating a new arrival, very much an extended family sort of thing. As far as anyone's been able to find out so far – at least in our area – the only time it's turned into anything darker has been the two occasions when there have been multiple births; ours and the one at Billinge.'

'That would effectively remove any chance of joint charges, by the sound of it, as this testimony would indicate that none of them knew or could have reasonably been expected to know that there was anything sinister about the Welcomings at all,' Ted agreed.

That was starting to sound more like the boss on true form, to Virgil's relief.

'I've made it an early afternoon interview today so there's time for Ali and Maurice to try for some more witnesses first, while they're on a winning streak. Even with what we have already, it's probably more people than Tonton would have expected to testify against him, from what we know about him. He probably assumed no one would say a thing, judging by the arrogance he shows.

'That's the overriding impression I get of him, the more I talk to him. Supreme arrogance and self-belief. Like he considers himself some sort of a latter-day Messiah, that no one would dare speak out against.'

'Be careful with presumptions, though, Virgil. I think we'd all agree that Tonton appears to be a devious character and one who considers himself above the law. But there may be much more to him than that. Something much more complex beneath the surface which we've not yet glimpsed.

'I would certainly expect him to be surprised that any of his flock are now willing to talk about him in any negative way. That could be his arrogance, of course. But he may possibly be naive enough to think no one would question his actions, let alone speak out against them.

'You're doing a good job with him. See if you can find out if he knew in advance that those two cases involved twins. If he could reasonably have been expected to know that. That's of course key to any question of premeditation.'

Virgil hesitated for a moment then said, 'Boss, this probably sounds daft, but I wondered. About Tonton and the mystery of his origins.

'We know Tonton means "uncle" in French so he might be from a French-speaking country, although he doesn't really have any accent. And I know Steve's been looking into that to find where he might have come from and how he got into the country.

'But what if he's here legally and was maybe even born here? We know he speaks good English. So what if someone else nicknamed him Tonton and he just took it up? Could it be another thing he's using to put us off the trail?'

'Virgil, you're a genius. And I'm an idiot,' Ted told him. 'My mother always calls me *bach*. But that's because she's the Welsh speaker, not me. So if ever I used the word about myself, it would be wrong for anyone to think I was a Welsh speaker.

'That was an elephant trap and I fell right into it. Please update Steve and make sure everyone knows that it's a potential red herring we all need to avoid.

'And now I think of it, there was a brutal secret police force called the Tonton Macoute, in Haiti, and they were anything but cuddly uncle figures. He might even use the name as a sick reference to their brutality and human rights violations.

' You made a very good point there. One I should have considered right from the start.

'Keep up the good work, Virgil.'

* * *

Rob and Jezza had an early start. Sergeant Duffy had decided to leave them in charge of the raid on the property which, through their work in finding the nature camera, was now thought to be where the two dogs who had killed the victim on their patch were being kept.

The dogs were key to any case against anyone, being in effect the murder weapons. Until they were found and their DNA tested for a match, the investigation couldn't get much further. Duffy had decided that until that link was made, there was no point moving any of his team down from Rochdale for the moment. They had plenty to get on with on their own patch, rounding up and questioning anyone they suspected of being involved at any level in the death of Turnbull.

Duffy had liaised with Ted and got his approval. If and when they found the right dogs, and their owner, he could look at sending officers to Stockport to work with Rob and Jezza on taking the murder case forward from there.

Ted had had words with both Rob and Jezza before the raid. Separately. He wanted to check that Rob was all right. He understood that having previously been stabbed, he might still have some anxiety issues in such a situation. Perhaps even without him knowing or suspecting they were lurking under the surface, ready to emerge at the worst possible moment.

'No heroics though, Rob,' Ted told him to end his little speech, reminding him of his expectations. 'You've got experts there to see to the dogs in the safest possible way, and to help arrest anyone on the premises.

'I'll be telling Jezza her fortune as firmly as I can but we both know she can be hot-headed, so make sure she understands that you're the senior officer on this. What you say goes.

'Good luck, and stay safe, both of you.'

Rob recounted his conversation with the boss to Jezza as they drove out to where they were meeting the support teams for the raid.

Jezza smiled at his words.

'How have I acquired this totally unjustified reputation for not following procedure?'

'This journey isn't long enough to list all the ways,' Rob told her with a grin. 'But I could start by mentioning the time you kick-boxed the boss to the ground in a puddle then sat on him to keep him there.'

Jezza laughed at his words.

'Oh, that. Well, ironically, that was me trying to prevent him doing a bloody stupid thing and drowning himself by being a have-a-go hero. So it's a bit rich to throw that in my face in the circumstances.'

Both switched back to professional mode as they pulled up next to where other officers from different sections were getting out of their vehicles ready for action.

There were two officers with dart guns to take down any dogs which might attack on sight. The darts contained enough tranquilliser to knock out animals which could potentially weigh nine stone or more. It was risky, but it had been decided it was better that way than to have the bad press of a raid gone wrong and claims in the media of the savage killing of soppy family pets who wouldn't hurt a fly. It had happened that way in the past, although not to date on their patch.

Once the dogs were immobilised and securely muzzled, their DNA could be taken and a court order obtained for their immediate destruction, if they were a match for the dogs which had killed Turnbull.

The biggest worry was not knowing if the dogs would attack on sight or if they needed a command from an owner or handler before they went on the offensive.

The instruction from the top had been to take no chances. Disable the dogs by whatever means available as a first priority, before attempting to search the property. The house had been kept under observation from the moment it had been found and identified as housing dogs which seemed to match closely both the film footage, although that wasn't totally clear, and the few witness statements they'd obtained, including the one from the café owner, Ruby Barnard.

In case for any reason the darting didn't work, or not to a sufficient degree, there were officers from the dog section in heavy padding and armed with hypodermic needles loaded with a substance strong enough to knock down something even larger and more dangerous than the biggest fighting dog.

As a last line of defence, there were marksmen from Firearms on hand to take the dogs down by lethal force, if that became necessary.

Rob, as designated senior officer, did a final briefing of all present: a firm reminder of the dangers and potential pitfalls. He wanted those dogs, and their DNA, but not at the expense of any officer under his temporary command being injured, or worse.

He made it generalised but his eyes were on Jezza for most of it. The two of them got on well. They were on friendly terms outside work. Plenty of banter and teasing. But this was serious, and they both knew it.

It was a dangerous raid. Rob's neck was on the block if it all went wrong and he wanted to impress on everyone, especially Jezza, the need to stick to the plan. The last thing he wanted was for her to do something daft which could get her or someone else killed or seriously injured.

The most dangerous role of all was that of the officer who made that first knock on the door, not knowing what could potentially come out at them. An older PC from Uniform had volunteered for that role. He was wearing a stab vest, which was routine enough not to raise the alarm, but he and everyone else knew that would be scant protection against dogs the size of XL Bullies, nor any wary or potentially aggressive person who might also be lurking behind that closed door.

As soon as he knocked, there was a palpable holding of breath from everyone present. For a moment, nothing happened. Then all hell broke loose in such a jumble and confusion that Rob had difficulty sorting out the order of events in his mind later on when he came to write his report.

The PC had assured everyone that he could move remarkably quickly when he needed to, and he certainly wasn't wrong. The instant the door started to inch open, two huge beasts, jaws gaping, hurled themselves through the gap, seemingly ready to defend their territory against all comers.

True to his word, the PC rolled himself up and dived to the side, his left shoulder hitting the hard surface of the driveway with a sickening crack which sounded ominously like bone breaking. But at least he was out of the way of those slavering jaws, and clear of the two large and heavy dogs who were quickly knocked off their feet by the fast-acting darts.

Jezza was the first to react by rushing to the fallen PC, whilst other officers, led by those from Firearms, were streaming into the house to flush out anyone inside and check for any other dogs on the premises.

Rob noticed her movement as he too was heading for the house. He'd have to have a word with her. Even after his pep talk she hadn't followed basic procedure and had potentially not only put herself in danger from the occupants of the house, she had been in the line of fire of the armed officers, dashing in like that, and she should have known better.

He'd need to go through all of the body cam footage available to be sure of the sequence of events before he could present his full report to Sgt Duffy and to the boss. He didn't want to drop Jezza in it, but he'd a feeling the boss was going to have a few words to say to her when he saw the footage.

All in all, despite Jezza's actions, Rob felt it had been a successful operation. The two big dogs, out for the count and now safely muzzled, in case, were on their way to get their DNA taken and tested. They had been the only dogs in the house, to the relief of most of the officers. Especially since they'd seen the size and weight of the two brutes which had been sent out to greet them.

Officers had also arrested a man – the presumed owner of the dogs – a teenage boy, said to be his son, and the woman who lived with them both. Rob had used various sections of the Dangerous Dogs Act for the initial arrest, but was hoping to be able to hit the man, at least, with a much heavier charge, once the CPS had decided what would be the most appropriate ones to bring, with the best chance of a successful outcome in court. If they could get it that far.

Once they'd finished at the site and were walking back to where they'd parked the car, Rob turned to Jezza, but before he could say anything, she interrupted him.

'Yes, sarge,' she said, in her seemingly innocent but most sarcastic tone, 'I know, I went off-piste, but there was an officer down and I thought someone should at least check on him. I was the nearest.'

She would never normally use his rank, so she was clearly taking the piss or making a point. But Rob had one to make, too, and he intended to do so.

'He was in no more immediate danger than any of us. Less, in fact, down like that. There was a chance the dogs wouldn't have attacked him, lying in a defensive posture like he was.'

Jezza made a noise like a snort.

'Seriously? You and I know exactly what those dogs were capable of. They'd previously half eaten a man on the ground. I could hardly leave him there right where they were likely to attack him.'

Rob was starting to sound angry now. Jezza was well in the wrong and he needed her to at least acknowledge that.

'What were you going to do, Jezza? Chuck him over your shoulder in a fireman's lift and run for cover? I'd put him at nearly twice your weight. He was safer on the ground, leaving clear line of sight for the shooters, without you getting in their way.'

Jezza sighed. Rob was right, and she knew it. She'd acted on instinct and done something potentially dangerous. It could mean big trouble for her, especially if the boss got wind of it.

Time to put her drama skills to good use.

'Sorry, Rob, you're right. It was a daft thing to do and I'm sorry. I was just worried for him, and I hope he's going to be all right.

'If I buy you a coffee on the way back, do you promise not to tell Duffy? Or at least give him the watered-down version of me only moving after doing a thorough and complete risk assessment. And definitely, please, don't tell the boss.'

Chapter Sixteen

'I am not a bloody PA for your officers, Ted. Can you make that clearer to them.'

It was retired Sergeant Bill Baxter's voice in Ted's ear when he picked up his phone, and he was sounding even more grumpy than usual.

'I have enough to do dealing with bloody stupid members of the public with no clue of what we're actually here for, and how under-resourced we are. Your lot should know better.'

Ted stopped himself from sighing – just. He was tempted to offer to swap shifts with Bill for one day to see if he still thought he had the tougher role.

Ted was trying to balance figures on a spreadsheet. Something he did often, usually with no trouble at all. He was never thrilled by the admin side of his role, but he didn't usually struggle with it as he was currently doing. His concentration kept deserting him at the critical moment.

'More flowers for Maurice?'

'Flowers, yes, but this time for that DC Vine. Send someone down to fetch them, will you? I don't want my reception area looking like a florist shop.'

Ted did allow himself a sigh as Bill hung up, still not sounding in the best of moods. He got up and went out into the main office. He would normally have gone downstairs himself, for the leg-stretch and the chance of a quick word with Bill, to try to smooth his ruffled feathers, if nothing else. He wasn't the sort of boss to consider himself above running an errand for someone on his team. But there was simply no way he could justify even the few minutes it would take. Not if he hoped to clear his desk by the end of the day.

Steve was the only one of the team in the office, working on trying to find any more links to cases anywhere in the country or further afield which might possibly have something to do with their own.

'Steve, can you do a little errand for me, please? Someone's delivered some flowers for Jezza and Sergeant Baxter wants them out of his space. Knowing him, he'll have given them a quick check to make sure there's nothing suspicious included in with them, like he did with Maurice's, but perhaps have a look yourself, too. Carefully, in case of anything sharp.'

It wouldn't be the first time someone had tried to seriously injure a copper, or worse, with a seemingly innocuous gift which wasn't what it seemed.

'Perhaps put them in a bit of water in a wash basin somewhere until Jezza gets back. I'm not sure how long these things stay looking good these days and I don't expect she'll be here until a fair bit later today.

'It's not her birthday or anything is it, and I've forgotten?'

'Not her birthday, no, sir.'

Well, if it's a special occasion of some sort, she'll no doubt share the information with us, if she wants to. Thank you, Steve.

'Any more developments with our case, before you go?'

'Not so far, sir. I'm still not sure how long Tonton has been in our area nor, of course, where he came from or what his real name is yet, which is hampering searches. I'll keep trying, though. He must have come from somewhere.'

* * *

This time the prison officer who had escorted Tonton to the station would stay with him throughout his second interview with Virgil in case of a further angry outburst. The suspect would remain handcuffed to the officer at all times.

Virgil had discovered at the previous interview that, despite the lack of a fully-formed hand on one side, the man had knuckles on his deformed side, which stopped the cuff slipping off him. After talking to the boss, Virgil had agreed to leave him to the prison officer to control, if he did anything similar this time.

'You are still under caution, and I have to inform you once again that you are entitled to have legal representation, although you refused that yesterday,' Virgil began, once the recording was on. 'I'll ask you again for the record, do you wish to have a lawyer present? And can you give me the name by which you are known on any official document, such as a birth certificate, passport, driving licence? Anything.'

One thing Virgil was struggling with was how to address the man. He refused to use the nickname Tonton, and didn't feel inclined to call him sir, which left him with nothing.

'As I have repeatedly told you, officer, Tonton is the only name by which I go these days. I had to leave the place where I was born in a hurry, without any form of documentation. I have not yet found the need to apply for replacements. I am here legally, but I currently have no means to prove that, and I live lightly in this country so I leave no trace. I am not sponging off the state. I have friends who kindly supply my every need, in exchange for the modest spiritual help I can offer them.

'And in anticipation of your next question, no, I haven't suddenly and miraculously gained an address since our last little chat. But to reiterate on the record, I do not wish for a legal representative, since I have done nothing wrong. Not in this, nor in any other country.'

'The trouble with that is that we are now accumulating more witnesses willing to testify that it was you who killed baby twin girls, and were then involved in the killing of their mother, at a recent Welcoming, as you apparently call such ceremonies.'

'I attended a Welcoming where twin girls were born. Yes. I don't deny that. Two beautiful little girls. A credit to their parents. I blessed them and their mother and then I left. If something happened to the little ones after that time, then I have no knowledge of it because I was not involved. I was not even present at that time.

'When you finally sort out your laboratory problems with my DNA, you will, of course, find my traces, since I laid hands on all three to bless them. Because that is my role. But I did no more than that, at any point.'

'The problem there, as I have said, is that we are finding more and more people who are now prepared to make statements saying that you were, in fact, the one who killed both the babies, and who then forced the father to kill his own wife.'

The prison officer caught Virgil's eyes and rolled his own. He thought he'd heard pretty much everything in his time in the job but this character really did take the biscuit. The officer's role was purely as an escort but it was clear from the expression on his face that he didn't believe a word of what the prisoner was saying.

Virgil kept it up for more than two hours. Gently probing. Asking questions which never got answered. Rephrasing them and trying again. Endlessly patient while all the time wishing he could simply thump a confession out of the man.

Virgil had never yet hit a suspect, although it had been tempting, on occasion. Even if he'd wanted to, he knew the boss would be behind the glass watching at some point, at least. He'd said he would and there was a moment when Virgil could almost feel his presence there.

The DCI had said he would only intervene if he felt he could add anything remotely useful to the agreed interview plan he and Virgil had gone over prior to the man's arrival from prison.

Tonton wasn't shifting from his resolve to deny everything and to volunteer nothing. He seemed, if anything, to be enjoying himself. Revelling in the verbal jousting. Not remotely concerned.

Much as he hated to admit defeat, Virgil eventually called a halt and let the prison officer take away the mysterious man with the beatific smile who didn't seem in the least concerned to hear that there were eyewitnesses now prepared to testify against him.

Virgil went straight upstairs to find the boss and update him. He started out by apologising for not having obtained a positive outcome.

'Not your fault, Virgil,' Ted assured him. 'I've no idea, yet, why he thinks he's untouchable, but he certainly seems to. It sounds like our witnesses are solid now, and growing in number, so I can't imagine what trump card he thinks he's holding, but he clearly behaves as if he has one.'

* * *

The prison officer was escorting Tonton back to his cell. It was still afternoon association time, so he would return the man there then leave it up to him what he wanted to do with his time. He never seemed to associate with anyone but he might choose to go for a shower, or simply to walk round the landings. With forty cells on each side, it was a decent enough leg-stretch, and a few laps round wasn't far off a proper walk.

The two officers on duty on the wing would almost certainly be locked in their office in the central section during association time, writing up their reports for inmates' files, with information on prisoner behaviour, self-harm, or any other points of note.

There was one prisoner walking slowly up and down the landing, reading a book as he went, as he so often did.

A lifer, fifties, short and slight, almost bald apart from a few wisps of a bad comb-over, the man looked an easy target for the other inmates. But nobody bothered with The Professor, as he was known. He could come and go as he pleased and no one would touch him.

'All right, Prof?' the officer asked him, after he'd returned the prisoner to his cell.

'Indeed, Mr Farrell. All Quiet on the Western Front,' the man replied, holding up his book to show the title. '*Im Westen nichts Neues*'. The German original.

The Prof was a clever man. Everyone knew that. And that wasn't all they knew about the quiet but unfailingly polite man.

He'd been a teacher, of English Literature and of German. And he'd had that holy grail which every teacher yearns for and few are lucky enough to find. A genuine genius. A young girl with a passion for learning, and especially for books. A certainty for Cambridge, with the right help and guidance.

But also a girl from exactly the wrong sort of background to get her where she needed to be. No money for books, no encouragement from home to help her realise her potential.

Yet somehow, whenever it came to paying for theatre tickets, trips to literary venues, or anything of that nature, her expenses were always covered, by an anonymous benefactor.

She should have thrived and blossomed. Risen to her full potential. But the opposite happened. She became more quiet and withdrawn than ever. Her work suffered, as did her attendance record. Letters had to be sent home, asking for an urgent meeting with her parents.

That never happened. Instead came the shock news. The star pupil was dead. By her own hand.

Rumours were rife, inevitably. The main ones centred around sexual abuse as a motive behind her action.

The Professor was beside himself. The school governors were falling over themselves to enact damage limitation for the possible risk to the establishment's reputation. They made it abundantly clear to all staff members that they should keep their distance from the family, and from the case, as far as possible.

But the Professor knew the truth. Knew it with a visceral certainty. One day at the end of his teaching stint he went round to the girl's house and beat the stepfather to death with a heavy hammer, then calmly walked into the nearest police station, carrying the bloodied weapon, and handed himself in.

Everyone inside knew his story, which was why he was one of the untouchables. Even the hardest of them had respect for the quiet man.

'You've brought back the Quare Fellow, then?' the Professor asked the officer.

The man knew of the nickname the Professor had bestowed on the new remand prisoner. Something from some book or song or something, he'd heard. Not anything he knew, but he'd certainly agree that the man had something queer about him. He'd quickly been dubbed 'the one-armed bandit' because of his deformity, but somehow the Prof's version had now been taken up by almost everyone.

'Aye, that's right. Still time for association, but I don't suppose he does much of that, does he? Maybe keep half an eye on him, Prof?'

'I most certainly will, Mr Farrell. You can safely leave him to me.'

As soon as the officer had left the wing, the Professor went to the nearest cell door and started to kick it, rhythmically, over and again. A marching rhythm. Martial. Menacing.

'Thud-thud; thud-thud; thud-thud.'

Within minutes, every prisoner within earshot appeared, chose a door and started doing the same thing. The sound built to a deafening and utterly distracting crescendo which reverberated through the old building.

Tonton appeared in the open doorway of his cell to find out what was going on, but was unceremoniously shoved back inside by two men, both big and broad across the shoulders.

As Tonton staggered backwards and half-fell onto his bunk, the door of his cell slammed shut – not that the sound could be heard above the beat of increasing numbers of feet against other doors.

Inside the locked wing office, the only two officers on duty on that level looked at one another. The younger one wore an expression of rising concern. It was the first time he'd ever heard such a racket and it was scaring the crap out of him, not knowing what it meant.

The other officer was a lot older, galloping up towards retirement and counting the days, with a 'been there, done that, got the T-shirt' look about him.

'What the fuck is that?' the younger one asked. 'Do we press the alarm, before it gets out of hand?'

'Could be something and nothing,' the older one told him. 'Maybe someone nicked and ate someone else's pudding at dinnertime. I've seen riots kick off for less. We're safe enough locked in here for now and they might get fed up and stop if they don't get the attention they want.'

Even as the officers were deciding there was no immediate cause for concern, Tonton was starting to scream as the two intruders into his space produced their arsenal.

The first weapon was a sock made heavy with a filling of batteries, which smacked him full in the face, breaking his nose with a sickening crack and making tears stream from his eyes. That at least meant that he didn't see the razor blade, expertly welded to a plastic handle, which opened up the blood vessels in his neck.

The life was already going out of him before the final weapon, a stainless steel teaspoon sharpened to a lethal point, started its journey down his ear towards his brain.

As the two men left the cell, they closed the door behind them. Then both of them said a respectful, 'All done, Professor. Thank you', before they went on their way.

Gradually, the drumming sound faded away to nothing and prisoners went back to making the most of their association time.

'There you go,' the older officer in the wing office said to the younger one. 'I told you it would all blow over in no time if we ignored 'em.'

Chapter Seventeen

'Duffy here, OCG,' the voice at the other end of the phone told Ted. 'Can I keep your DC Vine? She's a cracker! I'd take her for my team at the first opportunity. I can bribe you with chocolate biscuits, if that helps?'

Jezza and Rob had not yet made it back into the office to report on how the seizure of the dogs had gone. Well, by the sound of things, if Sergeant Duffy was prepared to barter in chocolate biscuits for Jezza. That was high currency in any nick.

'It went smoothly, then, the raid?' Ted asked him. 'They're not back in so I've not yet seen copies of their reports.'

'It went bloody well. The mutts are safely behind bars, where they belong, and probably on Death Row, once we get the DNA results through. I've been promised they're being fast-tracked, but we both know that doesn't always mean much. And I have someone standing by to whack in a destruction order application as soon as we have confirmation that it's the right dogs.

'The owner of the property, if not necessarily the owner of the dogs themselves – he won't yet admit to that – is singing like a budgie about anything and everything else and desperately trying to make deals. Protected witness and all that shite. "Don't know nuffin' about the dogs, just minding them for a friend, but the other stuff I could tell you ..." He watches too much telly.

'If even the half of what he's telling us is true he's already a dead man walking. For our own sakes, with the case, we'll protect him until he testifies, but I'm making him no promises yet for beyond that.'

'Sounds like a good result,' Ted told him. 'Especially if you want to poach one of my officers.'

Duffy laughed at that.

'I'd seriously take her on in a flash if she fancied a move. She has balls, too, the way she went in to help the officer who was down. I know he's already sent her round some flowers. Jammy bastard, his wife works in a florist shop so he gets mates' rates, but don't tell her I said that.'

'An officer was injured?' Ted queried. 'By the dogs?'

'No, it was the door-knocker, diving out of the way before the big brutes came out. Mistimed it and broke his collar bone, the silly pillock, but nothing serious. But Jezza went straight in to make sure he was all right. That took some guts.'

Ted wasn't going to voice what he was thinking – that he'd done enough armed raids in his time to know how dangerous such acts of bravado could be. Not just for the person carrying them out, but for everyone involved. He was going to have to have strong words with Jezza. That was another task which was going to slow him down and which shouldn't need doing, with an officer of her experience.

Between the admin tasks and a rebellious Jezza to deal with, Ted was not in the best of moods to start with. And then he got the phone call. From the prison. To tell him what had happened to their murder suspect on remand there.

He hadn't done it for a long time but on this occasion he couldn't help himself. Yet another wastepaper basket met a swift and ruthless end at the toe of his shoe.

Then he walked out through the main office and into Mike Hallam's to ask him to get all of the team together, if possible, as soon as he could, as he had something he wanted to announce, preferably to everyone at the same time.

Jezza was back at her desk, hastily shoving a large bouquet of flowers down behind it, out of sight, but not before she'd seen that the boss's sharp eyes had taken in their presence. It was obvious even from across the room that he was not in a good mood – at all – so she felt it best to do nothing to attract his attention in her direction.

Ted decided to walk downstairs to update the Super in person, rather than over the phone, to give time for Mike to get everyone together for an update and to give himself a chance of a leg-stretch and time to cool off a bit.

Superintendent Caldwell's usual poker face gave very little away as she asked him, when he'd told her, 'Have you updated CPS?'

'Sent them an email as soon as I heard.'

'And I imagine they are going to say that we don't have anything like enough evidence to charge any of the others, without a case against the main suspect. Does that about sum it up?'

'In a nutshell, I would say. I'm just about to tell the team, and they're going to be gutted, after all the work they've put into this. Especially Ali and Maurice, after they'd got more witnesses to start talking. Jo too, of course, as he got the first one.'

'What about the prospect now of proceeding against the husband and father for the killing of the babies and their mother?' she asked him.

'I'll have to see what CPS have to say on that. The witnesses who have talked so far all put the blame squarely at Tonton's feet. Certainly for the babies. And in the mother's case, they don't put the husband in the role of perpetrator at all, more of being an unwilling and forced participant. In too much of a state of shock to have fought against Tonton.

'The statements refer to Tonton coercing him, both verbally and physically. He may only have one fully functioning arm, but from what we've been told, he was very strong. Physically, and with a powerful, controlling personality.

'All of which means we simply don't have a solid case against the father on his own. Not so far, and I don't see that changing, to be honest.'

'Please pass on to your team that I am impressed by their hard work and diligence to get as far as they have, and that this result in no way reflects badly on their investigation.

'Do we know what happened in the prison? Should I be concerned that it occurred immediately after his return from here? The possibility of some sort of leaked information, perhaps?'

'I'd like to think that was highly unlikely,' Ted told her. 'We both know that baby killers don't get an easy ride in prison, any more than paedophiles do. Tonton's fellow inmates might simply have decided to be judge and jury on him. To save the taxpayer the cost of a trial and then keeping him in prison for years, is probably how they would justify it.

'Well, again, please let your team know that I would find it hard to believe that any of them had had a hand in any such leak. As you say, the most likely explanation is an inside job at the prison end, I would imagine.'

The Ice Queen had her faults. She could be stiff, formal. Awkward even, in her interactions. But she always tried to hand out praise where it was due. It was a crumb of comfort, at least, Ted thought as he went back upstairs to break the news to the team.

* * *

'Bloody hell!'

Maurice was the first of them to react aloud at Ted's news, although several of the others were muttering under their breath. There was an air of sheer disbelief from all of them.

'I wish I'd kept on at him for longer,' Virgil said, looking and sounding morose. 'At least we might have known the truth. Had some sort of closure on the case. I mean, I think we all agree there's little room for doubt that it certainly was him who actually did the killing, but it would have been good to have a confession, at least.'

'Don't beat yourself up about it, Virgil,' Ted told him. 'You did everything you could and stayed professional. That was no easy task in the face of his arrogance, and knowing what he'd done.'

'There's still the DNA result to come, though, isn't there?' Mike Hallam put in. 'If that comes back positive, that's something, at least. We'd know we had the right suspect. We could at least close the files, couldn't we?'

'And what about the twins' father now, boss?' Ali asked him. 'Have we got enough to get him to court? Maybe if Maurice and I go back to the witnesses who we were talking to and probe a bit further?'

'In a sense if we get a positive now on Tonton's DNA, it makes our case against the husband even weaker, because it would seem to bear out what the witnesses have said: Tonton was the instigator, who coerced and physically compelled the husband into participating in the killing of the mother, but he wasn't involved in the death of either of the babies. The most he was guilty of there is staying passive and not reacting to try to stop those killings.

'But again, I'm going to need a long conference call with CPS to know where we go from here. whatever the DNA result is.'

'How was he killed, boss?' Maurice asked him. 'Because I bet I'm not the only one here who hopes it was slow and very painful.'

'Maurice, I'm going to pretend I didn't hear that. Especially in a team briefing. Don't forget you're supposed to be convincing me you're ready to go back to normal duties. Making inappropriate remarks is not the way to go about doing that.

'Right, thank you everyone. As soon as I have any updates I'll let you know. Meanwhile please ensure that you have written up everything accurately, because the case files are likely to come under much more scrutiny than usual on this one.

'DC Vine, a word, please, before you do anything else.'

Jezza and Rob exchanged a glance. They both knew that tone from the boss was never a good sign. He must somehow have already heard of Jezza's heroics on the raid and been unimpressed. He certainly didn't sound like someone about to shower her with praise.

Jezza wondered fleetingly who might have dobbed her in, but she knew all too well that the boss had an uncanny knack of knowing things without anyone being able to tell how he did. She didn't think it would have been Rob. He'd soundly told her her fortune on the drive back to the nick, so she couldn't see him running to the boss as well. For one thing, he hadn't really had the time.

'Close the door, please,' Ted told her, going to sit behind his desk but making no move to invite her to take a seat. This was clearly serious.

'Would you like to tell me about your role in this morning's raid, please. In full detail.'

There was never any point trying to pull the wool over the boss's eyes, Jezza knew. He wouldn't be behaving like this unless he knew most of the facts already. Given the way he was looking at her, it could only mean that he knew all about her throwing caution to the wind to rush to the assistance of the officer on the ground.

'I think I know what this is about, boss. I broke procedure when the door-knocker went down and was clearly injured. I didn't wait for clearance before I went to him, and I should have done. Sorry, boss.'

If she was hoping to soft soap him, her words didn't seem to be having the desired effect. He still looked decidedly unimpressed.

Ted sighed aloud. He could really do without having to deal with a Jezza who had a ready off-pat explanation for everything.

'You put your own life at risk, behaving like that, not to mention potentially preventing other officers from carrying out their own roles, and you would certainly have been briefed beforehand on correct procedure.

'If I didn't already have to contend with Maurice on restricted duties, I'd send you off on a course or two to remind you of how to proceed in such operations. But I shouldn't have to. You're an experienced officer. You know the rules, and why they're in place. There really is no excuse for your behaviour.

'The next time you act like that, no matter how short of officers we are, you'll be off on a series of retraining courses faster than you can pack an overnight bag. Are we absolutely clear on that?'

This time he did at least feel she wasn't simply using her drama skills when she said quietly, 'Yes, boss. Sorry, boss.'

'Before you go, though, I have to tell you that, despite your reckless moment, Sergeant Duffy tells me he's very impressed with you. By your performance to date. He credits you with getting as far as finding and seizing the dogs, and for leading his team to someone who's finally talking to them and naming names. So well done on that.'

She brightened up visibly at that. She thought the world of the boss and took any criticism from him to heart.

'In fact, he thinks so highly of you he said he'd be pleased to have you as a member of the OCG whenever you wanted to make the move. He even offered to pay in chocolate biscuits for your transfer, and we both know that's a high opening bid.

'And if ever you did want to make the move, please know that I would never stand in your way, and would always give you an excellent reference.'

Jezza was staring at him as if he had just thrown her off his team, rather than telling her she'd made such a good impression that another team wanted to poach her.

'But boss, I don't want to go anywhere. I'm happy here. Happier than I've ever been on any other team. And besides, I can't work out of Rochdale. I just can't. All the extra travelling times would play havoc with Tommy. You know how he hates change, and I'd get to see less and less of him. I can't leave everything to Nat. He already does so much for me, I can't dump even more on him without wrecking our relationship.

'I really want to stay here. Unless you're telling me you don't want me on the team any more?'

'That depends on you entirely. The offer is there. If you want to accept it, I'll support you all the way. But if you choose to stay here, I expect you to follow procedure at all times. Are we clear on that?'

'Clear, boss.'

When Ted nodded at her to leave, Jezza scuttled out of his office and made straight for the loos. She didn't want anyone to see how close to tears she was.

Ted checked his inbox before making the brew he felt in dire need of after dealing with Jezza. One of the first things he saw was the lab results on Tonton's second DNA sample.

A full match. Beyond any doubt. They had the vital piece of evidence which would potentially have put the man behind bars for life.

At least they could now close the file, but with a feeling that justice had not been served.

This time the already mangled remains of his wastepaper bin didn't survive the fury of Ted's further assault on it.

* * *

Trev took one look at Ted as he walked into the kitchen and asked, 'As bad a day as that?'

'Does it show that much?' Ted asked him as he went to give him a hug. 'I have to admit it's one of those days when I really wish I still drank something stronger than ginger beer.'

'Is it anything you can tell me about? And would it help if I changed the planned dessert and made a quick golden syrup sponge instead?'

'That sounds like the perfect pudding. And I can tell you. You'll hear it soon enough, it's bound to be all over the news. Our prime suspect for the baby killings was murdered in prison this afternoon, by other inmates, it would seem. Not long before I got the DNA results back. Positive. So we could probably have got him on all three counts of murder, and possibly also another from outside our area, and he'd have got life. Quite likely a whole life tariff.'

'Oh shit, that is truly awful,' Trev told him, hugging him again, more fiercely this time. 'You must be totally gutted.'

'The team certainly are. They've taken it badly. We were so hopeful of a good result and no one saw that coming, for sure.'

'So now his killers will be charged with murder, presumably, if they're identified, which seems ironic in so many ways. Are you all right?'

'I will be. Case of having to. I need to get the team through this when morale is currently sub-zero.

'On a more positive note, the OCG want to poach Jezza because they're very impressed with her.'

'Jezza?' Trev looked surprised at the mere idea. 'And would you let her go? I thought you were very fond of her, and impressed by her work. She certainly idolises you. I've said before I'm sure she'd fancy you if she didn't know you were with me.'

Ted shrugged, but avoided eye contact by finding cats to stroke.

'It's an offer she won't get every day so I can't stand in her way if she decides to go.

'Anyway, have you had time to think any more about where we're going to let Mr Marston take us for dinner?'

Trev looked at him suspiciously.

'Hmm, evasive answer, clunky subject change, displacement activity involving cats. My detective skills tell me there's more to this than meets the eye, but I'll leave it for now. And yes, I was thinking Canal Street would be billirant ...'

Ted looked at him in horror.

'We can't take him there! What if your gaydar is really off on this one?'

Trev gave a wicked laugh, pleased to have broken the dark mood.

'I was teasing. I've actually booked that nice place in Heaton Moor that we like, where they seem to cater to most palates. I thought that would be the safest.

'But you've clearly had a rough day if you couldn't tell I was winding you up. So I'd suggest supper, no telly, because you'll only want to watch the news and finish up angry again about your lost case, and then an early night.'

Chapter Eighteen

Jezza managed to hold it together, after a fashion, until she got back to the flat she shared with her boyfriend, Nathan, and her younger brother, Tommy.

With his various difficulties, Tom didn't always recognise or identify all human emotions in others, nor react appropriately to them. But in his own way, he loved the big sister who had become his only family since the death of their parents in a road accident when he was very young.

He had carers to help with his needs, and his sometimes demanding behaviour. He got on well with Nathan, who was endlessly patient with him, and also appreciated the company of both Maurice and Steve. But Jezza was the one he recognised as someone significant in his life.

Through interaction with others at his school, he had some learned behaviours, and could sometimes produce the right response, though without necessarily the normal feelings associated with the emotion.

Jezza had done an emergency make-up repair in the toilets at the station, after her talk with the boss, so she didn't think she looked too bad. But her brother was lying in wait for her in the hallway when she got back from work, as he so often did, and he scrutinised her face as she came through the door.

'You look sad,' he greeted her. 'Don't be sad. It will all be better in the morning. I've devised forty-seven more questions for my quiz game today. Do you want to hear them?'

Nathan was back from work. As far as he could, he always tried to work his shifts around Jezza's so he could look after Tommy until she got back, and at least try to have something by way of a meal for her when she got home.

He heard her come in, to be instantly assailed by her brother, so he went out into the hall to greet her. A quick glance told him now was not the time for Tom to be pestering her. She looked like someone who would sooner be confronted by a gin and tonic.

'Tom, your sister looks as if she's had a rough day to me. I think perhaps it might be nice if you gave her a bit of time before trying out your questions. D'you think you could perhaps get up to one hundred new questions while Jezza has a sit down and a drink?'

Tommy looked from one to the other of them. He'd managed to pick up on her sadness but didn't have the ability to relate that to anything in particular. But he liked Nathan. They got on well together, so he was happy to do as he suggested.

'All right, Nathan, I will go and devise fifty-three more questions.'

As Tommy walked purposefully back to his bedroom, Jezza went to put her arms round Nathan and to lay her head against his chest with a sigh of gratitude.

'Thank you for that. Have I told you often enough that I really don't deserve you?'

'Not remotely often enough, but I'm keeping a tally. Come into the kitchen whilst I finish cooking. I'll make you a drink and you can tell me all about it. Whatever it is, in the context of how low you look.'

Once he'd made the drink and put it in front of her, Nathan asked 'How did the raid go? Did you get the dogs all right?'

Jezza took a long swallow from the glass before she replied, perching on a handy stool.

'We did, so at least they aren't going to half-eat anyone else. They're being tested for a positive ID but the way they behaved when they were let out of the house at us, they're unlikely to be returned to the owner, even if there isn't the evidence for a destruction order, which would be the favoured outcome.'

'Well, that's a good result, at least.'

He held out a mortar towards her in which he was using a pestle to crush garlic cloves into olive oil.

'How much garlic? Is that enough?' he asked her.

Jezza dipped a finger in and tasted it but made a face at the offering.

'You know Tom would want twice that amount of garlic and more. Chuck a bit more in. I'm really not up to him throwing a tantrum about anything tonight, if we can avoid it.'

'Your wish is my command,' Nathan told her with a smile. 'It sounds like you should be pleased with yourself over that result, though. Yet you don't sound as if you are. Not remotely. After all, it was mostly your work which led you to finding the dogs. Surely Duffy and the boss would have been happy with that result?

'Or is there something you did which you've not yet told me? Something you probably shouldn't have done?'

'There was an officer down. The door-knocker. He mistimed his dive and went down hard, so I went to assist.'

Nathan was frowning now, his assault on the garlic becoming heavier.

'That sounds dangerous. Should you have done it? And what did Duffy have to say about it, as it was his op?'

'Oh, he was thrilled. He honestly was, that's not irony. Apparently he phoned the boss, singing my praises and wanting to poach me for his team.'

Nathan stopped crushing the life out of the cloves and looked at her in surprise.

'Well, that's a good thing, isn't it? Duffy clearly thinks very highly of you if he did that. I imagine you wouldn't want to transfer to Rochdale, because of the extra mileage, and I imagine the hours would be even less predictable there. But surely it's great that he was so clearly impressed by you. Or am I missing something obvious?'

Jezza got up to make herself another drink. The first had hardly touched the sides.

'It was the fact that the boss actually sounded as if he wanted me to make the transfer. Like he thought he'd be glad to be shut of me. I thought he understood that I have no plans to move from his team. That I'm more than happy where I am. But he sounded as if he was all for me making the move.'

'Don't take this the wrong way,' Nathan began cautiously, knowing that a fraught Jezza could so easily fly off the handle, 'but might you possibly be misreading him? Is he simply doing what he thinks is right and not standing in your way if you did want to make the move? Surely he's the sort of boss who would think about what's right for you and encourage you if you wanted to make a change?'

'Nat, you didn't see him. I've never seen him like that before. He honestly did sound as if getting rid of me to another team would be a huge weight off his shoulders. And the worst of it is, I have no idea what I've done or said to make him feel like that, so I can't even try to put it right.'

The second G&T was going down almost as fast as the first one. Nathan rummaged in cupboards to find nibbles, which he transferred into bowls and put right in front of Jezza. The meal wasn't going to be ready for a while yet and Jezza was clearly going to need something to help soak up the alcohol.

'Are you sure it's not just his workload? You've said yourself, both the cases he's been overseeing are difficult ones and fraught with problems. That can't be easy for him.'

Jezza paused to put a few peanuts in her mouth and start chewing before she replied.

'It's getting a lot worse, too, although you didn't hear this from me. Our main suspect for the baby killings has been murdered in prison, probably by other inmates. Just as we were starting to get somewhere, with Maurice and Ali finding more and more witnesses finally prepared to testify.'

'I heard on the news about a murder in prison, but I didn't realise it was your suspect. So there you are, that's enough to put even your normally sunny boss into the blackest of moods, surely?'

He dipped a spoon into the sauce he was now preparing, blew on it, then had a taste.

'Good grief, I'm not sure you were right about the extra garlic. Just don't breathe on the boss tomorrow after you've eaten this or he'll definitely want to get rid of you.'

He held the spoon out to Jezza who took a taste and made an 'mmmm' sound of appreciation.

'Perfect! If we have to go seizing more dangerous dogs, we won't even need dart guns. I can just breathe on them and knock them right off their feet.'

At that moment, Tommy came padding back into the kitchen, looking worried.

'I haven't devised fifty-three more questions yet, Nathan, only forty-two. But I thought Jezza might need to have a hug. When people are sad they can feel better if someone gives them a hug and Nathan can't give her a hug while he's cooking.'

He looked so earnest, standing there with his arms out to her that Jezza nearly lost it. Tommy didn't do hugs in normal circumstances. Physical contact only happened on his terms. But his special school was helping him to learn about interaction and he was trying hard to understand it and apply the principles.

'I would like that very much, Tom-Tom, thank you,' Jezza told him, holding out her arms to him in turn. 'I can't think of anything nicer to make me feel better than a hug from my brother.'

* * *

'Right, even though our prime suspect for the murder of the babies and their mother is dead, there's still a lot of work we need to do on the file before we send it to CPS for their decision on what, if any, further action can be taken,' Ted began by telling the team at the Monday morning briefing, the first time he'd had them all together since the death of their principle suspect.

'As soon as the news came through about Tonton, I made some calls to see if we can get the father of the babies, who is now effectively our only suspect for the killings, put under special protection so the same thing doesn't happen to him. He's not in the same prison as Tonton was so there may be no risk where he is. But in case anyone else has the same idea, solitary is probably his safest bet for the moment.'

'Is there any news yet on who might have killed him, boss?' Mike Hallam asked him. 'Fellow inmates, or perhaps even prison officers who don't take kindly to anyone like him?'

'It's too early for anything like that,' Ted told him. 'The nearest suitable team will take it, and there'll also be an internal inquiry. I wouldn't hold your breath, though. I can't imagine any prisoner being willing to talk to the police, especially after such an incident.

'If it follows the usual pattern of others I've heard about, there will probably be recommendations for a minimum number of officers patrolling given landings at any time, for a start. And you probably all know that prison officer numbers are down as much as our own are, so that won't happen.

'I don't know yet all the details of weapons used on Tonton, but no doubt there'll be a recommendation for more frequent cell searches looking for concealed arms. There'll probably be a one-off sweep of everywhere by an outside team to see what that might turn up. Nothing at all, in all likelihood, as whoever's done this will be too smart to leave anything incriminating lying about.

'And of course, after the first flurry of activity, things will most likely be basically back to how they were before within about three months.

'I can ask for a pre-emptive sweep of the prison where the father is being held, but I doubt I'll get anywhere with such a request. There's probably not the manpower nor the funds to do anything like that without stronger intelligence to go on.'

Virgil was the first to voice what others on the team were probably thinking.

'Is it a coincidence that it happened pretty much right after he went back to prison from here? We know it wouldn't be the first time a prison officer had been involved in the disposal of a suspect for something as serious as our case, but might there have been a tip-off from here?'

'No point in speculating, Virgil,' Ted told him. 'The timing could have been coincidental. We all know the old "honour among thieves" thing inside. There are some crimes not even the hardened criminals will sanction, so anyone on remand, or convicted for something like this is always likely to be a target. And like I said, in the same way we're short of officers for sometimes pretty basic stuff, it's every bit as bad in the prisons, I keep hearing. At best just a couple of officers on duty at a time on a wing which might hold some very violent offenders.

'All we can do for now is carry on interviewing the witnesses, and talking to the father again. That's as near as it's possible for us to get to a positive outcome on this, in any sense of the word.'

* * *

Jezza and Rob hadn't been at the morning briefing as they were going straight out to continue their investigations as part of the OCG's case. Sergeant Duffy had told them to carry on the way they'd been working previously, as their methods had already produced dividends beyond his hopes

195

and expectations.

'Rob?' Jezza began, sounding unusually hesitant, for her. 'If I ask you a question, will you give me a straight answer?

Rob was driving. He threw a quick sideways look at her before he answered. Jezza was sounding unusually serious.

'Well, within the constraints of the Official Secrets Act, or similar legislation, of course I will,' he told her in a jokey tone.

'Did you tell the boss about me breaking procedures on the raid yesterday?'

He glanced at her again, briefly, as they were coming up to a line of vehicles stopped at a red light.

'You asked me not to tell him, so I didn't. Against my better judgement, it has to be said. But I didn't. Maybe it was Duffy?'

'He did mention it, yes. I just wanted to know if perhaps the boss had asked you to corroborate anything.'

'Hasn't said a word to me. But if he knows I knew and didn't tell him, I imagine my neck is the next on the block. I should have told him in the first place.

'So what exactly did Duffy have to say to him about it all?'

'Apparently he was very impressed. So much so that he was telling the boss he'd make room for me on his team, if I ever wanted to make the move.'

They'd stopped now at another red traffic light, this time for roadworks, so Rob turned to look at her in surprise.

'Wow, Jezza, well done, that's amazing. You're going for it, I imagine? It would be a hell of a good career move for you.'

'I can't,' she told him. 'I would have loved to, but I just can't. Not with my circumstances. With Tommy. It simply wouldn't work out. The longer commute, the even more unpredictable hours.'

'That's a shame, although we'd all have missed you, if you'd moved on. I hope you know that.'

The traffic was moving again, so Rob put the car in gear and concentrated on the road once more.

'I thought I knew that. I hoped it was the case. But ...'

'But?' Rob prompted her.

'The boss sounded like he really wanted me to go for it. But in a way that sounded like he just wanted rid of me, at all costs.

'I know I did a daft thing, going against procedure, but I really didn't think that would be enough for him to want to see me off the team. Never for a moment.'

'I honestly think you should cut him a bit of slack at the moment, Jezza, considering the pressures he's under. He barely had a break all weekend, for one thing, and it's not every SIO who works the kind of hours he puts in.

'I know he had Sunday lunch in The Grapes yesterday with Trev, but I'm pretty sure that was his only down time. I honestly wouldn't pay too much attention to him seemingly acting out of character, given the pressures he's under.'

Chapter Nineteen

Virgil was on his way to interview the father of the twin babies, who was, since the death of Tonton, their only remaining suspect for being involved in the killing of them and of their mother.

It had been decided that it would be safer not to move the prisoner anywhere until there was a clearer picture of who had killed Tonton, and if there had been any possibility that prison or police officers had been involved in the planning or execution of the attack. No one wanted to lose another suspect in the case.

Before driving up to the prison, Virgil had liaised by phone with staff there about arranging an interpreter and a legal advisor for the suspect, should the man require either or both. He'd been surprised to get a call back later to say the suspect had refused both. Clearly someone else who had been less than honest about their English-speaking abilities in the initial interviews.

Maurice and Ali were back out and about talking to as many potential new witnesses as they could. They wouldn't inform any of them of the death of Tonton, and they had no way of knowing which, if any of them, might know about it. They'd have to feel their way carefully with each one to try to find out what, if anything, they knew.

There'd been a brief mention on the local news of the death in prison of a person who was on remand. The only details given had been that it was someone who was facing murder charges and had been arrested in the Stockport area. But even that little information might be enough of a clue for anyone with knowledge of the case.

In theory there was no reason for the second suspect, the twins' father, in a different prison some distance away, to know anything about Tonton's killing. But as he drove up to interview him, Virgil was wondering if he might perhaps know, or at least have guessed, if he'd heard or seen any news bulletins. He would almost certainly not know which prison Tonton had been sent to, but any mention of Stockport in a newsflash might alert him.

But being suddenly moved into solitary confinement would almost certainly have set alarm bells ringing in the man's head, if he'd done nothing himself to merit such a sanction.

If he had seen or heard the news, he might then possibly have phoned someone on the outside to find out what had gone on. Virgil had no way of knowing until he got there whether any such knowledge would make the man more or less inclined to talk to him. It might make him talk, with the intention of putting all of the blame on Tonton, safe in the knowledge that the man could not now deny any allegations about him.

So far, none of the witnesses Ali and Maurice had talked to had spoken of the father as being in any way the instigator of what had happened to his family. Several of them had also said that when Tonton had picked up the first baby he had shown no signs of intention to hurt the child. He'd held her gently in the crook of his functioning arm and murmured words in a language most of them didn't recognise. It looked exactly as most of the witnesses might have expected some sort of ceremony of welcome to be carried out.

The second baby arrived very quickly after her sibling, and several of those present reported that her arrival seemed to be the trigger which changed Tonton from a smiling, benevolent holy man to a sadistic murderer.

From all the testimony they had so far, it would seem to be difficult to show that any of them, and certainly the father, could have known that the arrival of a second baby would be the catalyst which would trigger three such savage killings.

Once Virgil had passed through security at the prison, the officer designated to accompany him filled him in on various procedural points as he escorted him to a room where he could carry out his interview.

'First thing to tell you, in case you didn't get that message, is he doesn't want a lawyer present and he doesn't need an interpreter. He can speak English okay. He makes a few mistakes but not as many as I would trying to speak another language. Thank feck for phone apps, I say, when I take the missus on holiday. God knows what we'd end up eating without them when the menu's in foreign.'

'What's he like, as a remand prisoner?' Virgil asked him. 'Behaviour-wise, I mean. In case that gives me any ideas of how to proceed with him.'

'Good as gold,' his escort told him. 'Wish they were all like him. Nobody likes a baby-killer, not even the worst of the scrotes we get in here. That's probably what got your other bloke killed. But this one seems to be tolerated well enough. He's tended to be treated a bit more like a victim himself than anything else.'

'You heard about that, then? Us losing our prime suspect?'

'Course we did! Few secrets inside and word gets out very fast when something like that happens. Even from one nick to another. Someone knows someone who knows someone. I bet it's the same with your lot.'

'So what's the word on the grapevine about it? Inmates guilty? Or a bit of help from officers, if that's not too sensitive a question?'

'There'll be an internal enquiry, of course. I'd like to say there was no chance of officers being involved but we get rogue ones, just like you do with coppers. Probably not actively involved, so nothing could ever come back on them. But there would be some who would be happy enough to turn a blind eye to someone like that bloke getting what some would say was his just desserts.'

They'd reached a closed door now, with another prison officer standing outside it.

The one who'd escorted Virgil told him, 'Thanks, Charlie, I've got this now. How's he been, while he's been waiting?'

'Quiet as a lamb, John, as usual. Wish they were all like him. Not a peep out of him. And yes, he is still in there, all in one piece and breathing. I keep checking on him.'

As Charlie walked away, John went over a few details with Virgil before they went in to speak to the man.

'He's not cuffed at the moment. He's not considered a flight risk and he's never shown any sign of aggression. I'm another one who wishes we had more as docile as him. He just looks totally shell-shocked by the whole experience. Like he has no idea what happened or why.

'If you want me to, I can attach him to the table while you interview him, but I'd honestly be surprised if that was needed. I'll be in with you the whole time and it's on me if I've got it wrong.

'I know you can't go off appearances. I've been in this job far too long not to know that. But he's either an incredible actor or he really is what he claims to be – a man grieving for his lost family and struggling to understand how it all happened, and what he's doing in here charged with killing them.

'Excuse me going in first, it's procedure, not me being ignorant. My mam and dad brought me up better than that,' John told Virgil with a smile and a wink.

As soon as they both entered the room, the man who had been sitting waiting sprang to his feet. There was nothing at all aggressive about the move, it seemed to be simply a polite reflex. An almost deferential gesture.

'All right, Khan, sit down. This gentleman is a police officer. He's come to ask you some questions, like you were told. You're sure you don't want your brief here?'

He saw the look of incomprehension on the prisoner's face so he added, 'Your lawyer. You have the right to have one.'

Instead of answering the question, the man looked at Virgil as he asked, 'Is true? Tonton is died?'

Despite the small error, it was clear that the man could understand, and speak, English to some degree. Virgil would be interested to find out where the instruction to insist on interpreters for all the members of the group during questioning had come from, and why. But for now, he had far more important information to try to get from the man.

Virgil showed him his ID as he said, 'I'm Detective Constable Tibbs, Greater Manchester Police. Are you sure you're happy to talk to me without either a lawyer or an interpreter present?'

'Yes, yes, very happy. I tell you all I can. I hear that man is died. Tonton. So now I will tell you everything I can. It was all him. He was killer.'

Virgil took the seat opposite Khan and sat quietly for a moment, observing him before he began his questioning. He was trying to get inside his head. A man who had lost his entire family in a matter of minutes, in the most brutal fashion.

In a way, it was a shame that Khan already knew about Tonton's death. Virgil would have preferred to have been the person to drop that bit of information on him at a suitable point during the interview, to see what his reaction was like.

Virgil began by cautioning the man, checking carefully that he understood, that he knew everything he said was being recorded, and that he could still stop and ask for a legal representative at any time during the interview.

'Can you tell me exactly what happened on the day your wife and your twin babies died, Mr Khan, please? In your own words, and take all the time that you need.'

* * *

'You clearly do this sort of thing all the time so would know better than me, but what did you make of his testimony?' the prison officer asked Virgil, as the two of them were walking back to where Virgil had come in.

'Off the record, and not for public consumption?' Virgil asked him. 'And on the condition you share your thoughts with me afterwards?'

'Fair enough. Scouts' honour.'

'I thought he sounded genuine. He held it together pretty well, but he showed the emotion you would expect from an innocent man who'd lost his whole family, and his liberty. It would have been easy for him to turn on the waterworks and leave them running, if he was putting it on. The fact that he seemed only to break down at specific details, which I have to confess even I found harrowing, made me think he could be telling the truth. You?'

'I think a lot of us in here think the same thing, and we've seen some great acting in our time. Trying to convince us someone was innocent when absolutely everything pointed to their guilt.

'He hasn't done or said anything that fits with what he's supposed to have done, and believe you me, no matter how clever they are, the guilty ones almost always slip up.

'Not Khan. Not so far. He cries in his sleep most nights. Doesn't eat anything like he should do. Spends a lot of his time praying, although he must know that's not going to bring his family back. If he's putting it on, he's the best I've ever seen, in all my years of service.

'And what about this other fellah, in Manchester, who got topped? What was his involvement in it all? Was he the real killer and just took Khan down with him?'

Virgil was becoming uncomfortable with the way the conversation was going. He still had no idea who had killed Tonton, or how whoever it was got to him in a high security prison. He didn't want to appear rude, but he thought it best to make his excuses, blame pressure of work and get out of there, with his recording to discuss with the boss when he got back.

* * *

Jezza was still subdued the following day as she and Rob drove out to try to find more witnesses for the Turnbull murder case. They'd heard of another possible place with what might be XL Bullies on the premises. Duffy had authorised them to do a recce from a safe distance but had cautioned against any heroics without appropriate back-up.

'Duffy's certainly got your measure now, Jezza,' Rob told her as he drove. 'He may think you're the bee's knees and want to poach you, but he knows you need keeping on a lead.

'Have you thought any more about his offer of a move to the OCG?'

'I can't, though, Rob. I just can't. Not with Tommy. You know what he's like with change of any sort, and something as big as that would really unsettle him. It just worries me still that the boss seemed so keen for me to go, and I have no idea why.'

'Don't take this the wrong way, but have you just misread him? Are you sure he wasn't simply putting your best interests first and not wanting to stand in your way when such a good opportunity came along?'

Jezza's tone was sharp as she replied to that.

'D'you mean am I feeling hormonal and taking everything the wrong way? I know what I heard, Rob.'

'You know I didn't mean it like that, at all. It's just that we both know the boss well. He wouldn't want to stand in the way of what could be a good career move for you. Even if he didn't really want you to go. I'd be inclined to give him the benefit of the doubt.'

'But even without the problems with Tom, I don't want to move. I like it here. I like everyone on the team. Well, as long as they're not making sexist remarks and insinuations about my hormones.'

At least she was smiling at him now, calming down a bit.

'It sounds to me like Duffy is very keen to have you on his team. He really doesn't need to come down here today for a catch-up. We could do it by phone like we usually do, so I bet he's coming down to try to persuade you to think again about the offer.'

'I know it's a great offer and some people will think I'm mad to turn it down. I'd feel a lot better about the whole thing if I could just say thanks but no thanks and not have the feeling the boss is trying to edge me out.'

'I'd put money on it just being crossed wires between you,' Rob told her, then went on, 'but if it really bothers you that much, why not try talking to him again? He's always been approachable, at least. Why not take him round to The Grapes for a Gunner and a hotpot in the back room and try having a sensible discussion about it? It might all be just a misunderstanding that you could sort out between you.'

Jezza was quiet for a moment, considering.

Then she said, 'I have a strong feeling this is not something we can sort out over a drink. You know what the boss is like when he's in stubborn mode. It's easier to interrogate a clam. But I can think of someone I might be able to talk to about what's going on.'

Chapter Twenty

'This is bloody good work you two. Looks like you're spot on again with this latest address. We're turning up names well known to us in connection with the house. Not the very top brass, because they seldom leave Rochdale, where they think they're untouchable, but certainly some on the next rung down the ladder.'

Sergeant Duffy from the OCG was sitting in a car in a lay-by with Rob and Jezza, a short drive from the property they had been watching, with Jezza taking photos of anyone in the vicinity as they had sat there.

One photo in particular had brought Duffy driving over to see for himself. Someone he and his team had prior knowledge of in connection with organised crime.

'This is going to need to be a very carefully planned raid. Even more than the last one. Which is why I wanted to take a shufti myself. The dogs pose a threat again, potentially, but I'd rather go up against six of those than this bloke without being fully prepared.'

He held up his phone to show one of the photos which Jezza had taken and forwarded to him.

'This is the closest we've ever got to getting our hands on him, assuming he has reason to come back to this place, as we've no intel to suggest this is where he lives.

'The reason for the extra careful planning is that this bloke has been known to use any weapon at his disposal to evade capture, and that includes explosives. That's his speciality and he's an expert at it. So this next raid is going to be interesting, and challenging, but highly dangerous.

'So Jezza, much as I admired your guts going to help a fallen officer on the last one, this time there will be no heroics. At all. From anyone. I'm assuming the two of you want to see this through to its conclusion, since it's your work that's got us this far. But if you want in, I need to know that you've hoisted that in and agreed that no one plays cowboys on this. None of you. Is that clear?'

'Clear, sarge,' Jezza told him with an innocent-looking smile.

Rob contented himself with nodding his head and added, 'I'll try to make sure neither of us does anything daft, but I'm not making any promises where my learned colleague is concerned.'

Jezza laughed at that but Duffy went on, 'I mean it. Jezza, if you can't give me that assurance, and sound sincere, you're not going anywhere near this raid. Knowing this scrote like I do, I'm going to need bomb disposal, explosives experts, sniffer dogs, the full monty, and it's all going to need signing off at a much higher level than me.

'It's also going to need time and careful planning. We need to act as soon as possible but we can't just go steaming in trusting to luck. So the last thing I need to make it any harder than it already is would be anyone playing cowboys and putting lives at risk.

'It's a simple choice. Either say it and mean it, or you don't go anywhere near the action. Because this time, Jezza, the wrong move by you could literally blow the whole thing up in our faces, plus god knows how many of us as well.'

Jezza put on a suitably meek expression. Rob, knowing her acting skills, wasn't convinced it was genuine, but it did seem to appease Duffy.

'Sorry, sarge. I'd really like to be in on this raid, if you'll let me. And knowing the risk of explosives, I promise to behave and follow your orders at all times, without question.'

'Fair enough, as long as you mean it. I have to confess to wondering, when your boss seemed so keen to let you transfer to us, if that was his reason. You not following orders, perhaps once too often. But maybe he really was just thinking of your career and not wanting to stand in your way.

'So are you absolutely sure you don't want to make the move and join us in OCG?'

'Not don't want to, sarge. Can't. I look after my kid brother since our parents were killed in a car crash. He has special needs. Special, and very demanding. I just about manage in Serious Crime. The boss is very kind and accommodating, because he understands my difficulties. Which is why I was surprised he seemed to think I would want to make the move to join you. The extra travelling time alone would pose me huge difficulties.

'If it was just me to consider, I would jump at the chance. But I can't. I honestly can't.'

'So should I even be letting you be present for what is a potentially dangerous raid? More dangerous than usual, given the risk of explosives. If you're effectively telling me you can't transfer to us because of your domestic situation with your brother?'

'I'd like to see it through to the end, sarge. I promise to stay well away from any dangerous action and follow instructions at all times.'

'All right then. I'll have to risk assess the whole op before we go in, of course, like I said, and there's a possibility you won't make the final cut after that. That may not be my decision alone.

'But good work again, both of you. Stay away from here until we go in, unless I tell you otherwise. The fewer new faces that are spotted around and about, especially more than once, the better chance of success we'll have.

'I'll keep you posted.'

* * *

Ted listened to what Rob had to say about their discovery of another good lead, and the planned raid on the property, once the risk assessments had been carried out. Jezza had gone with him but let him do the talking.

'Good work, the two of you. And I concur with everything Sergeant Duffy has told you. On something like this, it's more important than ever that you follow instructions, to the letter and all the time, and don't get in the way of any of the specialist teams. Certainly not of those dealing with the explosives.'

As Rob turned and left the office, Jezza hesitated and said, 'Boss, could I talk to you at some point? Maybe over a Gunner and a hotpot in The Grapes? Just a few things I'd like to ask you about when you have time, please. Outside work time, I mean. Maybe one evening?'

She was still standing in front of his desk. Unusually he hadn't invited her or Rob to sit down whilst giving their report.

'Is it urgent? Where on a scale of one to ten is it?'

That didn't sound promising. Normally the boss would find a slot speedily for any of the team who specifically wanted a one-to-one with him.

'Well, probably not really on the scale at all if I'm honest, boss ...'

'Can we leave it for now then, please, Jezza? I need to get a file together for CPS on where we go from here, if anywhere, with the babies' father. And on top of that, I'm trying to finish off a report for Chief Superintendent Marston about recruitment procedures and how they can be improved. He's in the area shortly and he's a real details man, so I'm a bit pressed just now.

'I'm sorry, Jezza, I'm honestly not putting you off, just asking if it can wait a few days more.'

It certainly sounded like a brush-off, Jezza thought to herself as she left the room. But she knew the boss well enough to know he was stubborn as a mule. If he said not now, she'd have to live with that and wait until he could find time for her. If ever.

She went to find Rob as soon as she left the boss's office.

'It's definitely serious. Not even the offer of a Gunner and a hotpot on me could do the trick. It seems like almost anything at the moment is more inviting than spending time with me,' she told him.

'Jezza,' Rob began cautiously, 'at the risk of insulting your hormones or whatever again, d'you not think he might simply be up to his eyes in work-related stuff? With the killing of a prime suspect and the case against a second one now looking shaky in the extreme? It's not as if he's cleared your desk and put your belongings out of the door.

'Perhaps give him the benefit of the doubt? Maybe he was simply trying to let you know he wouldn't stand in your way if ever you did want to spread your wings and move on. And once we all know what CPS advises going forward from here, he might be back to the boss we know and love and eager to take you up on your suggestion.

'I'd honestly suggest cutting him a bit of slack in the current circumstances.'

* * *

Ted certainly looked a bit more fraught than he usually was when the team got together at the end of the day for a progress update.

'I've been talking to CPS. So far the late twins' father, Mr Khan, doesn't seem to want to make a fresh application for bail, now that the case against him is looking weaker every day, but it's probably only a matter of time before his legal team suggest it. I suspect he doesn't want to go back to his home which would be bound to remind him of the family he's lost. Especially if there are baby clothes and things everywhere, ready for what should have been the happy homecoming from the Welcoming ceremony, so-called.

'We all know there was no trace of him on either of the babies, so it looks as if he never even got to hold them.

'There were traces of him on the wife's body but that would be quite normal. And I think, Ali and Maurice, all the witnesses to date have said he was more or less forced into what happened to her, although Tonton was very much the instigator, which would explain any concentration of his DNA in the area where she was strangled.

'Is that still the situation, or has anyone said anything to contradict that?'

'No one we've spoken to has said anything really incriminating about the husband, boss,' Ali told him. 'An accessory at best, and an unwilling one. A physically coerced one, it would seem, at that, is what we've been told.'

Maurice was nodding his agreement with what she said.

'And his and Tonton's prints and DNA aren't on the system anywhere? Steve?'

'Nowhere so far, sir. Not in this country, so I'm widening the search, which will take time, since we still don't know his origin. Nothing so far, though.'

'So if Mr Khan does eventually make an application for bail, on legal advice, what solid grounds do we have to oppose it?'

Ted looked round at the team for suggestions. He was fairly certain there were no such grounds, but he hadn't been all over the case as much as he would like to so, it was possible he had overlooked something, maybe even something obvious.

'Nothing, boss, in a word,' Mike Hallam told him. 'Unless we've all missed it. And I can't believe all of us would.'

'That's pretty much what I told CPS but I just wanted to check I'd not overlooked anything.

'The other thing we probably need to prepare for, in the event of bail being granted, is the defence getting their act together and applying for protection for their client. There's already what happened to Tonton for them to cite as grounds for that.'

A murmur rippled through those present. The boss was right, as ever. It was a distinct possibility. The man remained innocent until proven guilty, something which didn't seem to be getting nearer to any sort of resolution.

'I know, none of us much likes that idea. But unless and until he's convicted, his safety is our responsibility, as with any other person, if he's granted bail, and that of the prison service if he's not.'

'But what was he even doing hanging round with a mad cult like that, boss?' Maurice asked. 'If you don't want to get arrested for something, why put yourself in such a position ...?'

The room went quiet at once. Even Maurice suddenly realised the irony of what he had just said.

'Maurice, considering you're currently on restricted duties for being in entirely the wrong place at the wrong time – and we all accept that it was with nothing but good intentions – I think you need to consider that Mr Khan thought, like many of the witnesses seem to have, that he was about to witness something good. A special ceremony for his new family.

'The defence team would have a field day with any suggestion that the word 'Welcoming' could in any way be interpreted as something menacing or remotely dangerous. We've no evidence, as far as I'm aware, of Mr Khan having attended any such ceremony prior to that of his own children ...'

He looked to Steve for confirmation as he spoke. Maurice had been trawling the statements to find potential witnesses, but Steve was the one for the fine detail, always.

'Nothing at all, sir,' Steve confirmed. 'No mention of him having previously attended a Welcoming, and none of the statements about the Circles contain any mention of discussion of what might go on in the birth ceremonies.

'Plus as far as we've found out up to now, this one was the first Welcoming on our patch. So I can't see how Mr

Khan, who lives in our area, could have been expected to know that anything sinister was likely to happen. And in case it's significant, sir, there's nothing to suggest, in any of the statements, that anyone other than the father, most probably, knew that the woman was expecting twins.'

'I know it's a big ask but we need to go over every single witness statement again in detail. We need to build a prosecution case against Mr Khan, rather than making the bullets for the defence to fire at us if we carry on opposing bail.'

* * *

'Sorry, I'm even later than I thought I would be, and I didn't get chance to phone again with an update.'

Ted was already in apology mode as he closed the front door behind him, before he'd even made it as far as the kitchen where Trev had music playing loudly as he sang along to it, missing almost every single note but clearly enjoying himself enormously.

His good humour was explained when Ted dodged and avoided cats, giving only a cursory gentle pull to waving tails, on his way to plant a kiss on his partner's cheek. The large wineglass in Trev's hand was nearly empty. From the look of the bottle, and judging by his partner's serene mood, it was unlikely to be the first of the evening.

'You're forgiven. I'm in a mellow mood as I've whiled away the time waiting for you by cooking more than we could eat in a week, drinking this rather nice Bordeaux and chatting away to another gay man.'

'Should I be jealous?' Ted asked him.

'Insanely, because he far outranks you. I've upped my sights. Raised my expectations. His salary may be more suited to my oenophile needs than yours is.'

'Mr Marston? You're convinced he's gay, aren't you? You could conceivably be wrong. He could just be a bit of a loner who doesn't know himself where he should be looking for company.'

'I am never wrong on such things. Trust me. And he really is an absolute sweetie. We chatted away for ages while I was waiting for you to come home, or even to phone to tell me when you would be back.'

'Sweetie' was not exactly the word which sprang first to Ted's mind when he thought of the somewhat pompous and officious chief super, but Trev had a way of seeing the best in people. Especially after a couple of large glasses of wine.

'Ironically, it's largely due to him I was later back than I intended to be. I've been desperately trying to put together some ideas, facts and figures for my meeting with him, which is growing disconcertingly close. I was adding in Mike's thoughts to my own, so it at least looks like a proper job, although I could have done with more time to work on it.'

'He seems to be thrilled at the mere prospect of seeing you again, not to mention meeting me in the flesh, and the meal out afterwards, bless him. He also seemed pleased with the venue, but I still say we should take him to The Gay Village as well, afterwards.'

Ted shook his head, smiling.

'Can you imagine the repercussions if you're wrong? Anyway, have I got time to change before we eat? I've had enough of being suited and booted for one day. I need to relax.'

'That sounds promising,' Trev told him with a smile. 'Time for a quick shower too, if you want. I'll lay the table and put everything on a low light until you're ready.'

Chapter Twenty-one

Ted was in early the next day, even by his own standards. He wanted some quiet time at his desk, before anyone else appeared, to go over the file on Khan yet again to make sure absolutely nothing had been missed.

He was becoming increasingly convinced that Khan was the wrong person to be held in prison for the killing of the baby girls and their mother. It wasn't Ted's job to do the defence's work for them, but from all the evidence he had read, and reread to check, he couldn't identify anything which he could imagine persuading a jury to return a guilty verdict on the husband and father, if it went to court and there was a not guilty plea.

He had a responsibility not to waste resources, or court time, by pursuing a case with little chance of success. It would be up to the CPS to make the final decision on whether or not there was a case, but that would be based on the file put together by Ted's team, and overseen by him.

The way things were at the moment, Ted was more and more convinced CPS would decide not to pursue the case against Khan, for lack of reliable evidence. A costly trial with little hope of success always had to be weighed up in the public interest.

The whole thing risked being a PR nightmare, if it did go to full trial and they'd got it wrong. The headlines didn't bear thinking about, for one thing, not that that was the most concerning aspect.

Ted needed to read through everything they had yet again, then talk at length to someone senior from the CPS to decide whether, at the next remand hearing, simply to offer no evidence and draw a line under the whole tragic affair.

In the meantime he was growing increasingly uneasy about keeping Khan behind bars with so little evidence to justify the action.

From everything he had read so far, thoroughly, sometimes more than once, all those present who were talking about it were now putting the blame squarely on Tonton, including him physically manhandling Khan to force participation in the killing of his wife.

It was the most remarkable murder case Ted could remember having been involved in. There seemed no doubt, from witness statements, that despite his disability, Tonton had been exceptionally strong, both physically, and in the psychological hold he seemed to exert over his followers.

Every so often as he worked, Ted kept having a pang of guilt about putting Jezza off the previous day. He knew he should make time for her. She deserved that. The problem was, he had no idea of how to broach the subject which had been niggling away at the back of his mind. He kept pushing it further onto the back burner, hoping it would go away of its own accord.

But it wouldn't. He knew that. If he couldn't find the way to make it disappear he should talk to someone about it. To Jezza, for sure, eventually, but to someone impartial first. Someone who would laugh in his face, ask if he was mad and tell him to forget all about such rubbish. Then he could simply let the whole thing drop, go for a drink and a hotpot with Jezza, apologise profusely and put his recent behaviour down to the stresses of such a complex case.

He'd normally talk to his old boss, Big Jim Baker, for advice on anything like that. But on this occasion he could imagine Jim seriously doubting his sanity. There were times when he'd done that himself.

Trev was always his first choice of confidant but again, the idea was so far-fetched, he hesitated even to raise the subject with him.

He kept telling himself he'd deal with it as soon as he'd spoken to CPS for guidance on what to do now with the Khan case, and then finished his proposals for Mr Marston.

At the same time, he knew he wasn't being honest with himself. After those two jobs, there would be something else. Then something else again. And his concerns would still be there, festering away, unsolved.

* * *

With at least some inroads made on his workload, Ted could now find the time to phone the Senior Crown Prosecutor for advice on where to go next with the case against Khan. It wasn't something which could easily be decided on at lower level. For one thing, it was the first time Ted could remember himself having been in the position of not only being unable to see a case through to court, but of being more and more convinced that it would be the wrong course of action to even try.

'I don't know, Ted,' the prosecutor told him cheerfully, 'you do like to test us with some of your cases. But if someone of your experience is saying you don't think there's enough evidence there to proceed, I'm inclined to take your word for it. Although of course, as arse-covering is my special responsibility, I will have to go over every single dot, dash and hyphen of the paperwork on file myself. Sooner rather than later, please.

'And you say Khan refused legal representation last time? Was it made clear to him he was entitled to have someone with him, and is that on the record somewhere? Because I think we both know that if he'd had someone with him, based on all the circumstances, they would have been making every effort to get him out on conditional bail straight away, and that in all probability it would have been granted, subject to strict conditions. Despite the seriousness of the original charges against him.'

Ted had a mug of green tea in front of him and took a hasty swallow while the prosecutor was talking. He'd heard him do the same earlier on with whatever he was trying to drink between phone calls.

'I think what you should probably do, as soon as possible, is to send someone back to talk to Khan but this time ask someone at the prison to strongly advise him to have a lawyer present with him for this next interview.

'Who interviewed him last time?'

'One of my DCs. Solid, reliable. DC Tibbs.'

'Hmm, well, no offence to DC Tibbs, but I think you need to send someone more senior to see Khan, with his legal representative, and spell out what's what. Ideally, I'd say go yourself but I'm sure you're going to tell me that's impossible.'

'To put it bluntly, if I run up and down the stairs, I might just have chance of a pee at some point today but that's it.'

The prosecutor laughed.

'I know that feeling and I feel your pain. So who's your 2IC?'

'DS Mike Hallam is second to me and experienced enough to stand in for me on something like this, with a thorough briefing.'

'Right then. Give him the tightest possible brief you can. Make sure there's a solicitor present when he talks to Khan and tell him not to take no for an answer on that one. Then get him to spell out to both client and lawyer that if they were minded to make further application for bail, in the light of the usual "further information which has recently come to light" bollocks, the prosecution would not oppose such an application.

'Just make sure he stops short of admitting we appear to have bugger all evidence to offer against his client if and when it does go to a committal or they'll hang us all out to dry.

'By the sound of it, you're telling me we won't have anyone left to prosecute for this case if we do that, which is a bit of a bugger because it's already high profile. But I do still think that might be preferable to trying to send an innocent man down for life when he's already lost his entire family.

'I know he's currently in solitary for his own safety but the media might try to misrepresent that as psychological torture or some such. Such headlines don't bear thinking about, for one thing. Not to mention the inevitable appeal in the unlikely event of getting it to court and obtaining a conviction, and all the further publicity which would go with that. Not in the public interest and other such platitudes would appear to apply in this case, I think.

'I know you can do diplomatic, Ted. I've seen you in action. But to protect all of our careers, and our future pensions, make sure everyone who goes near this case is singing from the same hymn sheet. Sticking strictly to the script.

'Something as potentially career-breaking as this I'm sure you'll need to take to your super, and she's almost certainly going to want to run it by executive level. It's a ticking time bomb which definitely needs expert dismantling before any of us goes up in smoke.'

* * *

'If you don't mind covering for me, Rob, there's somewhere I'd quite like to sneak off to before I go back in,' Jezza told him as they were getting ready to call it a day. 'I won't be long, honestly, and it's not work. There's just someone I need a quick word with and I'd prefer to do it face to face. Are you okay with that?'

'Can it not wait until after we finish? And if not, what do I tell the boss when he asks, as we both know he will?' Rob asked her.

'Well, you're the one who was claiming my hormones were making me irrational, so just drop a few hints about me being hormonal and he'll soon quieten down. He'd definitely list that as too much information,' she told him, smiling.

'And you can't do it after work because ...?'

'Because, sarge,' she told him ironically, 'I need to catch this person at their place of work, for which I have the address, and not at their home, where I daren't intrude.'

Rob was still looking at her suspiciously, but they were getting closer to the nick, so he was going to have to make a decision soon. He was assuming Jezza would want to slip away to wherever it was she was intent on going without anyone seeing her and perhaps asking where she was off to.

'And you're definitely not going to do anything bloody stupid involving organised crime gangs, bomb-making terrorists or big killer dogs when you go off by yourself, are you?'

'Perish the thought!' she told him with a grin. 'Honestly, it's nothing to worry about. Just someone who can probably help me with a personal dilemma, so at worst, I'm nicking off work for an hour or so. And am I ever going to live that incident down when every man and his dog, pun intended, keeps throwing it up at me?'

'It's only that we care about you and don't like seeing you put yourself in danger. And go on, then, I'm probably going to regret this, but drop me on the next corner and I'll walk from there. Just don't take the piss, Jezza. Don't go doing anything stupid that's going to drop both of us well in it. You for doing it, me, as the more senior officer, for letting you.'

Jezza gave him a cheery wave as she pulled away from the kerb, then made a couple of turns at junctions so she was heading north away from the town centre.

She'd found the address online. Nice and easy to get to, so she was there in no time.

She parked her car outside the premises then went in. As she opened the door, instead of the traditional bell, there was the sound of an accelerating motorbike, sounding its horn.

It was Trev who came striding across the otherwise empty shop, smiling broadly to see her. He leaned over to give her a kiss of welcome on each cheek.

'Jezza! This is a lovely surprise. Don't tell me you've decided to join the biker community. You've come to the right place, if you have.'

'I haven't, no, sorry. But I do need your help and advice please. About the boss. He's being all weird, as if I've done something awful, but I don't know what. I've tried asking him but he keeps giving me the cold shoulder. I even offered to take him for a Gunner and a hotpot after work but he turned that down, too.

'I really am sorry to bother you, Trev, honestly, but I didn't know who else I could ask for help.'

'Well, it does sound serious, if he turned down the offer of hotpot. Come into the sales office and I'll make us both a cuppa. I have choccy biccies, too. I should warn you it's a bit of a tip, though. I get used to Ted tidying up after me at home, and I'm not very good at that side of things myself. In fact I'm an unashamed slob.

'But I am a good listener. So you can tell me everything, and then I'll tell you what we can do about it.'

* * *

Ted was with Superintendent Caldwell in her office, the two of them on a video call with the Assistant Chief Constable (Crime) Russell Evans, discussing the latest developments in the triple murder case.

'It certainly sounds as if we need to allow Khan out on bail, at the earliest opportunity. After all he's been through, if we've banged up an innocent man, we're going to get slaughtered in the press and media, for one thing.

'He'd need to surrender his passport, of course, if he has one, but subject to that, and strict reporting conditions, I think we need to do that as soon as we can.

'What's happening with the PM on this Tonton bloke? I'm just thinking that if we could get Professor Nelson to do that, and soonish, or at least to oversee the results in some way, that could work to our advantage. It would certainly help with our case if she could confirm whether Tonton would have been capable of physically coercing Khan into the killing of his wife. Assuming it's not been done already?'

'Not yet, sir, no, although she has already checked and confirmed the feasibility of him killing the babies,' Ted told him. 'And I have put through a call to the coroner's office to see if it's even a possibility to get Professor Nelson. She's the closest Home Office pathologist so it would be logical, if she's available.'

'Let me know if you need any strings pulled for that,' the ACC said. 'I know Leo socially. I know he can be a stickler for procedure and is someone who's not always obliging.'

You can say that again, Ted was thinking to himself. He'd always had a rather stiff and strained relationship with the coroner. He was finding it difficult to imagine the man having any kind of a social life, so it was good to know there was a way round if he was making difficulties.

'Right, if that's all for now, I have at least two other places I should be at the same time, so I'll leave things in your capable hands, Ted. Just let Vanessa know if there's anything else I can do to facilitate things and she'll fix you up with an appointment. She always knows where to find me.'

* * *

'You look absolutely knackered, to put it mildly,' Trev greeted Ted as he got home, went into the kitchen and immediately put the kettle on.

'I feel it today,' Ted admitted. 'It's been a bit full on. We've lost one suspect already for the triple murder. Now we're probably going to have to let the other one out on bail, so we've got the sum total of bugger all to show for a lot of hard work, at the moment.'

'But the OCG case, with the murderous mutts – that's going a bit better, isn't it?'

Ted never discussed cases in much detail with Trev. Not that he didn't trust his discretion, simply that usually the last thing he wanted to do when he got home from work was to talk about the job.

'Yes, that's making good progress. We might at least be able to wrap up the related suspicious death case on our patch, which will help with statistics.'

'And you've nothing else bothering you at the moment?' Trev probed. 'Don't forget you can always talk to me. You know that. I know what you're like at bottling things up, and it never ends well. You do seem a bit distracted lately.

'Perhaps as soon as you can find the time we should take the bike out and go for a walk up to Kinder Downfall, with a picnic, and chill out. And you can tell me anything you want or need to. Could you make some time for that? Otherwise I'll only worry you might be about to blow a gasket.'

'I honestly can't see it happening soon, the way things are going. But I promise you, it'll be my first priority as soon as I can find the time.'

Chapter Twenty-two

Ted had asked Mike Hallam to come in earlier than usual so he could brief him on visiting Khan in prison, based on the latest advice on the case. He didn't know how soon it could be arranged so he wanted Mike up to speed for whenever it could happen.

'It's not that I don't trust Virgil, of course. He's done a very good job with Mr Khan so far. But it's getting a bit tricky now so it calls for someone with a bit more experience. And a higher rank, as suggested by CPS.'

'No pressure then, boss?' Mike asked him cheerfully.

'None at all, Mike. I trust you with this one. I know I don't have to spell it out for you, but the main thing is there needs to be no hint that we've knowingly had the wrong person on remand. Someone who's now having to be held in solitary confinement for their own protection.

'He may possibly still be culpable in some way, even a minor one, but I won't be satisfied we know that for a fact until after the PM on Tonton. Hopefully, we'll be getting Professor Nelson on that one, and I'll probably attend myself, if I can find the time.

'I don't even know if it will be possible to deduce what Tonton was and wasn't capable of, physically speaking, as regards the killing of the mother, although she managed to do that with the babies. But if anyone can do that it will be her, and it might make taking things any further with Mr

Khan unwise. It might stop us proving beyond reasonable doubt that he was involved in any way.'

'And what about finding out about who killed Tonton, boss? Is there any mileage there?'

'I've spoken to the prison and they're carrying out their own initial investigations. They've promised to keep me posted. What we don't know yet is if there is any suggestion of prison officer involvement. His death came very soon after his return from being questioned here, almost as if the killer or killers knew of his movements.'

'Which in turn probably turns the spotlight onto us here, in this nick. It could theoretically have been a copper here who tipped someone off that he was on his way back. We both know that even a lot of hardened criminals don't like baby killers, and a lot of coppers certainly don't. Should we at least be looking into that possibility?' Mike suggested.

'In our spare time?' Ted asked him ironically. 'I agree with you, Mike. In an ideal world we'd turn our own house upside down at the same time as looking elsewhere. We both know we don't have anything like the time or the resources to do that, though. Unless we brought someone in from outside, but do we yet have enough even to consider that?

'It might well need to happen in the future and then it would almost certainly be with someone neutral being brought in to show impartiality.

'I've got this session with Chief Superintendent Marston coming up later today where, as you know, we're meant to be discussing, amongst other things, how we can improve the selection process for the police service. I'll try at least to raise with him the issue of having enough officers to do a proper job, on all cases. He'll no doubt tell me that's up to the Home Office, but he just might agree that further

229

representation needs to be made to show how inadequate the police funding settlement is.

'Despite his faults, Mr Marston does at least seem to be trying to bring about improvements in the service where he can, hence this meeting with me. Speaking of which, after morning briefing, can you please make sure everyone understands I'm a definite "Do Not Disturb" for the rest of the day. Unless, of course, the ship has actually hit the iceberg, the stern is up in the air and you're still away at the prison.'

* * *

Rob and Jezza weren't with the team for morning briefing. They'd gone straight out to liaise further with the OCG in preparation for their next planned raid.

The new target property was being kept under constant covert watch, any and every visitor being recorded and identified, where possible. The gang's explosives expert was also under round-the-clock surveillance, with regular changes of those watching to avoid rousing suspicions.

He was someone the OCG had had in their sights for a long time, but he'd always managed to slip through their fingers. This time they wanted nothing to go wrong which could tip him off to their presence. He was one of the big fish in the gang, although still a rung or two below the very top, and had so far proved too elusive to have been landed.

He was certainly a frequent visitor to the target house but it wasn't yet known if he was living there or had some other connection to the property.

Sergeant Duffy was certainly all over this one like a rash, in constant phone contact with any of his own officers, now including Rob and Jezza on a temporary basis, to minimise all risk of them being spotted by any gang members, whose surveillance would no doubt be as thorough as theirs.

Inevitably, some of the gang would become familiar with a few faces from the OCG, at least, which was where Rob and Jezza were a valuable asset to the operation. Even if anyone had clocked either of them on the last raid, Jezza was always careful to change her appearance each time, and to help Rob to look different. His lack of hair was distinctive, so Jezza oversaw a selection of headwear for him, different in some way each time they went out.

Their cover was easy enough. Any onlookers would probably see a happy young couple, perhaps checking out various neighbourhoods in search of somewhere to set up home together.

They had one nerve-jarring moment when they turned to walk into the road parallel to the target property, checking out access and egress points, when they spotted the gang's bomber, walking briskly towards them, head down, but visibly scowling. It was their closest sighting of him to date. Unplanned and unwelcome. Too close for comfort.

Jezza was the quicker of the two of them to react. She turned to Rob, flinging her arms round his neck and pulling his face down towards her almost as the man drew level with them.

'Oh, darling that's a fabulous idea!' she said, loudly enough to be heard. 'I like that house best of all. The apple tree in the back garden would be just perfect for a swing.'

The bomber barely glanced at them as he walked past. If he registered them at all, he would have seen nothing but a young couple of house-hunters. Nothing remotely suspicious. Not even on his radar.

Jezza had positioned them so Rob still had eyes on the man to see where he was going and what he was up to, until he reached a side road and turned off, the first of two right-angle turns which would bring him round to the front of the target house.

'Sorry about that,' Jezza told Rob with a grin. 'But I think it paid off. He didn't look remotely interested in a lovestruck young couple looking for a home to call their own. Were we convincing enough to go back the same way, looking for the house with the apple tree so we can keep an eye on him and see what he's up to? I haven't actually seen any apple trees anywhere, so I hope our man's not a tree expert or he might notice the lack and get suspicious.'

'Not our op, Jezza, remember. I need to check with Duffy on what he wants us to do.'

Rob already had his mobile phone in his hand and was pulling up the OCG sergeant's number.

'He's the one in charge on this, so we need to liaise closely on the slightest detail. The last thing he'd want now is us crashing in and scaring the gang off. So we do whatever he says on this one. Without arguing either. Got that, Jezza?'

This time she gave him nothing but a meek smile as she replied, 'Yes, sarge.'

* * *

Ted had asked Bill to let him know once Chief Superintendent Marston arrived in the building, so he could go down to meet him in person. He knew the man was a stickler for protocol and would expect no less.

Because his visit was only short, hopefully Marston was not expecting to meet all of the senior officers in the station, but Ted had arranged to at least take him to exchange civilities with Superintendent Caldwell on arrival. He didn't have time for much else himself and he was sure Marston wouldn't either, if the two of them were to go over in detail the report which Ted had prepared, just in time to email it to the chief super so he might have had chance to at least glance at it on his train journey up to Stockport.

Ted knew Marston wouldn't travel up in his uniform, even if he came first class. It could be asking for trouble, with hate crimes against the police on the increase. But he also guessed that the stiffly formal senior officer would want to be in uniform for their meeting. He would probably have allowed himself time to visit his hotel to change before making the short walk from there to the police station.

Once they were both in the modest-sized office which was the DCI's and he had offered his visitor a seat, Ted started with the niceties.

'Have you had chance to look at your hotel, sir, and is it acceptable?'

'I have, thank you, and it is indeed. Certainly very clean, and that's always a worry with unknown hotels.'

Without judging or stereotyping the man, Ted had had a hunch he might be fastidious over cleanliness. He was pleased his accommodation had passed muster. Marston was never exactly easy-going and the prospect of going out for the evening with him if he'd been in the mood to moan and grumble about his hotel hadn't appealed. Ted wasn't exactly thrilled by the whole idea as it was. He always preferred to keep work and social life separate when he could.

'Would you like coffee, sir? Or tea, perhaps?'

'I prefer not to drink stimulants of any kind whilst on duty, chief inspector,' Marston told him in his somewhat prissy tone. 'And it really isn't necessary to call me sir in every sentence, but thank you for that courtesy.'

'I have green tea, if you would prefer that? Trev says it's good for balancing chakras, although I'm not quite sure I believe in all that.'

'Ah, now that sounds delightful, thank you.'

Once he'd brewed up and sat back down, Ted was relieved he'd been even more meticulous than usual in preparing his report for Marston, and had fleshed it out with statistics for every point he had made, helped by Mike's input.

'We both know there have been instances where people have got through background checks and the usual procedures to join up and have gone on to commit crimes as bad, if not worse, than those committed by the criminals who are our main target,' Ted told Marston.

'It's possible – probable, even – that there are other such cases waiting in the wings to come out to bite us in the future.

'Again, I'm not telling you anything you don't already know when I say that often the people who are capable of the worst crimes have no moral compass, so it's hard to find them out with the usual methods employed. Especially as some are above average intelligence so they're unlikely to give themselves away solely by how they respond to stock questions.

'I don't imagine asking them something like "Are there any circumstances in which you think killing someone could be justifiable" is going to get a truly honest answer, for example.'

Marston was studying him appraisingly, then asked, 'It does sound rather as if you're speaking from personal experience, chief inspector. Have you ever met such an officer, and what course of action have you taken regarding them?'

His question was more direct than Ted had anticipated. He was probably way off the mark with what he had been pondering recently. Luckily he was nothing if not a quick thinker.

'We had an older, experienced Uniform sergeant here. Mickey Wheeler. Seemingly solid as a rock. Good friends with my predecessor, Chief Inspector, later Superintendent, Jim Baker. No one knew that Mickey had a serious gambling habit which he was trying to fund – largely by getting paid for any tip-offs to the media on ongoing cases.

'It came to light when his computer needed an overhaul. He'd not been tech-savvy enough to wipe away his digital footprints. Instant dismissal, of course, just shy of his pension, so he walked away with nothing. No one's heard much about him of late, not even Jim Baker.

'The thing is, none of us knew or suspected anything untoward about Mickey. Not until the computer incident. We couldn't have known, without running financial checks on him. So my point is there could conceivably be other officers I know who are sitting on equally dark secrets of things they may have done in the past. Far worse things, possibly. And I have no idea what systems we'd need to pick up on anything like that.'

* * *

The transformation in the stiff and formal Chief Superintendent Marston came as a complete surprise to Ted when he and Trev went round to his hotel on the station approach to find him waiting outside for their arrival.

He wasn't wearing the three-piece suit Ted had expected to see him in. Instead he was sporting a blazer with a badge Ted didn't recognise, teamed with a cravat which looked like silk, chinos, and leather boat shoes. He even had a smart leather man bag hanging from one shoulder.

Far more casual than Ted would have imagined, and it made him feel slightly overdressed in the suit he'd gone for, convinced Marston would also be wearing a formal suit. He was glad he had at least rebelled and shoved the tie Trev had waved at him back into the wardrobe.

Trev was also casually dressed but looking, as ever, stunning. He could have got away with jeans and a tie-dye T-shirt at any formal event and he would still have stood out.

Trev had travelled down to the hotel in the front passenger seat of Ted's small car, but leapt out to offer it to Marston, moving to shake the man's hand. It was the first time the two of them had met, having previously only spoken on the phone.

'No, no, I wouldn't dream of it,' Marston insisted. 'You're much taller than I am. It would surely be utter torture for you in the back of this, erm, somewhat compact vehicle.'

Trev laughed at that. 'Don't diss da wheels, Mr Marston. Ted is very fond of his little Dinky toy.'

That set the tone for the evening. Ted had been rather dreading it, expecting Marston to be as pompous as ever. Instead he found him to be good company. Polite, surprisingly amusing, and clearly very intelligent.

Ted always said of his partner that he could charm anyone, but he was still surprised at how well he and Marston seemed to be getting on. The chief super kept reminding them that he was picking up the tab for the entire evening, and seemed genuinely pleased at the amount of good wine Trev was, as always, putting away.

Ted's one worry for the evening was that Trev would suddenly insist on the threatened visit to Canal Street, and that could ruin what had been a far more pleasant evening than Ted had feared. He was more than a little relieved when Trev made no suggestion of going on anywhere.

When Ted drove Marston back to his hotel, the man insisted on shaking hands formally with both of them and thanking them for their company. He and Trev had already exchanged mobile phone numbers in what seemed to have the makings of some sort of a friendship.

'You see,' Trev said as Ted pulled out onto the A6 to head south for home. 'He really is a sweetie when you get to know him. I still think he's gay though, even if he's not yet admitted it to himself.'

Chapter Twenty-three

Ted hadn't even got into his car to go to work the following morning, never mind reached his office, when his mobile phone rang, the screen telling him that the incoming call was from Home Office pathologist, Professor Bizzie Nelson.

'Leo informs me that you have need of my supposedly specialist skills on a murder victim, Edwin. Is that so?'

She was never one for the niceties. Always straight to the point.

'Good morning, Bizzie. And yes, please. I know how flat out you always are, but it would really help me enormously if you could take a look at our body from the prison killing, please. The mysterious so-called holy man we know only as Tonton, killed in his cell while on remand. And up to now, our prime suspect for all three murders.

'You'd probably get one like this anyway, but I was rather hoping it could be a priority. In brief, as you will know, we have someone else on remand for the same crimes – the husband and father of the three deceased – and we're coming more and more to the opinion that he was probably innocent, physically forced to participate by Tonton.'

'Theoretically, it would probably have come to me anyway, as you say, on a geographical basis. I'm assuming there are special factors which you feel my modest skills could help with?'

'Definitely. Again, as you already know, our deceased had a withered arm – which is probably not the correct medical term, so I apologise. I don't even know if this is possible but it would really help the case to know if it had any function at all, and also whether or not the other arm may have been stronger in some way, as compensation.

'You helped to show he could easily have killed the babies, but now I need a definitive answer on whether he would have been physically capable of forcing the husband to participate in the killing of his wife. Which you might be better able to give me now you have the chance of getting him on your table.'

'Aaaaah.'

Bizzie made a little sound of contentment.

'This all sounds absolutely fascinating. Too much so to pass up on it. But as it's so important to you, I sense I have room to barter.

'I will make time for your monobrachius case this very day, at the end of my usual working hours, if he can be delivered to me by then. But strictly on the condition that I may bring a carefully selected handful of my eager students with me to observe as part of their training.

'Do we have a deal, Edwin?'

'We definitely do, and thank you. It might just be what my team needs to finally get somewhere with this case. Particularly to avoid a miscarriage of justice.

'We don't even have the man's real name, which of course means we've not been able to trace any next of kin, so, unless someone turns up out of the blue, there's no one to raise any objection to your students being present. I certainly won't.

'I'll take this one myself so I'll see you later, and thank you, Bizzie.'

Before he drove off, Ted fired off a quick text to Trev to apologise and to tell him he'd be late home because of the PM. No point going back into the house to tell him in person. Trev was never fully functioning as early as Ted was. He was even less likely to be so after the quantity of wine he'd put away the night before.

Somehow he always managed to drag himself up, take a shower, eat copiously, dress and get to work, sometimes even quite close to the time he was supposed to arrive. He was an equal partner in the business so was effectively his own boss.

The other partner, Geoff, sometimes tried having a word about him setting an example to the staff they employed, but Trev's sales success was simply outstanding so he could get away with murder. He could sell the proverbial coals to Newcastle and his skills had kept the business afloat in lean times more than once.

Ted was forever warning him about keeping a check on his blood-alcohol levels and made sure he always had a spare breathalyser kit in the house. He'd told Trev that not only could he not intervene if he got booked, he'd be obliged to arrest and book him himself in the interests of public safety, if he was driving over the limit.

Jezza was just parking her car in the station car park as Ted pulled up and parked his a couple of places away. She and Rob would attend morning briefing to touch base and report on the OCG's progress and plans.

The smile of greeting Jezza gave him had something tentative about it, which gave Ted a bit of a guilty feeling.

He really did need to find time to make things right with her, if he could. She deserved that, at least.

'I honestly haven't forgotten you want to talk, Jezza. It can't be today, unfortunately. For one thing I have to attend the PM on Tonton, which the Professor can fit in later this afternoon. Once we make some progress on sorting out that case, I will make some time, I promise.'

'Thanks, boss,' Jezza replied.

She made a show of getting something out of the boot of her car as he walked away to go into the building. She watched his retreating form disappear inside and said under her breath, 'But probably not before the next Preston Guild, the way you've been ignoring me up to now.'

* * *

Ted asked Rob to go first with his report, knowing that he and Jezza needed to get off back to the OCG to prepare for the next stage of their operations. They'd already brought Duffy up to speed with their sighting of the bomber.

'And you're sure he didn't clock you for what you really are?' Duffy had asked Rob when they'd caught up by phone at end of play the previous day.

'As sure as I can be,' Rob assured him. 'Jezza's drama talents were put to good use yet again. She was so convincing I half-believed myself that I was engaged to her,' he added, with a wink in Jezza's direction.

Duffy chuckled at that, but soon became serious once more.

'The two of you better stay well clear of the area for now. You got away with it once, but a second sighting would be just too much of a coincidence, and we don't want the whole op to turn to worms because our man gets suspicious.

'How's the CCTV gathering going on? Can you chase up any that's outstanding? I want us to have every possible advantage and element of surprise on this before we even think of going in. The bomber was enough of a surprise to fall into our laps like he has, so it's vital we know about anyone else who might present more of a real and present danger than your average scrote in that gang.

'Keep me posted on anything you find and stay in close contact. We might need to go in at very short notice if we get the feeling they're spooked and about to do a runner.'

* * *

'No heroics, either of you,' Ted reminded Rob and Jezza after they'd finished their update and were getting ready to leave. 'Follow instructions to the letter and if in doubt, always consult Sergeant Duffy, then stick to his script.'

Jezza was often impetuous but Rob had managed to get himself stabbed on a previous case when he'd waded in without checking for the possibility of a weapon. Ted didn't want a repeat of anything like that incident.

Once they'd left, Ted asked Mike Hallam for an update on the situation with Khan.

'I managed to set up a meeting with his lawyer present, boss, late yesterday. I told them both a further application for bail would not be opposed by us. Naturally, the lawyer wanted all sorts of cast iron guarantees for the safety of his client, given what happened to Tonton. Because of course every man and his dog knows about it, in great detail. I thought a nick was a gossip mill, but it seems prisons are even worse.

'I'm afraid I passed the buck a bit and said I'd need confirmation from higher authority, but I did promise him we'd put things in motion as soon as we could. Understandably, knowing what happened to Tonton inside, both the brief and his client are keen for him to be out and somewhere safer as soon as possible. Which is probably almost anywhere other than where he currently is.'

'I'm trying not to get my hopes up but there's a chance Professor Nelson might be able to add to the mounting evidence that Tonton was very much the instigator all along,' Ted told him. 'She'll be doing the PM on him later today.

'I'm still waiting to hear who's going to investigate Tonton's killing. In an ideal world, we'd get it as it's so closely entwined with our own cases, but we're flat out as it is. It will probably go to an MIT from Nexus House, with Forensic Services from Chadderton, I imagine.'

Although it was linked in to their own cases, it would certainly ease pressure on Ted's team if a Major Incident Team took over the prison killing as a case on its own.

'I for one would be reassured if we knew for certain about the possible involvement of prison or police officers in what went on. Even if it was only in the form of a tip-off, it's still a very serious breach of professional conduct at best, a criminal act at worst. I'll liaise with the MIT about that aspect of it.

'There's a lot riding on what the Professor can tell us from this evening's PM, but I hope I'll have something with which to update you all at morning briefing tomorrow.'

* * *

Ted was ahead of the time Professor Nelson had given him for the start of the PM on the man known only as Tonton, but he wasn't at all surprised to see the eager faces of five young students, her chosen few, sitting in the gallery, already craning their necks for a glimpse of anything which was going on.

There was no one else present, other than the coroner. Ted wasn't surprised at that. No next of kin could be traced without the deceased's real name, or any information at all about where he came from. Theoretically, had any relatives been traced, they could have asked for a family doctor to attend on their behalf.

Bizzie came to speak to him whilst he was getting changed.

'This sounds like a very intriguing one indeed, Edwin,' she told him.

She'd revert to formal mode as soon as they were in earshot of her students, Ted knew.

'Thank you for fitting this one in at very short notice, Bizzie. We're struggling a bit with everything about this case. With Tonton dead, we're just left with the husband, and I personally don't think he's guilty. I certainly don't think we can make a case to prove that he is.'

'I've had a very quick and cursory glance at him and it's left me eager to begin,' Bizzie told him. 'The extent of his fatal injuries suggest that he was definitely not flavour of the month with his killer or killers, and I'd certainly suspect more than one person at work.

'Again, this is only going on first impressions, and because someone was sensible enough to leave one of the murder weapons in place – a sharpened spoon, which is a favourite weapon of prisoners. Metal ones are not allowed inside, for obvious reasons, but apparently unthinking civilians sometimes take them in, mainly through educational sessions or workshops and they get overlooked and then purloined.

'They have ended up being used as murder weapons previously. But then, if a prison officer or officers wanted to do away with this person, perhaps because of the gravity of his actions, they may mimic the way a prisoner might act, to turn attention away from themselves.'

'As I said, the main thing I'm really hoping you can tell me, if it's even remotely possible, is how strong Tonton might have been, with his functioning arm, thinking now of the killing of the mother. Whether that had full normal function, or perhaps even some enhanced ones, as it was effectively doing the work of two. Enough to force the husband to act against his will.'

'Ah, Edwin,' she told him with a smile. 'I do sometimes wonder if you think I have supernatural powers. That would only happen in crime fiction, or one of those ridiculous supposed crime drama series on television.

'However, luckily for you, my eager young things have recently been studying the musculoskeletal system and its functions, and my chosen few for this evening are the brightest in the subject, so I hope they might possibly have some valuable input for you.

'And yes, I have, of course, threatened them with excommunication and worse should they breathe one word of what they see and hear within these hallowed walls, so you need have no worries at all on that.'

Professor Nelson had the rare knack of effortlessly gaining the total respect of her students. She didn't do second chances, except in the most extreme of circumstances. Places in her group were at a premium, hard won and fiercely guarded. Ted knew the risk of them saying anything was minimal.

In fact their input turned out to be helpful. They were part of the same group who had already helped the Professor to determine whether or not Tonton would have been capable of killing the twin babies in the way in which it had happened, using life-size models.

They had established beyond reasonable doubt that it would have been within his capabilities, so it was a logical progression to allow them to be part of the next stage: could he also have manhandled Khan, the father, into any sort of participation in the death of his wife, the babies' mother, possibly against his will, using only one arm?

The Professor had asked for, and been supplied with, details of Khan's height, weight, physique, and anything else which could be of relevance in determining whether he could have been a passive participant.

It was one of the longest PMs Ted could remember attending. The Professor was nothing if not thorough and she wasn't going to waste the opportunity of allowing her best students to be involved in such an interesting and unusual case.

He was glad he'd had chance to send Trev a text warning him that he might be quite late home. He'd fire off another quick one when he was on the point of leaving.

It was well worth the time. Subject to written confirmation in her report, which Ted knew would be reliably swift in getting to him, the Professor was confident enough to state that she could detect nothing which would have prevented Tonton using his valid arm in much the same way as anyone else. She also added that given the muscular development of the functioning limb, he could well have been someone of above average strength.

In terms of a result for Ted's team, it wasn't much to get excited about. It made it less and less probable that there was any kind of a charge which could be brought against Khan with a likelihood of success. They would at least be able to mark the case as No Further Action on the basis of Tonton now being the only likely suspect for the killings, subject to the agreement of the CPS.

It would be the ultimate irony for Ted's team if they did finish up having to investigate Tonton's killing for any reason, and to bring someone to justice for that. If they did, Ted was determined to get to the bottom of how his killers had apparently known exactly when he had got back to his cell. And heaven help any copper who had had any sort of a hand in that, if Ted got wind of them.

* * *

'Sorry, sorry, I'm much later than I hoped I would be. And would you mind if I have a quick shower before we eat? You know I don't like sitting down at the table when I've just come from Bizzie's lair.'

Ted was already apologising before he was halfway through the door. Trev stuck his head out of the kitchen to reply to him.

'Was it a disgusting one? Do you want me to get your suit cleaned for you this time?'

'Not that bad, thanks, quite a fresh one. I'd just prefer a wash and a change of clothes, if that's all right?'

'More than fine by me. I've already eaten part of mine and I've kept yours warm. I was starving, so I couldn't wait. Oh, and Roy phoned me, full of effusive thanks and singing your praises. You have a new fan there.'

'Roy, is it? It sounds as if you're the one with the fan if he unbent enough to go to first name terms.'

Trev laughed at that as he said, 'I wish you hadn't said unbent in his context because I remain convinced he's a secret gay who, with the right encouragement from people like us, might finally come tiptoeing out of the closet.

'Oh, and phone your mother. She says she's hardly heard from you since Germany and you playing paratroopers up the mountains with Mr Green. I told her not to hold her breath. You barely talk to me these days, and certainly not enough to tell me what's currently bothering you so much.'

Chapter Twenty-four

Jezza's muted mobile phone, on her bedside table, started to vibrate and move around on the polished surface. She groaned quietly as she reached for it with one groping hand. The screen told her it was barely four o'clock in the morning.

She picked up the phone, accepted the call and said a somewhat groggy 'Hello?'

She was not yet fully functional enough to hoist in the caller ID.

'Jezza? Duffy. We've had a reliable tip-off. We're going in. Very soon. Something's about to go down, and with the bomber on site, we can't afford to sit around waiting to find out what.

'If you want in on this, get here in half an hour, and give Rob a shout to come with you. And make sure it's low key.

'Are you up for it?'

'Already up and getting ready, sarge.'

It wasn't strictly true. So far she only had one foot out of the comfortable warmth of the bed, but it wouldn't take her long to get herself dressed and off out.

Duffy gave her the address of the RV point and reminded her again, 'Low key, maximum alert, remember,' before he rang off.

Jezza's partner Nathan was stirring on his side of the bed, making a low groaning sound under the duvet.

'Don't tell me – you've been called in,' he said as his head emerged.

'I'm really sorry, sweetie, but I have to go. The planned raid has been pulled right forward so if I don't go now, I'll miss it. I'm sorry to lumber you with getting Tom up, dressed and ready, with all the horrors that will entail, with a change of routine. Do you mind and can you manage?'

As she was reaching for clothes to throw on, she was calling Rob to give him the news and arrange for him to pick her up.

Nathan yawned widely as he asked, 'What time is it, anyway? Apart from obscenely early?'

'Around four, so you've time to go back to sleep for a bit, if I can creep out without waking Tom. Will you manage, and are you sure you don't mind?'

Nathan was sitting up now as he said, 'Let's face it, if I'm late for work because Tom kicks off, the worst that's likely to happen is that someone doesn't fill up the baked bean shelf before the ravening hordes descend. I don't think Stockport will grind to a halt because of that. Whereas if you're late, you might not get the baddies, which is far more serious.'

Nathan had been a high-flying financial trader until a catastrophic error had seen him sacked, made penniless and out on the streets. He now managed a large local supermarket, having started there as a trolley collector.

'Tom and I will be fine. We'll have some lads' time together and he'll hardly notice you've gone out early. Just please promise me, Jezz, you won't do anything daft and put yourself in danger. No mad heroics that might impress your Sergeant Duffy but will certainly not impress me. Nor your boss, if he gets to hear of them.

'If you think he's being a bit off with you now, just imagine what he'd be like if you do anything stupid on this raid, hot on the heels of your stunt on the last one.

'Take care of yourself, Jezz. Tommy and I both need you to come home safe.'

*　*　*

Rob arrived in good time to pick Jezza up. She had barely fastened her seatbelt before he launched into a repeat of the lecture on her not playing heroics or taking any risks, and following orders at all times.

'With possible explosives to contend with, just remember that we're both outside our knowledge base on this one. It's more important than ever to follow all instructions. Clear?'

'Yes, sarge,' she told him, in a tone dripping with irony. 'I'm really not daft, you know, so can you please give it a rest with all the lectures. I've finally found a decent bloke who's happy enough to accept the complicated package of my job and Tommy, and I do rather like going home to him. Especially when he does the cooking.'

'And you were thinking of him, and of Tommy, when you ran in front of Firearms officers to go and check on the door-knocker on the last raid, were you?' Rob asked her, sounding disconcertingly like the boss.

'Am I ever going to be allowed to forget that?'

'No. And for good reason. You're lucky the boss didn't chain you to your desk for the foreseeable future. Keep reminding yourself that his reaction to it was to try to persuade you to change to OCG. Do you think he'd even give you a choice in the matter if you do anything as reckless as that again?

'And I keep repeating it as that's actually my role as DS. Not to mention being rather fond of you, though I do sometimes wonder why.'

Jezza sighed.

'Fair points. Anyway you don't have to worry. We've got a bomber to contend with today, and the only thing I know about explosives is that they're loud, scary and unpredictable, so I've no intention of going anywhere near until the all-clear's been given.'

They parked up where Duffy had instructed, well away from the target house, and went to find him. He was looking understandably edgy, with such a big and potentially dangerous operation to run.

Not all of the attending vehicles were parked in the same place, so as not to draw attention to something big going on. One of the ones at the meeting point was a dog van.

Duffy saw Jezza's eyes on it and said, 'We sent a couple of little woofers and handlers in first. Black springers, they are. I didn't know they came in solid black, but it's a great asset for working in the dark, without alerting our targets, hopefully.

'One at the front, one round the back, and the handlers tell me they should be able to pick up any traces of explosives from that house. I just hope they're right about that, because it's the explosives that worry me more than anything. Even more than the thought of what big brutes of dogs they've got inside, and it's likely there are some, although they're staying quiet for now.'

'Maybe ones with their vocal chords cut, sarge?' Jezza suggested. 'Might the springers show a reaction to other dogs on the premises?'

'Not according to their handlers, no, unfortunately. Apparently they're so focused on what they're trained to detect they'll ignore almost any other scent, including titbits.

'We've got bomb disposal standing by, just in case, and whatever the dogs indicate from the exterior, they'll go in first, just to be on the safe side. They'll have close Firearms support, too, because if our bomber is still in there, the slightest move from him which could be interpreted as him about to trigger a device, we have Gold Command clearance for him to be taken down. We can't afford to take any risks on this one.'

Duffy paused to look hard at Jezza as he went on, 'I know I told you I admired you for having the balls to help a fallen officer on the last raid, Jezza, but this is a whole different ball game, with things ready to go bang if anyone pisses about.

'The intel may be wrong about the presence of the bomber on site. The explosives may be being stored elsewhere. But I have to proceed as if there are bombs there. So nobody, and I mean nobody, so much as breathes without my say-so on this one. I know your boss seemed quite happy to let you move on and join us, but I've a fancy he might be less than pleased if we gave you back to him in a box in little pieces.'

As with so many such operations, there was a lot of hanging about getting cold, a lot of checking and double-checking everything. Quite a few false starts, sending adrenaline levels soaring before plummeting when the 'Go' command was immediately rescinded.

But finally, they were going in and it was all over in minutes. No explosives found, let alone detonated. More XL Bully dogs safely immobilised and removed from the scene.

Several arrests made, including the bomber and a couple of other satisfyingly big fish from the gang. As Duffy had said, no one from the top echelons was ever considered likely to be there.

Duffy and the rest of his group who'd been present were jubilant. One of the best results they'd had so far.

'Bloody good show, everyone. Bloody well done. Debrief next over at Ashton.'

He looked round the assembled members of his team as he produced his wallet.

'Jake, get the sticky buns in, on me, and we'll see you back there shortly.'

* * *

Rob O'Connell waited until a civilised hour before phoning the boss to tell him where they were and what they'd been doing. No point waking him earlier than necessary just to tell him they were going to a debrief at Ashton and would be in later.

'And you're both all right? No heroics from Jezza this time?' Ted asked him.

'None at all, boss, she was as good as gold.'

Rob risked adding, hoping he wasn't overstepping the mark, 'So hopefully you don't still want to get rid of her and dump her on the OCG instead.'

'I don't want to get rid of her. I hope neither of you think that for a moment. I just wanted her to know that if she did want to make the move, I wouldn't stand in her way. Being head-hunted by OCG doesn't happen to everyone, and certainly not every day.

'I'm flat out at the moment but I'll try to find the time to reassure her I was only thinking of her career prospects when I suggested the move.'

Rob was frowning to himself as he ended the call. He'd got Jezza to drive so he could report in. The boss was usually absolutely on the level at all times, but something about what he'd said this time didn't quite ring genuine.

Rob couldn't for a moment think what Jezza could possibly have done to make the DCI want her off the team. He remained convinced that the whole thing was simply crossed wires somewhere along the way. Hopefully, once they'd debriefed with Duffy and his team and got back to their own nick to report in full to the boss, whatever the misunderstanding was might just sort itself out.

But first the prospect of sticky buns sounded good, after all the tensions of the morning so far.

* * *

Ted kicked off the morning briefing with news of the success of the OCG raid Rob and Jezza had attended earlier, before reporting back on the post-mortem results from the evening before.

'The Professor's conclusion was that Tonton probably did have above average strength in his valid arm, which would certainly seem to be in keeping with what most of the witnesses have now told us and Khan being seemingly in a state of total shock. Most of them have spoken of Tonton practically forcing him to participate in strangling his wife.'

'But boss,' Maurice said, his face creased in a frown, 'what about the bairns? I can just about see him being physically made to do that to his wife by someone who might have been a lot stronger. But what about the babies? I know no one has said he was involved in any way with killing them, but how could he just stand there and watch them being murdered like that in front of him?

'The first one, perhaps. Taken totally by surprise, no idea of what was going to happen, even though any dad's instinct should be to look out for their children, all the time, from the moment they're born. But then what about the second one? He must have known what was going to happen to her. Why didn't he do something? Save that second little bairn, at least?

'There must be something he can be charged with, boss, surely?'

'CPS are looking at every angle, Maurice, believe me. If there is anything there which could be proved against him, they'll find it. But in the meantime we're going to have to let Mr Khan out on strict conditional bail. There simply isn't enough compelling evidence to justify keeping him in custody. The defence will without doubt want a full psych evaluation of him and in the circumstances, that's likely to be the clincher to getting him released for now.

'Ali, while Jezza's currently tied up with the OCG, can you please liaise with the Merseyside officer she spoke to previously about the similar case at Billinge. We'll need to keep them in the picture. For a start it's possible – likely, even – that they haven't heard Tonton is dead, so they definitely need bringing up to speed. It affects them too, with their case.'

'So that's another innocent baby killed by this bunch of whatever they think they are and no one brought to justice for it,' Maurice said morosely. 'Can we at least do something to break the group up, boss? To stop them getting together and doing something similar in the future, at least? Otherwise what have we achieved?'

'We live in a free country, Maurice,' Ted told him patiently. 'We're all free to worship as we choose, including not at all. Nobody is free to commit crime, and certainly not murder, but if the group stays together and becomes peaceful and law-abiding, there's nothing at all we can do about that.

'Don't forget we once had to arrest a Home Office pathologist and get him sent down for life. You're surely not telling me that means all pathologists are murderers?

'I know it's disappointing. We badly wanted a result, but sometimes we can't get one. At least Rob and Jezza had a good one this morning. That will have to do for today."

* * *

Jezza smiled fondly at Nat as she walked into the kitchen at the end of the day. Whatever he was cooking smelled delicious and he poured her a glass of wine as soon as she appeared.

'I really don't deserve you,' she told him, planting a kiss on his cheek.

'You've had a long and difficult day, and I haven't. Mine was mostly fairly boring. Besides, I like looking after you. You're worth it.'

Tommy had heard her arrive and did his usual trick of walking into the kitchen, saying his stock phrase with little intonation then sailing back out again.

'Hello Jezza did you have a nice day at work and please may I have spaghetti for my supper thank you.'

'Hello, Tom, I did, thank you, and no, you will eat whatever Nathan has very kindly cooked for us, which smells wonderful,' Jezza called out affectionately to her brother's retreating back.

'It went well, then? I heard on the news about a successful raid so I hoped that was yours. Did you enjoy yourself?'

'I'm not sure enjoy is the right word. It was exciting, certainly. Scary, too, with the risk of explosives. A bit of an adrenaline rush. Duffy's good to work with. A good skipper. He bought all the sticky buns for the debrief. The rest of the team are okay too. They didn't make Rob and me feel like outsiders, for one thing.'

'You know, if you did decide to transfer, we'd find a way to make it work with Tom. I could maybe get another job. It's not as if it was my life's ambition to manage a supermarket. I can't go back to trading. I'm barred. But I am good with figures. I could maybe work from home. Be a sort of part-time house-husband to look after you and Tom. What d'you think? If it's what you want?'

She kissed him again, more lingeringly this time.

'That really is so sweet of you. But I honestly don't want to move. I love the team. I love the boss, when he's not being grumpy and trying to elbow me out. Besides, what about Maurice? You know he's my very best friend, after you, and I love him to pieces. Look what happened to the silly big lump when I wasn't around to keep him in check. I can't abandon him.

'If I could just persuade the boss to sit down sometime with me and tell me why he seems intent on elbowing me out, we could perhaps sort out what must be a misunderstanding, and go back to how things used to be.'

Chapter Twenty-five

Jezza hadn't told Nathan that Sergeant Duffy had had another go at poaching her before she and Rob had left. She didn't want him making some misguided gallant gesture of resigning from his job to let her make the move, without thinking through all the possible consequences.

'I hear what you say about your personal circumstances, Jezza, but if ever things change and you're looking for a move, make sure I'm the first person you call,' Duffy had told her before they parted.

'It's very flattering, sarge, but there's the simple issue of ordinary childcare, then there's the care of my brother Tom. It can be unbelievably difficult. Do you have children yourself?'

'I did have. A little girl. Sadie. A drunken driver took her away.'

Instinctively Jezza put a hand on his forearm and gave a gentle squeeze of compassion.

'I'm so very sorry, sarge. What a terrible thing to have happened. I hope the driver got the maximum sentence, at least.

'My father was well over the limit in the crash that killed him and my mother,' she told him. 'I've still no idea why she was in the car with him that night. She usually refused to travel with him if he'd had more than a glass of wine, and blood tests showed he'd had way more than that. She must have known, I'm sure.

'They were going to visit old friends so she must have thought it would be worth the risk. That's the only reason I can think of for why she would have gone with him when he'd had so much more than the legal limit. She didn't drive, so it's not as if she could have taken over from him if she thought he wasn't in a fit state to carry on. And after all, they'd have been having more drinks when they got there.'

'The driver who killed Sadie got fourteen years,' Duffy told her. 'He's still inside. Sadie never even got to live to fourteen.

'Anyway, enough bonding, I think we both know we got on well enough before we shared our life histories, so remember what I said. If ever the circumstances are right for you to make a move, give me a bell.'

* * *

'I know it feels like an anticlimax. I know how much you all wanted a nice clean conclusion to the Tonton case, with at least one solid conviction. But we know now that's not going to happen,' Ted told the team at the first full morning briefing after the weekend, now that Rob and Jezza were back with them.

Even with such a heavy workload, Ted always tried to make sure everyone got some time off at the end of the week. It wasn't just a budgetary consideration with him, either. He genuinely tried to look after the welfare of his officers, all too aware that if any of them succumbed to the stress of too heavy a burden at work, he'd struggle to get replacements for anyone who needed to take any time off.

'CPS need the full files as soon as possible to double check we've not overlooked anyone who could be prosecuted for anything. There's an emergency bail hearing for Mr Khan later today, then he's going to be spirited away out of the public gaze, because once the gutter press start up with their usual tricks – and they're bound to on a case like this – he's not going to be safe anywhere. Even if and when all charges against him are dropped, as they are very likely to be, as things stand at the moment.

'And we can't, of course, second guess which way the media will spin this. It could be "dangerous baby-killer let loose on the streets", or "tragedy of grieving father kept locked up in police bungle".'

Ted could see that Maurice was once again winding himself up to say something so he stepped in to stop him.

'I know, Maurice, I know. It's wrong. All of it. It shouldn't be like this. Especially not after all your hard work as a team. But that's how it is and there's absolutely nothing we can do about it.

'And speaking of the press, they're going to be all over this one, trying to get quotes out of anyone and everyone. Whichever way they decide to spin it. I shouldn't have to say it, but I'm going to, if only to cover my own backside, for one thing. None of you speaks to the media, or anyone else outside this enquiry. No one.

'If that's not clear enough for any of you, let me stress that anyone who does will be off this team faster than they can clear their desk. Have you all got that?'

Steve, the least likely of any of them to speak to anyone without authority, went bright red to the tips of his ears at the stern warning. His history with a bullying father still had an effect on him.

The boss was looking hard at Maurice, who still had a mutinous expression on his face.

'Maurice? Clear?'

'Clear, boss.'

'Good, because I've just had the dates for your next update training, and I think that's your last course, isn't it? So make doubly sure all your paperwork is up to date before you go off on that. It's next week, so once you have that under your belt, you're back to full unsupervised duties.'

A cheer went up from the rest of the team. They were all fond of Maurice and had every sympathy for him. He'd not followed correct procedure, but he'd certainly acted for the best of motives.

'Right, Rob, I'm relying on you and Jezza to build the file for your "death by dangerous dog" case, for want of a better phrase. That's going to be an extremely complex one, probably involving litigation issues none of us has come across before, so don't hesitate to check with me on anything you're not sure of. And certainly give me enough time to go through the full file before it goes to CPS, please.'

'Boss, before we finish, can I just say something?' Virgil asked, then went ahead at the nod from Ted. 'I'm going to be a dad again. The wife's expecting. So I'd like to buy you all a drink in The Grapes, perhaps just before the weekend. That's at least something to celebrate, even if we didn't get the results we wanted on the case.'

This time the cheer was even louder. Another bit of badly needed good news.

'Excellent idea, Virgil, but the first round's on me. Now, if anyone needs me, I'll be in my office having fun with spreadsheets once more. Let that be a lesson to any of you wanting to go for promotion.'

Jezza watched him go. He seemed in slightly better spirits now they were nearing closure of sorts on some of their cases. It might be the ideal opportunity to try once again to have some sort of discussion with him, which they both still clearly needed to do.

She debated with herself for a few minutes, then decided against. She'd concentrate on getting all her notes written up on the killing by dogs on their patch. At least they'd now had a positive result on the DNA sampling of them, as a match to the crime scene. Then once he had that full report, and was satisfied with it, maybe then she could renew her offer of a Gunner and a hotpot, plus a chat to clear the air. And perhaps this time he would agree, so that things could go back to how they always used to be. If not, she still had her Plan B up her sleeve as a way of bringing things to a head and getting a resolution.

* * *

Rob and Jezza had been given the task of interviewing the presumed owner of the two dogs which had killed Frank Turnbull. The man, Clive Martin, had been identified and arrested on the first raid. A subsequent search of his house had thrown up sufficient DNA traces matching those of the dogs to suggest he'd certainly had custody of them, even if, as he claimed, he was not the owner and had simply been looking after them for 'a mate' whom he refused to name.

The same thought went through both Rob and Jezza's minds as they had their first proper look at the man. He looked not unlike the dogs himself. Quite short and squat but with bulging muscles which didn't look entirely natural. There was, too, an aggressive set to his lower jaw.

He'd certainly put up a considerable fight during the police raid on his home. He'd thumped one copper in the face and broken their nose. Sufficient in itself to warrant him being remanded in custody, with bail refused. As well as those assault charges, he was also facing one of manslaughter in connection with dogs under his care having killed someone.

Jezza kicked off the interview, as the two of them had agreed.

'Mr Martin, as you've been told, you've been arrested on a charge of manslaughter because you are believed to be the owner of two dogs which forensic tests show were the ones which killed a man called Frank Turnbull.

'Did you know Mr Turnbull, and can you tell us what your dogs were doing at his house?'

Martin had a solicitor with him. Not one either Rob or Jezza knew. She looked young, and Jezza couldn't help hoping she was not one of the squeamish ones because a lot of the information they were going to have to put to her client was gruesome in the extreme.

'I was looking after them for a mate, like I said, then I asked Frank to look after them for a couple of days when I had to go away unexpectedly.'

'Yet you've so far refused to name the mate who did own them,' Rob told him, then went on, 'And were those dogs good with other people?'

'Lightning and Grizzler were big soppy family pets. Wouldn't hurt a fly, and you bastards murdered them. My kids are heartbroken. Loved them dogs, they did.'

'I thought you said they weren't yours?'

'We looked after them quite often. That's why my kids got so fond of them. They treated them like their own.'

Martin was visibly angry now, working himself up into a state of outrage. Jezza, a performing arts graduate, wasn't remotely impressed by his bluster. As well as being certain that all it amounted to was play-acting, and not very convincing at that.

The man's solicitor tried putting a pacifying hand on his client's arm, in an attempt to get him to calm down. He shook it off with such violence that Rob half-rose from his seat, ready to intervene.

Jezza's voice remained neutral as she told Martin, 'It might be best if you try to remain calm, Mr Martin. You're not creating a very favourable impression of yourself. As has been explained to you, the destruction order on the dogs was lawfully obtained and carried out because they were judged to pose a real and present danger to anyone around them. Especially after what happened to Mr Turnbull.

'You say he was looking after them for you. Yet the post-mortem examination revealed that the only contents of your dogs' stomachs were parts of Mr Turnbull's body.'

For an anxious moment, Jezza thought the young solicitor was about to throw up all over everywhere. She was certainly swallowing hard.

'From the expert advice we have been given,' Jezza continued, 'that would mean that not only had your dogs not been given any suitable dog food whilst with Mr Turnbull, they probably had not eaten anything for some significant time before you handed them over to his care.

'Was there a reason for that, Mr Martin?'

The solicitor leaned closer to her client to give him some quiet advice. Cautiously, Jezza noticed, not only because of his flare-up but because his body odour was pungent and not at all fresh.

His 'No comment' was ground out through clenched teeth with seeming reluctance.

Jezza's next question, 'There was also no sign of any dog food in the house anywhere – not even empty tins in the bin – so how long was Mr Turnbull supposed to be looking after your dogs, what was he meant to be feeding them on, and how often?' was met with the same response.

There was a folder on the desk next to Jezza. She opened it as she spoke to the solicitor.

'Apologies for the late disclosure on this, Ms Marks,' she said. 'It only came into our possession immediately before we began this interview.'

It was a single sheet of A4 paper, covered in typing and heavily redacted in places.

'Mr Martin, this is a statement from one of your near neighbours, whose name is being withheld at present for fear of reprisals. It declares that you previously got into a heated dispute with this person over a minor incident involving a parking space.

'This witness has attested that you threatened them with setting your dogs on them if they didn't, and I quote, "stop leaving your fucking rust bucket in my parking space". And that you did indeed go into your house to bring your dogs out, then made a show of – again using the witness's words – "psyching them up until he could hardly keep hold of the leads and they nearly pulled him over".'

The solicitor opened her mouth to jump in, but Rob was quicker.

'Again, my apologies also for late disclosure. I have also only just received these photos from Rochdale. Mr Martin, I'm showing you a number of photographs taken by colleagues from the Organised Crime Group there.

'They were taken by officers keeping observation on a house believed to be used by members of a known gang wanted for a number of serious offences, many of them of a very violent nature.

'I would suggest to you, Mr Martin, that the person in these photos – here, here, and here – is in fact you. Can you confirm that for me, please?'

Martin jumped to his feet so quickly this time that he took his own solicitor by surprise. She shot out of his way and scuttled to a corner of the room, looking nervous.

Jezza hit the alarm as she and Rob went into action as one smooth unit.

By the time other officers came through the door as reinforcements, they had their suspect overpowered, restrained and snarling like one of his own dogs.

* * *

'Nice work, both of you,' Ted told Rob and Jezza when they went to his office to report. 'With a bit of luck and a following breeze, we might stand a chance of a conviction on Mr Martin. We should at least get it to court. And who knows, if he thinks he stands any chance at all of a more lenient sentence if he cooperates – subject to being kept safe – he might just start to be a bit more helpful. Well done.'

The two of them were just about to leave his office when Jezza hesitated and turned back.

'Boss, is this evening a good time for that hotpot and a Gunner in The Grapes?

Ted shook his head.

'I'd love to, Jezza, I honestly would, but there are spreadsheets standing between me and any such offer, until

I can get my head down and finally start to make a bit of progress of my own.'

As they walked back to their respective desks, Jezza looked at Rob as she said, 'You see? The mere idea of some non-work time with me, even over a hotpot, is about as attractive to him as a dose of the clap.'

'Give him a break, Jezza. I really don't envy him the admin. It must be a real grunt. Especially when he's been a proper front-line copper in the past. I didn't take that as a brush-off. Just a man drowning under admin stuff and going down for the third time.'

Jezza's suggestion had put an idea in Ted's mind which wasn't going to go away, though. He got his phone out to call Trev.

'If you've not got anything already cooked, shall I get Dave to plate us up a couple of hotpots and bring them home with me? Jezza just invited me to go and eat one with her this evening, and it's really given me a taste for it.'

Ted could hear the frown in his partner's voice as he replied, 'You seriously should go with her, Ted. It sounds as if she really does want – perhaps even need – to talk to you if she asked you that. Putting her off is probably making her worried she's done something really serious that she doesn't know about.'

'I will, I promise, as soon as I can. I'm just currently suffering death by admin and I really don't have the head space for anything else just for the moment.'

'Ted, you're her senior officer. Her line manager. If she's asking for a one-to-one with you and you keep avoiding it, what's going to happen if it really is something serious and your refusal has dire consequences?'

'I don't think it's that serious. It doesn't sound it. And I promise I will talk to her, just as soon as I've finished the latest reports and projections.

'So, a hotpot supper?'

Trev gave a sigh of resignation. There were mules less stubborn than a Ted with his mind made up.

'All right, hotpot. But at least get a date in your diary to talk to Jezza, before something bad happens.'

Chapter Twenty-six

Nathan's head appeared from under the duvet as Jezza was trying to slide quietly out of her side of the bed to get ready for work. It was still early and so far there was no sound nor sign of life from Tommy's bedroom.

'Are you all right, Jezz? You were very restless last night. Like you were having a nightmare. Talking in your sleep, too. Luckily not loud enough to wake Tom. I didn't want to wake you. I had some notion you're not supposed to wake someone from a nightmare. Or is that for when they're sleepwalking?'

'Was I? I wasn't aware. What was I saying? Nothing compromising, I hope?'

'You just kept repeating "why were you there?" over and over. Can you remember what you were dreaming about?'

'Not remotely, but I think I can rationalise that one easily enough. You know this latest case with the not so happy-clappy cult is really getting to all of us. We all keep asking ourselves why anyone other than family was there at the birth, even if they didn't know there was going to be murder committed.

'Why would people want to be in the room when a person they might not know well, or possibly not at all, was giving birth? It's such an intimate family sort of occasion. Why would anyone else want to go along and gawp?'

'You're sure there's nothing else bothering you? Anything I could help you with? I was wondering, would you like me to try to have a word with your boss? To tell him how it's clearly troubling you that he won't sit down and discuss any issue he might have with you ...'

He got no further before Jezza interrupted him, gazing at him wide-eyed.

'Oh, god, no, please don't do that!' she exclaimed, clearly horrified at the mere suggestion. 'I mean, it's really kind of you to offer to ride into battle for me, but it would feel like asking your dad to go into school to threaten to duff up a teacher you didn't get on with. Not that mine ever did anything like that for me but I know there were others who did.'

She walked round to perch for a moment on Nathan's side of the bed and plant a kiss on his cheek.

'But I absolutely love it that you even made the suggestion. It's a very kind thought, but please don't. I'm working on a way to back the boss into a corner so he will have to talk to me. Whether or not I'll like hearing what he has to say for himself is another matter altogether, of course. But I'll cross that bridge if and when I come to it.'

* * *

Ted had just set off for work when he heard the item on the local news.

'A police officer has been taken to hospital after a road traffic incident in Stockport earlier this morning. The officer is said to be local and suffering from what are being described as potentially life-changing injuries.'

Ted swore under his breath and put his foot down. Whoever it was, one of his team or someone else from the station, he wanted to find out. The last thing he wanted was to get stopped for speeding, but he needed to know.

He sprinted from the car park to Kevin Turner's office. Whoever was involved, Kev would know. If it had been one of Ted's own Serious Crime team, he was sure he would have heard by now. Kev, of all people, would have got a message to him.

It was clearly something very serious, to judge by the look of him, dishevelled and worried, clearly someone who'd been at his desk for a good few hours, as duty inspector.

'Are you all right, Kev?' he asked him first, knowing the toll it took on any senior officer when something like that happened to one of their own team. 'And who is it?'

'Bloody marvellous, Ted, turning bloody cartwheels. And it's young Gavin, the daft ha'p'orth. For once, not his fault. He and PC Lyons, Mair, were despatched to deal with a potential public order offence. A woman shouting and swearing, getting aggressive and violent with anyone who came near to try to get her to calm down.

'As soon as they got there they could see it was a regular. Martha, she's called. Serious mental health issues and prone to violent outbursts, especially as she's not capable of taking her medication unsupervised. By rights she should be in a secure hospital because when she gets like that she's a danger to herself never mind to the public.'

Ted had pulled out the spare chair and sat down. He had so much he needed to do, but clearly Kevin needed someone on whom to offload, so for now, that would be his priority.

'She was really on one, too. Ranting and swearing, spitting and lashing out. Mair tried to talk to her, to calm her down a bit, while Gavin called for an ambulance. Once he said it was a mental health crisis not physical injuries, he was told there wouldn't be one available for at least eleven hours.

'Eleven bloody hours, Ted! I ask you. What were they supposed to do for that length of time? It certainly wouldn't be safe to try to put her in their car and take her to A&E, and even if they did, and got there safely, they could have been tied up for hours, waiting for someone to assess and treat her, then preferably find her a suitable bed.

'And we always try to avoid bringing her in here and locking her up when she's like that, because she's a serious self-harmer when we've tried that in the past.

'She got her ambulance in bloody double-quick time when it happened a while ago and we took her into custody, because she put her head down and ran full tilt into the wall of the cell she'd been put in. Gave herself a hairline fracture.

'Anyway, Gavin and Mair tried talking her down, trying to get her quiet enough so they could at least try to put her in the car and take her somewhere safe. They were starting to succeed a bit, too. Then some twat in the crowd started shouting at her. Not nice stuff. So she's totally flipped and gone for the head butt thing, but this time her target was Gavin because he was the nearest.'

Kevin paused for a drink from the coffee mug on his desk before he went on.

'He's gone staggering backwards into the road, right in the path of an oncoming car which was caning it a bit. It's hit him in the legs and flipped him up and over and down onto the road on the other side with one hell of a crack, Mair told me.

'Thank feck there wasn't an eleven-hour wait for the ambulance this time. He didn't regain consciousness at all and still hasn't, from the updates I've been getting. Talk about wrong bloody place at the wrong time. Our officers aren't trained for shit like that.'

'What's the prognosis? The news on the radio said possibly life-changing injuries. Have you heard what they are?'

'All anyone knows so far is "bloody unlikely to be a copper any more" sort of injuries. That's all anyone's saying at this stage, as far as I know.

'It's not right, Ted. It's not bloody right. "Policing by consent", they keep telling us. But what about us? Our consent? Did any of us sign up to be mental health carers and get seriously injured in the process, largely because of inadequate training, and no professional help when needed? Did we bollocks!'

'And where's Martha now?' Ted asked him.

'Ran off in a total panic as soon as she saw what she'd done. Disappeared completely and on her usual form, she won't resurface for days. She knows enough to understand she'll be in deep shit when we find her, and she has hidey-holes all over the place that we don't know of.'

Ted let him rant for a bit longer. He clearly needed to. Ted agreed with a lot of what he was saying. With a healthcare system in crisis and not enough beds for people like Martha to be properly cared for, it wasn't the first time Ted had heard of such incidents involving her, or others like her, though never as serious. The burden of looking after them was falling on the wrong people. Ones with little to no training in a complex specialist subject.

'And I'm feeling really bad about it because I had to give Gavin a massive bollocking last week for turning in reports that were so bad your cats could have done better. I told him if he didn't bloody buck himself up he could forget being a copper and go and do something else instead. And now he'll have to. Always assuming he survives at all.'

Ted could have trotted out endless platitudes but he wasn't about to insult Kev's intelligence. They'd known each other too long and were friends outside work as well as colleagues on very good terms within. He said the best thing he could come up with.

'Lunchtime. Me and you. The Grapes. I'll phone Dave to keep the back room free for us. I'll stand you a pint and something to eat and we can talk about what a bitch of a job ours can be on days like this. And with any luck, by then, the news might have improved a bit, at least.'

* * *

Ted kicked off morning briefing for his own team with news of what had happened to the injured officer. Most of them had heard already. News of one of their own so badly injured had swept through the nick like wildfire, but Ted wanted to make sure they had the full facts, not just the gossip.

'We know these incidents are on the increase and the way things are going, there's no sign of an end to them. So when you're out there, look out for yourselves, and for one another. Don't go anywhere on your own unless it's been thoroughly risk assessed as low to minimal. Even then, be on your guard and make sure Mike or I, or someone else, knows where you are at all times, and what your ETA back here is.

275

'This is not the appropriate time for anyone to go off playing the lone maverick. Not that it ever is, but certainly not at the moment. I hope I've made that clear enough.

'Hopefully most of you will be heads down over your desks for much of the day writing up all your various reports. But think on if you do have to venture off out anywhere. Don't go alone if you can avoid it.'

Ted's mobile was ringing as he walked back to his office. Trev. Sounding anxious.

'I just heard the local news on the radio. A seriously injured police officer. Not one of your team, I hope? What happened?'

'One of Kev's lads. Youngish. Not equipped to deal with what he was confronted with. We're still waiting on an update of his condition but it's not sounding very hopeful at the moment. The latest I've heard suggests he could survive but his policing days will be over.'

'Shit, Ted, that's awful. Listen, I know you're going to say it's totally impossible, but I want you to make sure you find the time to get to kids' club tomorrow, and to stay on for judo. You know the kids always love seeing you, especially Flip. Even more so after a break. And a proper physical workout is probably just what you need with all the stress you've been under lately. To stop you blowing a fuse.

'Will you do that for me? Please?'

'You know I can't promise, the way things are at the moment.'

Ted was looking at all the accumulated work on his desk, mentally trying to calculate how long it was going to take him to clear, even without interruptions. Ideally he'd have ordered in something to eat for a working lunch, but he needed to make time for Kevin, as he'd suggested. When Ted had lost a team member, a good few years ago now, it was Kevin who had helped him through that, so he needed to return the favour.

'If it's remotely possible, I'll be there for the kids, but I can't guarantee I'll be able to stay on for judo. I'll have to see how the day goes.'

* * *

Not only did Ted make it in time for the children the following evening, he was actually there before some of them. Even before Flip, which was unusual. He was normally one of the first to arrive.

Ted hadn't exactly cleared his desk but he'd at least made enough progress for him to decide he was entitled to some down time.

The news from the hospital about young Gavin had been guarded before Ted and Kev went round to The Grapes to eat.

'As well as can be expected,' Kevin had scoffed as they sat down at their reserved table in the back room. 'What the bloody hell does that even mean? How well should you expect to be after you've been thrown over a moving car?'

'It's the stock answer, Kev. You know that. It's probably too early to say much, and it wouldn't be right to raise hopes. We'll probably hear more by the time we get back to the nick. We might as well eat while we can.'

There was news when they got back, but not the sort any of them had wanted to hear. The young officer was now expected to survive, but surgeons would have to amputate one lower leg which was damaged beyond all realistic hope of repair.

That was the catalyst for Ted to decide that Trev had been right. What he needed was time spent with their young pupils, including some vigorous exercise as the two of them demonstrated moves. Even if he couldn't stay on for judo, for some unforeseen reason. He was determined to stay if he could. It had been too long since he'd had a proper workout.

'This is fantastic,' Trev told him. 'I'm so pleased you managed to make it, and nice and early, too. And you are going to stay on, aren't you? You're not suddenly going to get a phone call and have to dash away, are you?'

'I've left my phone in the car boot, switched off,' Ted told him. 'Today of all days, I feel I'm due some off-duty time. If there's anything really critical, Mike knows where to find me, and I'll check it between sessions, justin.'

Ted's usual verbal shorthand, and his philosophy. Just in case. Always have a Plan B, at least.

'But I fully intend to stay to the end, if I can.'

At that moment, young Flip came into the gym, in front of his adoptive mother. Instead of the usual smile of anticipation on his face, he was looking unusually subdued, his face flushed.

As soon as he saw that his hero, Ted, was already there, he forgot all correct protocol and came running towards him, without even stopping to take off his outdoor shoes. When he reached him he flung his arms around him, buried his face against him and started to sob.

'Flip,' Ted told him gently, 'whatever the problem is, you shouldn't be in here in your shoes. Take them off, please, then we'll go over to the side where your mother is and you can tell me what's the matter.'

Flip lifted his head, his eyes flashing anger, as he spat, 'I don't want to talk to her. I hate her. She says I can't be a copper and I have to leave cadets.'

Ted threw an apologetic look at Trev as he said, 'Sorry, I better see what I can do to sort this. Can you start without us, please?'

It was the last thing Ted needed, after the day he'd had. He could sense the hostility in the woman by the door, even before he got closer. He'd paused to make Flip take off his shoes and carry them. The boy was already in his judogi so was ready to start the session, but he would clearly now be late joining in. Whatever was going on with him and his adoptive mother, Ted felt an obligation to try to help.

'Mrs Atkinson? Would you mind if we stepped out into the corridor, so I can close the doors and let Trev start the class?'

'You won't change my mind though. I heard on the radio what has happened to that poor young police officer, and I don't want Philip to be facing such a dangerous job.'

'Isn't that rather up to Flip? He might have gone off the idea by the time he's old enough to apply to join. Not all cadets go on to join up. Far from it.'

'I won't change me mind, Ted. I want to be a copper, like you.' He looked mutinously at his mother as he said, 'And you can't stop me.'

'A bit of respect, please, Flip,' Ted told him, then continued, to his mother, 'Technically, Flip is right. By the time he would be eligible to join, he would be of an age where he doesn't need parental consent. And Flip, believe me, you might well have decided against becoming a police officer by then.

'Why don't you go and join the group now, and remember to apologise to Trev and to the others for your behaviour, which wasn't acceptable.'

His mother watched as Flip went back towards Trevor and the others, looking thoroughly subdued.

'I probably overreacted,' she told Ted. 'But I worry for him, you see. Very much. I love him every bit as much as if he was my own flesh and blood. That's why I'm afraid for him. I only want to keep him safe.'

'Will you at least let him carry on coming here, and going to cadets? I promise you it's not some sinister recruiting arm of the service. No one will put pressure on Flip to join up. After all, it's up to him what he wants to do with his future life.'

Chapter Twenty-seven

Ted was quiet and subdued on the drive back home from the dojo. He'd been his usual professional self with the youngsters, not allowing any hint of anything which might be troubling him to show in his behaviour. But it was obvious to Trev that all was not well with his partner.

They both knew how vital the weekly sessions were, to some of the youngsters more than others. Some attended because they were victims of bullying from other children, perhaps at their school. Others might be there because of violence in the home. It was a chance for all of them to learn not just how to protect themselves but also about respect. To understand how to show it to others but also to know that they were entitled to be shown it themselves.

'Are you all right?' Trev asked him, as they turned onto the A6. 'You're in one of your quiet and brooding moods. I thought a session at the dojo might have cheered you up a bit. It usually does.'

'Sorry. There's just so much going on at work I'm a bit run ragged.'

'But you've wrapped up two big cases between you and the OCG, haven't you? Even if you've not got exactly the result you would have wanted on your own case.

'I was hoping you might perhaps reach the stage where we could at least think about doing that trip up to Kinder

Downfall. Maybe this weekend? I really think you need something like that. It would do you good.'

'It's too early to say at the moment. I don't want to tempt fate, for one thing.'

'But theoretically, if you did manage to push the boat out and take a whole half day off work, for instance, which would be your preference – Saturday or Sunday?'

'I can't promise ...'

'Ted, I'm not asking you to sign a contract in blood. I know plans could change at the eleventh hour. I understand that. I should do, living with you for as long as I have. I just want a rough idea of which you would prefer. I'm not going in to work this weekend, it's Geoff's turn, so either day is good for me. But I'd like to make us a nice little gourmet picnic, so it's a real treat for us both, as well as a time to talk, and that will need planning and shopping for.'

'All right, then. I have to confess that it sounds very tempting. What if I say Saturday afternoon, then if I have to cancel that for any reason at the last minute, I could try again for Sunday? As long as that wouldn't ruin the picnic food?'

'Ted, you can sometimes be very obtuse for a police officer. We could, of course, eat the picnic on Saturday night, at home, if needs be, and I'll make another fresh one for Sunday. But do please try to make one of them. Unless there really is a major incident.'

'Sssshhhh, don't tempt fate like that. That's bound to make something big drop on my desk which will tie me up for the entire weekend, at least.'

Trev smiled as he shook his head in disbelief.

'Not to mention you being illogically superstitious for a supposedly logical copper. But don't worry. I shall have words with my undercover spies on your team to make sure you shall go to the picnic, Cinderella, no matter what fate throws up.'

* * *

Ted's first port of call the next morning, before briefing, was to see if Kevin was on duty and to find out what the latest news about Gavin was.

The nick was always a rumour mill at the best of times and Ted had heard just about every possible scenario being bandied about, but he wanted to know the truth.

Kev looked marginally better than the day before but was still clearly worried and, Ted was sure, still mentally kicking himself that his last contact with the young officer had been to pull him up on poor standards.

'Unravelling the hospital-speak as best I can, they think now that he should survive, but his injuries are significant enough that he can definitely forget his coppering days. They're behind him, and so is football, which was his sport of choice. He wasn't bad at it, either. Played on a couple of local teams. So that's his career and his favourite hobby down the pan just like that. I don't suppose there's much more call for a one-legged striker on his team than a copper like that.

'And all from being in the wrong place at the wrong time, and not being able to hand over to people who could have dealt with Martha properly, before it all got this far.'

'Which brings us to the thorny question of what action can be taken if and when Martha resurfaces, after what she did to Gavin,' Ted said. 'I'm assuming, from what you've said, that she's unlikely to be in any fit state to plead, never mind stand trial, even if you find her and can manage to bring her in safely, without a repeat performance.'

'God knows, Ted. Honestly, I know I shouldn't say it because it's not the poor woman's fault, but there are days when I seriously wish I could just shove her in my car and drive her right off our patch. A long, long way away, then dump her there. Then at least she wouldn't be our problem any more. But then I bet every patch has its own Martha, these days. What the hell are we supposed to do with them all, eh?'

* * *

Ted updated the team with all he knew to date about the wounded officer then went on, 'Inspector Turner also told me of a suspicious death report which came on via the night shift which we at least need to take a first look at.

'So, Mike, whoever you can free up first to transfer to that one, please, in case it does turn out to be one for Serious Crime.'

'Any connection to our existing ones, boss?' Mike asked him. 'Scores being settled because the gang has taken a clobbering from us of late? And before I decide who to send, do we have any intel on such things as the likely presence of any more of those big woofers on the premises? I don't want to send anyone in blind if there's the slightest chance of a close encounter of the worst kind with any of those big brutes.'

Ted looked across at Rob O'Connell to take that question, as he'd been working closest with the OCG.

'Rob?'

'As far as I know, boss, from the debrief with Sergeant Duffy, all of the dogs seized on the OCG raids have either already been destroyed, like the two that killed Mr Turnbull, with the positive DNA results, or are in safe police custody, awaiting assessment of their fitness to be returned to their owners, or not. From what we've heard, it doesn't sound like any will be going back into circulation. They don't exactly seem to be cuddly family pets.

'That's not to say there may be others about that we don't yet know of, so that's always worth bearing in mind. But the worst offenders, as far as we're aware, are no longer at large.'

'Thanks, Rob.

'So can you all please ensure everything is written up as it should be for all of our cases? I'm hoping, if we get ahead of ourselves, to be somewhere on Saturday afternoon, so I'd appreciate your cooperation in getting all your notes to me asap with a view to me being able to pass complete and hopefully watertight files to CPS by Monday.

'Thank you, all.'

As soon as Ted had cleared anything pressing from his desk, he went downstairs to find Superintendent Caldwell for a catch-up. He wanted to tell her, for one thing, of his hopes of taking time off on Saturday afternoon.

'Chief inspector, I shouldn't need to remind an officer of your length of service that we are all entitled to time away from the job. In fact it's essential we avail ourselves of whatever is due to us in the interests of our own health and sanity.

'Pushing yourself so hard you risk jeopardising your own health is a hangover from the olden days and should not be necessary. If you really feel you have no one you trust in charge in your absence, then we need to look at the structure of your team.'

'It's not that at all, ma'am. I have every confidence in Mike, and in Rob. It's just that I feel responsible for what my team does collectively and I like to see things through to the end myself.'

'All of which is very commendable. But not at the expense of your own welfare.

'So, do you have something in mind for your half day off? If that's not too personal a question?'

Coming from her, it was positively intrusive. She was always so wary of boundaries. Never wanting to cross lines. Ted had seldom seen her anything other than stiffly formal in the workplace. The very epitome of her nickname, the Ice Queen.

'Probably not everyone's idea of an exciting time but Trev and I hope to be able to head for the Peak District. A walk up Kinder and hopefully, if it's not blowing so much we risk getting drenched, a picnic by the Downfall.'

'That sounds absolutely delightful,' she told him, sounding as if she actually meant it. 'Not a walk I've yet done, but it sounds like a good idea for a family outing, so I shall propose it to mine on my next day off. Enjoy yourself and rest assured, you have a good team who are perfectly capable of managing without you. And should there be a crisis, I am at the end of a phone.

'It goes without saying that I firmly hope you won't be at the end of yours.'

* * *

'I thought we were going to take the bike,' Ted told Trev

when he got back late on Saturday morning after a quick run through anything he needed to deal with before handing over to Mike Hallam for the rest of the day. He was looking at the size of the picnic banquet Trev was putting together.

Trev put on a mock-offended expression as he said, 'I've spent all morning shopping for and preparing a gourmet picnic fit for royalty. If you think I'm going to stuff the fruit of my labours into the box on the back of the bike, you can certainly think again!'

The kitchen, as ever after one of Trev's special meal preparations, looked like ground zero, with various members of the feline family climbing all over the sink, draining board and work surfaces, searching for the smallest crumb of anything edible which might have been left lurking somewhere.

'Is half my team joining us, looking at the amount you've prepared? Not that I'm complaining. It looks like a real treat. Thank you.'

'You won't thank me when you see your credit card statement. I couldn't put it on mine, it would have been declined for reasons I won't bore you with, so I borrowed your second one,' Trev laughed.

Ted shook his head in mock despair, then said, 'I'll just go up and get changed, then I'd better clear up some of the chaos in here before we go out, or the cats will be all over everything. I won't be long.'

'You better not be! I've been looking forward to this little outing and I don't want to be coming back down from the summit in the dark because we were late going out. You did enough of that sort of thing with Mr Green and it doesn't appeal to me in the slightest.

'I'm sure this little trip will do us good. So don't even think of accepting any incoming phone calls from work. You have two DSs now who are more than capable of deputising for you, so cut them some slack and let them.'

* * *

They were lucky with the weather. It was better than forecast, with some sunshine and a light breeze. Perfect walking weather. The traffic was in their favour, too, with few major hold-ups so they reached their destination within the hour.

As they pulled into the car park they usually used for their planned walking route, Ted spotted a distinctive car. A limited edition VW Golf.

He was instantly on the alert, his voice suspicious as he asked, 'What's this? Have I been set up? What is Jezza doing here? Did she put you up to this, or was this your idea?'

'All my own idea. No blame at all on Jezza. Park over there, next to her. Because you are going to talk to her, Ted. She's been worried sick about why you're giving her the cold shoulder and putting her off all the time, as she sees it, and trying to move her on from the team she loves. She came to see me, in desperation, because you wouldn't talk to her, so I promised to help.'

'I thought you said how much you'd been looking forward to this picnic?'

'I was, but not for the reasons you thought. You need to talk to Jezza, Ted. She really is in an anxious state and you've been behaving very strangely. At least my little bit of subterfuge has got you here. So off you both go, and talk, for goodness sake.'

As Ted opened his mouth to say something else, Trev cut across him, in a tone which brooked no argument.

'And don't tell me you've been too busy to talk to her, Ted. You're her senior officer. You have a duty of care to her. For her welfare. I shouldn't have to remind you of that, any more than Jezza should have had to come to me for help in the first place.'

Jezza had got out of her car and was watching the exchange between them, suddenly with a horrible feeling that she'd done entirely the wrong thing in asking Trev for his help. The boss didn't like any kind of subterfuge, and certainly nothing that impinged on his private life, which he was bound to think this was.

But he was here. He'd taken time off, so she hoped she could profit from that. Hoped, too, he would not be so furious with her he would be even less inclined to talk to her. Or worse, decide he really did want her off the team for dragging Trev into work stuff.

'DC Vine, this isn't at all appropriate ...'

Ted got no further before Trev cut in once more.

'Appropriate or not, Ted, here we are, and you are going to talk to Jezza. Give me the car keys, take the picnic and off you go. Both of you. And don't come back until you've sorted out whatever is going on between you. Jezza can drive you home, Ted, and when she does, or at some point in the very near future, I want to hear her say everything is as it should be and harmony is restored.'

Chapter Twenty-eight

'Boss, I'm really sorry about going behind your back, but you couldn't find time for me at work ... '

'And that's really all it was, Jezza. Lack of time. You know we've been flat out recently. I'm sorry if I didn't make that clear enough.'

'But then you seemed to want to offload me onto the OCG when you know I couldn't make a move like that, because of my home circumstances. I just couldn't. Even if I'd wanted to.'

'Jezza, I promise we will talk. As soon as we sit down for this picnic Trev has made for us. You'll have my full attention to tell me exactly what's bothering you. I think such a conversation between us is long overdue and I'm sorry I couldn't make time for it sooner.

'But for now, we're walking in beautiful countryside, on a route you perhaps don't know ...' he looked at her quizzically as he said that, and when she shook her head, he went on, 'So for now, can we please just walk, and take in our surroundings. Maybe chat about the view, and if you have any questions about the area, I can perhaps answer some of them, at least.

'Then, when we get to the Downfall for our picnic, which Trev went to great lengths to prepare for us, we can sit and talk to each other. Each ask our own questions and give honest answers. How does that sound?'

<Like another brush-off> Jezza's inner voice was screaming at her. But she had no choice. She would just have to hope that between where they were and the top of the waterfall, the boss wouldn't have had the time to come up with some seemingly valid reason why he couldn't allay her fears.

She sighed as she said, 'It sounds like my only option, boss.'

* * *

Trev may have left the kitchen in its usual bomb site state after his picnic preparation but the contents of the rucksack which Ted had carried up to the top of the Downfall could have come from the best delicatessen in any major European city.

There was even a piccolo of a fairly decent wine for Jezza and a can of an elderflower drink for Ted, complete with unbreakable camping goblets.

'This is absolutely amazing!' Jezza exclaimed at the sight of it all. 'Much as I do want us to talk, I also can't wait to get stuck into this. Your Trev is definitely a keeper.'

They ate in silence for a while then Jezza began to talk.

'Boss, when I heard that you seemed all in favour of me transferring to OCG, I wondered what had made you think it was even workable for me, let alone a good idea. So that set me thinking about what I might have done to pee you off to the extent of wanting to get rid of me.

'I tried to talk to you about it but the more you shut down and fobbed me off, the more convinced I was that you thought I'd done or said something so bad you just wanted rid of me. At any cost. But I couldn't – and I still can't –

think what I could possibly have done to make you feel that way.

'So please will you tell me? Now? I'm sure it's just a misunderstanding. Wires crossed somewhere. But as long as I don't know what it is, I can't begin to set your mind at rest and show you that you've got the wrong end of the stick.'

Ted finished his mouthful before he spoke, his tone as neutral as if he was telling her about their return route back down to the car.

'You're a good officer, Jezza. Impetuous, sometimes, but intelligent and dedicated. I've been glad to have you on the team.

'But I have a copper's brain. It sometimes goes off wandering down roads others might not know, let alone follow.

'When I saw recently that you clearly know your way well round the insides of a car, something I didn't know previously, I remembered that you lost your parents in a car crash. Remembered, too, that night when you were raped and you confided in me that your father had also raped you.'

Jezza had just taken another bite from her blini with cream cheese and smoked salmon. She took a sharp intake of breath at his words which immediately set off a paroxysm of coughing, tears streaming down her face.

Ted got to his feet, moved quickly behind her, pushed gently to lean her forward and gave five firm slaps to the centre of her back.

Part of the blini made a reappearance which meant she could at least draw in some air as she used her paper napkin to wipe her eyes and mouth.

When she had recovered enough to speak again, she told him, 'Good god, boss, are you accusing me of murdering my own parents while you nearly kill me with the shock of an allegation like that? Oh, the irony.

'Are you actually serious or is this some weird manifestation of how much stress you've been under lately? And if you really did think that, why the hell didn't you simply ask me if it was true?'

'Would you have told me the truth if you had been involved?' Ted countered.

'Well, the truth is I didn't do it, so yes, of course I would have told you the truth. I have nothing to hide. I had nothing at all to do with that crash. The verdict was misadventure. My father was three times over the limit and speeding dangerously in a poorly-maintained car. An accident waiting to happen.'

'I know. I read the reports.'

She gaped at him as he said that.

'You read the reports? Why on earth would you dig them out and look at them? Do you seriously think I'm a murderer? That I killed my own parents, for god's sake?'

'That's how a copper's brain works, Jezza. You know that. Get all the available facts first. Basic starting point in any enquiry.'

'So I'm a suspect now? Is that it? Surely we should be having this conversation at the nick, you should caution me and I should have a solicitor present, in that case.'

Jezza shook her head in disbelief.

'Boss, I need another drink of my wine, so please don't say anything else outrageous while I do that. I don't want to choke for a second time. I just can't believe what you're telling me.'

Ted waited for her to finish drinking then went on, 'I saw how confident you were with Maurice's car, and with mine, and you said you used to work on your father's car. The crash report indicated some problem with the steering but it was impossible to say whether that pre-dated the crash or happened during it.'

'In spite of myself, I'm intrigued as to your logic, boss. I'm pretending we're discussing any other case, not you telling me your reasons for thinking I murdered both my parents. Or at least engineered the crash which killed them both.'

'Policing basics, Jezza. Means, Motive, Opportunity. You had all three, as someone who had worked on the vehicle of the person who had raped her.'

'This is me seriously humouring you now, boss, because I've reached the stage of thinking you've completely lost the plot and wondering if I'm actually safe up a mountain with you. A mountain with a great big drop down a waterfall, so I'm hoping this isn't going to be my Sherlock Holmes at the Reichenbach Falls moment.

'So please do tell. Of course I had a motive for killing my father, in theory, after what he did to me. But what was my motive – all of this being purely hypothetical, of course – for killing my mother? Factoring in that I had no idea she would go with him that evening because she must have known he'd been drinking heavily and she wouldn't normally get in the car with him when he had.'

'Jezza, you've been a copper for long enough to know that in many cases of rape, and especially of incest, the victim often holds any other close family member – especially their own mother – complicit, at least in part, for what happened to them.'

Jezza drank some more of her wine before she spoke again.

'And another thing. If I had done something deliberately to the car, why would I have shown you, of all people, that I had some basic – and it is very basic – knowledge of mechanics? I know how sharp you are for details.

'I thought at first this was a wind-up. In pretty poor taste, but maybe just a hypothetical thing where you were testing my powers of detection, using me and my family circumstances as an example.

'Because yes, when you lay it all out like that, I'd suspect myself, to be honest. But as we both know, what with the inquest verdict of misadventure, with recorded evidence to back that up, and all trace of the vehicle long gone, there would be no way of proving anything either way. Oh, and not forgetting those very damning blood-alcohol results. Three times over the limit was going it some, even for my father, especially coupled with excessive speeds.'

Jezza ate another blini and drank more wine before she said any more, aware of the boss intently watching her every move and gesture.

Then she said, 'Or, another explanation is that you've decided to enter the world of crime fiction writing. Weaving fiendish plots around things you've come across in your time in the force, and you want my opinion on whether this one has legs as a book.'

She said it in a light-hearted way, with a smile in his direction, as she went on, 'Well, sorry, boss, I think it's pants. It's unbelievable, cliché-ridden and it's probably been done to death, pardon the pun, many times over. I'd stick to the day job, if I were you.'

'All I want from you, Jezza, is for you to look me in the eye and tell me you had nothing at all to do with the death of your parents. I don't want to spend the rest of our professional time together with me always wondering what if. So convince me, and we'll say no more about it.'

'Well, that's easy enough, boss.'

Jezza's light blue eyes locked onto Ted's hazel gaze as she told him, without a flicker, 'I did not murder my parents. Nor did I intend to, or even attempt to. I was in no way involved in the incident which cost them their lives. The crash, as the coroner ruled, was caused by my father's excess drinking, his excessively high speeds, and his failure to keep his vehicle sufficiently serviced to be safe and roadworthy.'

* * *

'Well, thank you for a lovely day, boss,' Jezza told Ted as she pulled up outside his house, leaning over to give him a fleeting peck on the cheek.

'It's all been very interesting. Please give my compliments to the chef and good luck for the future as a crime fiction writer. Don't forget I'll always be available to read through your first draft, when it's ready. See you on Monday morning.'

She said it all in the same teasing tone she often used with him and gave him a cheery wave as she pulled away from the kerb and disappeared off up the road.

Trev had clearly been on the lookout for Ted's return. He had the front door open and was waiting for him on the doorstep, the youngest cat, Adam, carefully cradled in his arms to stop him going off adventuring.

The first thing Ted had done when he and Trev had moved into their house together was to fence the back garden as securely as possible to stop inquisitive felines straying too near the road, and denying them easy access to the front of the property.

'How did it go?' he asked anxiously as Ted reached the door. 'You're here, so clearly you didn't make Jezza angry enough to throw you off the top of the Downfall. Bear in mind I will be phoning her later for corroboration of anything you tell me.'

Ted sat down on the bottom stair to take off his boots and put them on the mat, as he said, 'Before I tell you everything, I want to say that I'm going to contact Carol to see if she can fit me in for some more therapy sessions in the near future. I think, with all I've had on my plate recently, I might need a bit of help to get things back into perspective.'

Trev's eyes widened at that. It was so unusual. So unlike Ted to be the one to admit he might need some professional help.

Ted headed for the kitchen, the rucksack with what little remained of the picnic over one arm so he could empty it and wash everything.

'Jezza was seriously impressed by the picnic. She told me to thank you very much. It was excellent. Just what we both needed.'

Trev put little Adam down and followed Ted into the kitchen, where he was putting the kettle on and starting clear-up operations with the empty food containers and the various things Trev had dumped in the sink since his partner went out.

'That's a bit of a bombshell to drop on me without any follow-up, you voluntarily seeking help. I'd be worried it was you who pushed Jezza off the top, if I hadn't just seen her driving off. So what on earth was the problem between you that you think you need therapy for?

Ted paused in what he was doing and turned to face his partner.

'I asked Jezza if she'd murdered her parents.'

Trev was staring at him now as if he didn't recognise him.

'Ted, that isn't even funny. Not even in a very black humour sort of way.'

'It's me being honest. I had totally convinced myself that I had a murderer on the team. One who'd been hiding a secret all this time and had never told anyone. Presumably. But the alternative to that is that other team members knew. Maurice, probably, for one, and they've been involved in a conspiracy of silence all along.

'I must be under more pressure than I realised to even be thinking any of that. That's why I'm going to ring Carol first thing on Monday, to see if she can unscramble my brains for me and help me get back to some semblance of normality.'

* * *

'I'm here, in the kitchen. Shall I put the kettle on?' Nathan's voice called out as Jezza paused in the hall to take off her boots and coat before going to find him.

'I've had the most amazing picnic! There was even a dinky bottle of wine for me. Trev had really pushed the boat out. But I'd love a coffee, if you're offering.'

She moved to kiss him, then leaned against a granite work surface as he started to make it.

'How have my two favourite men been today while I've been yomping up mountains with the boss?'

'Tom's school really do seem to be working hard with him on the subject of empathy. I saw the results of that this morning when he decided he wanted to go to the park to play football.'

He laughed at Jezza's expression of disbelief.

'Yes, I know, but he's seen or read something about it being good for you. First step, of course, was to buy a football, since we don't possess such a thing. And unfortunately he took a shine to the most expensive one in the shop.

'Fast-forward to the park, where he wanted to learn to score goals. Nothing else. None of the basics, like ball control. Just goals. So, two attempts, no goal scored, and you can imagine the rest. I was poised for the meltdown but to my surprise, Tom picked up the ball, walked calmly over to where there was a little lad on his own who'd been watching and told him "This ball doesn't work properly so you can have it if you want".'

'Oh bless! I wish I'd been there to see that. I hope the other kid was pleased?'

'Thrilled skinny. I decided to whisk Tom away after the littleun had kicked in three cracking goals in rapid succession. But it was good. A nice feeling.

'So, how was your afternoon with the boss? Did you even get close to finding out why he's got his knickers in a twist about you?'

'Oh yes. Are you ready for this? He asked me outright if I'd killed my parents.'

'What?' Nathan was staring at her now. 'And what did you say to him?'

'I told him the facts. The coroner recorded a misadventure verdict because my father was, as usual, as pissed as a brewer's fart, speeding, and hadn't had the vehicle properly seen to, despite me telling him repeatedly that's what it needed.'

Nathan had made the coffee now and put Jezza's mug within reach of her hand then folded his arms round her.

'And are you all right? That must have come as one hell of a shock to you. Dragging all that stuff up again after so long. Did he accept what you said to him?'

Jezza put her arms round him in turn and hugged him close, nestling her head against the reassuring warmth of his chest.

'He had to. There's absolutely nothing he can prove, whatever his suspicions tell him. Besides, never forget I'm an actorrrrr.'

She drew out the word outrageously, looking up at him, her eyes twinkling.

'And a bloody good one at that, even though I say so myself. I think I convinced him. And I also think I made him feel so bad about even considering it might not be as simple as the verdict would suggest that he'll let it drop now.'

Nathan hugged her back. Fiercely, protectively.

'I hope so, Jezz. I really hope so.'

From the Author

Thank you for reading the latest volume in the Ted Darling Crime Series. I hope you have enjoyed it. If so, do please consider leaving a review on Amazon. And please do tell your friends about the series. Thank you.

A couple of points to note before reviewing. Firstly, the books are not written in real time so may lag behind recent changes in legislation, as well as detail such as using Her Majesty, not His Majesty. Also, they are set in Stockport, and Greater Manchester in general, so the characters use local dialect and sayings.

Seemingly incorrect grammar within quotes reflects common speech patterns. For example, 'I'll do it if I get chance', without an article, or determiner, is common parlance, as is 'should of' instead of 'should have'. Ted and Trev also have an in joke between them – 'billirant' – which is a deliberate 'typo'.

If you have any queries about words or phrases used, do please feel free to get in touch, using the contact details in the book. I always try to reply promptly to any emails or Facebook messages.

Thank you.

L M Krier

Discover the Ted Darling

Crime Series

If you've enjoyed meeting Ted Darling you may like to discover the other books in the series. All books are available as e-books and in paperback format.

The First Time Ever
Baby's Got Blue Eyes
Two Little Boys
When I'm Old and Grey
Shut Up and Drive
Only the Lonely
Wild Thing
Walk On By
Preacher Man
Cry for the Bad Man
Every Game You Play
Where the Girls Are
Down Down Down
The Cuckoo is a Pretty Bird
Dirty Old Town
The End of the Line
It's Oh So Quiet
A Woman's Heart
No Way to Say Goodbye
Everybody Hurts Sometime
Sweet Little Lies

The First Time Ever is also available as an audiobook, brilliantly read by Christopher Corcoran, and is translated into French by Jean Sauvanet, under the title of 'Darling.'

Printed in Great Britain
by Amazon

41454182R00172